"You think I can do this?" Annja asked.

Vic laughed. "We[...] strong motivatio[...]

"I do?"

"Yeah, if you don't hold your own, I'll leave you behind. These woods are about to turn ugly on me as well. The people I annoyed last night will be out in force looking for yours truly. I'm not hanging aro[...] longer than I have to."

"You'd leave me behind?" Annja asked.

"In a heartbeat, sister. I've got my own age[...] to. Sorry to break your heart and all."

Annja frowned. "You're not breaking my he[...] said.

Vic smiled. "Let's get moving."

Annja stood and rubbed on some more mo[...] repellent. Vic hefted his rifle and then stopped. "Here," he said, holding out a small-caliber pistol. "You know how to use one?"

Annja took the gun, dropped the magazine and racked the slide. As the bullet in the chamber spun out, she caught it in her hand. Then she topped off the magazine, rammed it home and racked the slide again.

"Yeah, I think I can handle it," she said.

Vic nodded and grinned. "You're not exactly a damsel in distress, are you?

Titles in this series:

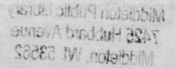

ROGUE Angel

Alex Archer

SACRIFICE

A GOLD EAGLE BOOK FROM

WORLDWIDE®

TORONTO • NEW YORK • LONDON
AMSTERDAM • PARIS • SYDNEY • HAMBURG
STOCKHOLM • ATHENS • TOKYO • MILAN
MADRID • WARSAW • BUDAPEST • AUCKLAND

Recycling programs
for this product may
not exist in your area.

First edition May 2009

ISBN-13: 978-0-373-62136-1
ISBN-10:   0-373-62136-1

SACRIFICE

Special thanks and acknowledgment to
Jon Merz for his contribution to this work.

The
LEGEND

...THE ENGLISH COMMANDER TOOK
JOAN'S SWORD AND RAISED IT HIGH.

The broadsword, plain and unadorned,
gleamed in the firelight. He put the tip against
the ground and his foot at the center of the blade.
The broadsword shattered, fragments falling
into the mud. The crowd surged forward,
peasant and soldier, and snatched the shards
from the trampled mud. The commander tossed
the hilt deep into the crowd.
Smoke almost obscured Joan, but she continued
praying till the end, until finally the flames climbed
her body and she sagged against the restraints.

Joan of Arc died that fateful day in France,
but her legend and sword are reborn....

1

The air was so thick, Annja Creed felt she could use her sword to slice it open. But doing so wouldn't affect the extreme humidity that seemed to surround her every second of the day. Even when the blistering sun didn't penetrate the thick canopy of the jungle, she could still feel the heat of its merciless rays burning down. Something as simple as taking a breath felt as if she was swallowing thick porridge.

She'd already resolved herself to the one simple fact about being in the jungle—she would never be dry. Her clothes clung to her, accentuating every curve of her body. They were soaked through with sweat and the twice-daily rains that haunted her new home.

It wasn't a home she wanted to live in. But, for the moment, she had no choice.

She worked her hands behind her back, trying to relieve some of the pressure on her wrists. The handcuffs didn't help matters.

She stretched to get her hands under her, hoping she'd eventually be able to slide them under her legs so her hands ended up in front of her rather than behind her. A stream of sweat ran down her face for her efforts.

Annja took a deep breath and sighed. How do they stand it here? she wondered. She'd been in the Philippines for less than a week and she still hadn't acclimated to the tropical environment.

Of course, she hadn't come here thinking she would end up as a prisoner of the dreaded Abu Sayyaf, the notorious terrorist group with links to al Qaeda. Annja was supposed to be researching a new story for *Chasing History's Monsters*. But a contact hadn't turned out to be who he said he was. Instead, Annja found herself looking down three gun barrels, and when the small Toyota van had rolled to a stop in front of her, the wisest move was to get inside.

She smirked. If she was being totally honest with herself, part of her wanted to see where things led. She was getting used to unexpected adventures and the truth was she usually enjoyed them. She was pretty good at getting herself out of tight spots.

Her smile faded. I should have considered all the options beforehand, she thought. Before she was forced to endure a bumpy flight away from Manila, and then a riverboat ride to some desolate part of the country.

And there was also the fact that she had no idea where on earth she was. The Philippines comprised over seven thousand islands. Annja could be on any of them.

With no real way home.

She racked her brain. What do I know about Abu Sayyaf? Not much. Just what had made it to the news. She knew they were notorious for their cruelty. They hadn't pulled off much in the way of actual terrorist attacks—a stray bombing here and there. But what they lacked in a track record, they made up for in terms of their lucrative side business—kidnapping.

Abu Sayyaf operatives had resorted to kidnapping over the past ten years to help finance their various other operations. Normally, the kidnappings took place at expensive resorts frequented by wealthy Europeans. But in the past few years, Annja knew that Abu Sayyaf had also kidnapped several missionaries. The results weren't always positive. If the ransoms were paid, by and large most of the victims were released. In the case of one missionary, however, he was beheaded.

Annja wondered what they hoped to achieve by kidnapping her.

She looked around the makeshift camp. There were several huts built a foot off the ground on stilts. Their rooftops had been painted and thatched over to help conceal them among the other plants of the jungle canopy, probably to discourage them from being seen from the air by the military units that hunted the terrorists.

She wondered if it was true that U.S. special-operations troops were involved in the hunt for Abu Sayyaf. She supposed they could be, and the thought of them attacking the camp cheered her.

The reality of it seemed unlikely, though. Annja hadn't heard any type of aircraft in the area since she'd been here.

The jungle, she knew, could be utterly impenetrable. Walk in any direction and within ten yards, you'd be totally lost unless you knew exactly where you were going and how you were going to get there.

She heard a chicken clucking off in the distance. They were one of the few animals that Abu Sayyaf members seemed to keep around the camp. She was grateful they at least fed her well enough. Last night she'd had a chicken-and-rice dish that had filled her stomach and set her at ease for the first time in a few days.

They kept her well hydrated, too. Of course, they had to.

In this heat, even just being leashed to the wooden pole a few feet away, Annja could dehydrate fast. Someone stopped by about once an hour and forced her to drink water.

The dark skin of her Filipino hosts suggested they were indigenous to this area, rather than city transplants. She knew that Abu Sayyaf, like many terrorist groups, preferred the disenfranchised lower classes to the middle class or wealthy. It was easier to recruit them, easier to get them to commit to suicide missions if they believed their families were going to be taken care of after they were gone.

From her vantage point in the camp, Annja had seen a total of twelve men and four women. Each one of them was dressed in camouflage fatigues. And even Annja was wearing fatigues. Her own clothes had been unceremoniously stripped off when she'd first arrived. Annja wondered if her nakedness might have aroused any of her guards, but they merely looked away while she put on the new clothes, which smelled of mothballs.

She heard the tramping of feet and looked up. One of the guards, a guy she'd named Big Nose because of the bulbous snout he had, approached with her hourly ration of water.

"Drink."

Annja tilted her head back and opened her mouth. The water was cool. Annja wondered if they had a refrigerator somewhere, and if so, what sort of power it was running on. A generator out here would be too noisy and would require a supply of gasoline to run. She didn't think they would opt to trade their concealment for a creature comfort. But who knew?

She swallowed some water, pausing to take a breath before finishing off the water off. She felt a few drops run down her chin and smiled at the guard. "Thank you."

He frowned and walked away.

So much for making a friend, she thought. I don't think I can count on him as an ally.

She continued the struggle to get her hands around to her front, but couldn't make it work. She slumped forward, straining to stretch her back muscles. She'd already worked on keeping her legs flexible, but her arms had pretty much gone numb.

She sighed and took another deep breath. Now what? Annja closed her eyes and looked inside of herself. The sword she'd somehow inherited from Joan of Arc hung in its ready position. All she had to do was reach in and take it.

But how could she do that when her hands were cuffed?

She was still learning about the powers of the sword and what she could and couldn't do with it. Maybe I don't need my hands free in this plane to do it in that plane, she thought. Perhaps she could reach into the otherwhere and then, when she opened her eyes, the cuffs would be gone. All she had to do was see it so.

Annja saw her hands as free as she reached toward the sword.

She felt the hilt and wrapped her hands around it.

She opened her eyes.

Her hands were still cuffed behind her. The sword was nowhere to be seen.

Annja frowned. So much for that.

She knew she had to get her cuffs off before she tried to do anything at all that might spring her from this place.

The problem, she realized, was that even if she did escape, where would she go? She had no idea where she was. They'd blindfolded her until she arrived in the camp. And stumbling through the jungle wasn't the smartest thing she could do.

There had to be another way. But what?

Annja looked up. Somewhere in the camp, there seemed to be some sort of commotion. She heard more voices. They spoke loudly. Was it an argument? Annja strained to listen, but her knowledge of Tagalog was minute. And there was no way of knowing what particular dialect these terrorists were using.

The voices seemed to be getting closer. Annja sat back, trying to feign disinterest.

The guard with the big nose came into view. The AK-47 assault rifle he wore dangled from its strap on his shoulder. The gun looked large in his smallish hands, but he kept it fixed on Annja.

She wanted to smile. Like I'm any type of threat right now, she wanted to say. But she kept her mouth closed.

Big Nose knelt behind her and untied the leash binding her to the tree. He stood and gestured to Annja with his gun. "You will come with me," he said.

Annja nodded and the guard motioned back the way he'd come. Annja took a few stumbling steps, waiting for the blood to flow back down her legs. She tried flexing her arms, but the cuffs really restricted her movement.

The man led her to a large hut. As Annja walked toward it, she saw other members of the terrorist cell peering at her intently. Did they know who she was? Was this why they'd kidnapped her? Did they even get *Chasing History's Monsters* out here? And if they did, Annja would still be surprised they might know who she was. Since she didn't make a habit out of wearing skimpy clothes, her fan base was significantly smaller than her buxom cohost's.

The guard walked her up the steps of the hut. Annja's feet felt the rough-hewed wood flooring under her. It felt good to be standing again after sitting for so long. She ducked under a palm frond opening and walked inside the hut.

It was much darker inside. But a small fire kept it just shy of total darkness. The heat was worse in here and Annja instantly felt herself sweating even more than she had outside.

"What is your name?"

The voice wasn't one she'd heard before. It sounded quite cosmopolitan.

"Annja Creed," she said, looking for the source of the voice.

"Where are you from, Annja Creed?"

"Brooklyn."

Annja strained to make out any details, but she could only see that he had close-cropped hair. There was also a vague tinge of some sort of cheap cologne on the air. He'd obviously showered recently. Or maybe he'd rolled around in the cologne sample inserts that they stocked magazines with these days.

"What brings you to our country?"

"I work for a television show. One of the story ideas brought me here," she replied.

"You're a reporter?" he asked.

"Sort of."

"What does that mean?"

"I'm not with the news. It's more of a history show. Like documentaries."

"You don't have a camera crew with you?"

Annja shook her head. "I came over first to see if the story was legitimate. Only then would the camera guys come over so we could film it."

"I see."

Annja heard the rustle of papers. "We have your passport here."

"They took it from me when I was kidnapped," she said.

"Yes, and it's a shame they didn't bother to look at it. Otherwise it might have saved us both from the embarrassing situation that now confronts us."

"Embarrassing?"

"Yes. You see, my colleagues are sometimes a bit, shall we say, overzealous in their work? It's a stressful thing—I'm sure you can appreciate it. There are all sorts of logistical elements to planning a proper kidnapping. Emotions run high. People make mistakes."

"Mistakes?" Annja wondered where this was going.

"Yes. You were not our intended target, Annja Creed."

"You didn't mean to kidnap me?"

"No."

Annja smiled. "Oh well, that's cool."

"It is not…cool. It is a bad mistake," the man said calmly.

There was movement behind Annja. A guard pushed another man through the doorway. His hands were bound behind him and he was gagged. But Annja recognized him as the terrorist who had kidnapped her.

Annja looked back into the darkness. "Well, like you said, everyone makes mistakes."

"Mistakes are not tolerated in our organization. It would set a bad precedent if I allowed such behavior to fester within our ranks."

The gunshot sounded like an explosion and Annja jumped. She looked behind her and saw her kidnapper facedown on the floor, a pool of blood rapidly pooling around his head.

Annja turned back. "So, we're all through here, then? I'm free to go?" she said quickly.

"Unfortunately, no. You've seen too many things here."

Annja shook her head. "I didn't see a thing. I was blindfolded until I got here."

"Even still…"

Annja shook her head. "I have no issue with what you do

or who you do it, to. You said this was a mistake. So let's correct it. Let me go," she spoke confidently, hoping she was persuasive enough.

"No. I think you'll be able to help us out, after all," the voice said.

"Oh?"

"Indeed. But it will, most unfortunately, mean your death."

2

The guard with the big nose steered Annja out of the cloistered environment of the thatch hut and back down onto the muddy ground. He deliberately pushed her fast enough so that Annja's legs had trouble keeping up with the momentum, causing her to stumble and trip most of the way down. At last he shoved her and Annja had to turn her head at the very last minute before she crashed to the ground.

She sat up and spit out some dirt. "Thanks for the help, jerk," she muttered.

The guard grinned and took his pistol out. Annja frowned. This was not good. The guard thumbed the hammer back.

"Stop."

The guard and Annja both turned toward the veranda of the hut she'd just left. The man standing there lit a cigarette. He exhaled a thin stream of smoke into the dense jungle air and regarded Annja.

"Are you scared about dying?" he asked her.

Annja got to her knees and stared at him. "I've faced death before."

The man nodded. "I can tell. You have that look about you. My friend here doesn't intimidate you much, does he?"

Annja smiled. "Who are you?"

"My name is Agamemnon."

"You're joking, right?" Annja said.

Agamemnon grinned. "My parents. What can you do? They grew up with this fixation on Mount Olympus. They named us all after the gods and goddesses of mythology. My brother was named Midas."

"Was?" Annja asked.

"Government troops killed him while he slept. Him and his young bride. They were but twenty years old."

Annja flexed her wrists. The cuffs still held her tight. "I'm sorry for your loss. Really."

"Thank you," he said quietly.

"Is this really necessary?" Annja asked, hoping she could talk her way out of her predicament.

Agamemnon shrugged. "Is anything we do ever really necessary?"

"You tell me—you're the one in control right now."

"Yes." Agamemnon nodded. "I am indeed. And unfortunately, your death will help to convince the government we are truly serious."

"Since when have you had trouble with the government thinking you aren't serious?" Annja asked.

Agamemnon came down the steps. Annja could see he looked to be in his late thirties. His close-cropped hair was still jet-black. His eyebrows hung over his dark eyes like heavy velvet drapes. The way he walked reminded Annja of some of the more ferocious fighters she'd met in her lifetime. Agamemnon was thin, but he resonated with strength and cunning.

He stopped just short of coming into range if Annja had

decided to try to kick him. "Ever since the American troops started hunting us, the government has considered us a has-been organization," he explained.

"I didn't realize the U.S. forces had done so much damage to your organization," she said.

Agamemnon stepped on his cigarette butt and ground it under his foot. "They hunt us when they can find us. Their special-operations troops are quite skilled at navigating the jungle. Even though we know it like the back of our hand, they are quick to adapt and learn our tactics. I have lost many soldiers since they started combing the islands for us."

"And so now you've taken to kidnapping?"

Agamemnon shrugged. "We kidnap high-profile targets in the hope that our cause gets publicity, drives more recruits to us, and that the ransoms get paid. That money helps fund our operations in Manila and other places."

"I see." Annja saw that several other members of the impromptu village had come out of their huts. Agamemnon certainly seemed to hold sway over them; they seemed to be hanging on his every word.

"These are my people," he said spreading his arms as if about to hug them all. "I've led them through some harrowing incidents. They trust me completely and I do believe they would follow me straight into the depths of hell itself if need be."

"I don't doubt it," Annja said. "And I have no doubt they trust you completely. But I still don't see why you need to kill me."

"Because our intended target was not picked up. The plan cannot be canceled just because of that one simple flaw," he said.

"I won't get you any type of respect. I'm a nobody," Annja said.

Agamemnon shook his head. "Nonsense. You said it yourself—you're a television personality. I'm sure a woman as lovely as yourself has thousands of devoted fans."

"I don't think the number's that high. It's just an offbeat history show on cable."

Agamemnon frowned. "I don't follow."

Annja shook her head. "The show is a bit of a joke. No one takes it seriously," she said.

"We will videotape your beheading and then broadcast it all over the world. Your death will help us reestablish ties to our friends in other regions. It will also serve as a call for others to join us and help overthrow the government."

"Beheading?" Annja asked, horrified.

Agamemnon unsheathed a large knife hanging at his side. "Unfortunately, the world has grown desensitized to shootings. People see thousands of them on TV and in the movies. Simply shooting someone has no impact. But decapitation, well, that is something else again."

Annja swallowed hard. Having her head sliced off wasn't what she'd imagined coming to the Philippines would entail. And the thought of that knife cutting into her neck sent adrenaline flooding into her veins.

I have to get out of here, she thought. She closed her eyes and saw the sword hanging where it always did when not in use. If she could just get it and get free of her cuffs, she could cut these butchers down and then disappear into the jungle.

But where would she go?

She frowned. It didn't matter. Anything was better than staying here and waiting for her head to be lopped off.

"Annja?"

She opened her eyes. Agamemnon was staring at her intently. Annja coughed and cleared her throat. "I wasn't expecting to be killed in that fashion. You don't strike me as being that barbaric," she said angrily.

Agamemnon laughed. "Oh, but I am. Trust me."

Annja flexed her wrists. There was no give in the cuffs. If she didn't get them off, she was as good as dead. And by the sound of it, beheading wasn't exactly a quick and painless event unless done by guillotine. Being hacked off with a knife sounded extremely painful and messy.

"I need to pray," she blurted.

Agamemnon frowned. "What?"

Annja looked at him. "I need to pray. Surely you wouldn't begrudge me a final chance to make amends with my god before you kill me?"

Agamemnon lit a fresh cigarette. "Forgive me for saying so, Miss Creed, but you don't exactly strike me as the religious type. I've killed missionaries before. They walked with much more an air of God than you do."

"And you've never heard of people finding religion right before they die?" Annja said.

"I have."

"Then you should have enough respect for me—if only for what my death will represent to your cause—to grant me a few final moments of inner peace."

Agamemnon sighed. "Very well. I will give you five minutes to pray. I suggest you use it well."

Annja turned herself slightly. "I need the cuffs removed, please."

"Why?"

"My religion dictates that my hands be free when I pray. In order to make the proper signs of my god, I must have both hands free."

"What religion is this? I've never heard of such a need before."

"I'm not exactly orthodox in my religion," Annja said. "I belong to a new church that incorporates the teachings of many religions into its values," she said.

Agamemnon took a deep drag on his cigarette. He gestured to the guard. "All right, you may have your hands free. But I warn you not to try anything. My friend there will have his gun trained on you at all times. And he will shoot you if need be."

Annja bowed her head. "Thank you for the consideration."

The guard knelt behind her and Annja heard the key slip into the lock. In another moment, the pressure on her wrists vanished. Annja took a deep breath and rubbed them, trying to flush some blood and feeling back into them.

"All right. Your time starts now," Agamemnon said.

Annja brought her hands together in front of her. I have to make this look good, she thought. They'll expect me to make a move immediately if I'm going to try anything at all. So let's give them a show when they least expect it.

Annja raised her hands overhead and opened her mouth. She called out in an imaginary dialect and mixed it with a bit of Swahili slang she knew. As she did so, she moved her hands around her, gesturing first to the sky and the sun and then to the ground and the trees.

She let her head loll around as if she was possessed. She got off her knees and squatted, drawing a circle on the ground and then dancing in the center of it.

Her words grew louder. Annja felt her body responding to the sense of freedom for the first time in days. Adrenaline pumped through her veins. She felt energized and alive.

With her eyes closed, she saw the sword.

She reached for it with her hands.

Felt the hilt of the sword slide into her hands.

She instantly dropped to the ground and pivoted, slicing as she opened her eyes.

A gunshot rang out, but Annja knew that the guard would have fired above her head. She heard the bullet ricochet but

then felt her sword cut into something even as she continued
to spin.

The guard grunted as the blade bit into his midsection,
slicing him open.

Annja yanked her sword free and rushed toward Agamemnon. He looked utterly unfazed by the sudden appearance of
the sword in Annja's hands.

She was just thirty feet from the hut. Agamemnon disappeared inside.

A volley of gunfire exploded across the camp. Annja felt
hot lead zipping past her head. She ducked and zigzagged
across the compound. Agamemnon's people must have had
their weapons closer than she realized.

I have to get out of here!

Annja took a hard right and ran between two huts, the
sword leading the way. A young man stepped in her path and
aimed his AK-47 at her. Annja leaped into the air and screamed
as she came down, swinging the sword.

The man dropped dead and Annja ran on.

Ahead of her, she could see the thick jungle. She ran for
the twisted vines and warped tree trunks as if the devil himself
was on her tail.

She entered the foliage.

Under the dense canopy, the air grew even thicker. Annja
didn't think the terrorists behind her would stop. She needed
to put some real distance between them.

Annja pressed on, using the sword to cut a swath through
the dense jungle.

Suddenly she stopped. They'll track me if I keep doing
this, she thought.

She sighed. As much as she hated doing it, she closed her
eyes and returned the sword to the otherwhere.

Annja opened her eyes again and took a deep breath. From

here on out, it gets tough, she thought. I'll have to take my time and creep through this jungle if I have any hope of getting out of here alive. The more I fight it, the quicker it will win.

Annja parted a blanket of vines in front of her, carefully moving them out of the way just enough for her to get past. Once she did so, she turned and slid them back into position.

She hoped her pursuers would think she had magically disappeared.

Annja looked overhead and all around. The color was the same anywhere she turned. Green.

How in the world am I going to get out of this mess?

3

Agamemnon watched as his men scampered about the camp collecting themselves and their weapons. The carcass of his man lay in the dirt, staining the ground with dark blood and gore. The air stunk of his death and it only made the rage growing in Agamemnon's chest swell even further. Already hundreds of tiny flies and mosquitoes fed upon the corpse.

One of his men noticed the sudden invasion of bugs and came over. "Shall we dispose of Jojo's body?"

Agamemnon watched as the flies seemed to form one undulating mass as they crawled over Jojo's body, eagerly feeding. He watched for another full minute and then finally shook his head.

"Leave it."

"Sir?"

Agamemnon faced him. "I want him left where he died. Let the bugs eat him for all I care. His death is an object lesson to you all. You can never, ever let your guard down. Not for one instant. If you do, the same will happen to you."

His man blanched. "I understand, sir."

"Do you think that is cruel of me?"

The man's eyes never met Agamemnon's. He was far too scared to look his boss in the eyes. "I understand your intentions, sir."

"Further," Agamemnon continued, "if your search parties do not come back with the woman, then all who failed will meet the same fate as Jojo. Am I making myself perfectly clear? I will not tolerate failure."

"Yes, sir." The man jerked his hand up in salute and then excused himself.

Agamemnon watched him run away, corralling the other men who would assist him in the search. He could hear the hushed tones they used as they discussed the urgency of the mission before them. Of course, Agamemnon wouldn't kill them all. That would be foolish of him. There was little sense killing his own troops. But with the image of Jojo's body still so fresh in their heads, he knew the threat of another death would make his men work harder. It would drive them to turn the jungle upside down.

And then they would find Annja Creed and bring her back to the camp, where Agamemnon could dispose of her properly. After all, her death would play a key role in the events that were about to unfold in Manila.

Agamemnon smiled and turned away from the corpse. He wandered over to his hut. At the steps leading inside, he paused and watched the various search parties fanning out to enter the jungle.

Good luck, he thought to himself.

Inside, he sat down at the small radio console and opened up the channel. A screech of static punctured the humid air, and then he heard the voice he wanted on the other end.

"Yes, sir?"

Agamemnon leaned into the microphone. "Is everything ready, Luis?"

"The package has been delivered as promised. We are in the final stages of preparing it for delivery now."

"Excellent. And how long do you anticipate it taking?"

"Perhaps the rest of the night. If all goes well, we will leave with it tomorrow morning and have it in position the following day."

Agamemnon smiled. Luis was his most trusted man. If he set a task before him, he knew Luis would always get it done. Unlike Jojo, Luis would not have let himself be taken so easily.

He leaned back and took a breath. Who would have ever expected that the son of a beggar could have risen so far as Agamemnon had? Certainly not the worthless souls who called themselves his family. They'd forsaken him years ago when he'd revealed his plans to them. The idiots—they were content to stay in the slums he'd grown up in, scavenging a meager existence while the wealthy aristocrats and new entrepreneurs drove past them, oblivious to the children running barefoot in the late night traffic hoping to beg a few coins off of them.

The inequity of the classes had drawn Agamemnon to the promise of change that a revolution offered. And Abu Sayyaf seemed just the organization to grant this chance at making things better.

The problem, as it always seemed to be, was that no one in the upper class would listen to rhetoric. All the protests and words would never make them open their eyes and see the hell that the majority of the population lived in on a daily basis.

Something bigger had to be done. And Abu Sayyaf made the people listen with its bombings and violence. A body count guaranteed news coverage. And it made the people in power pay attention.

Now Agamemnon stood poised on the brink of his biggest accomplishment to date. There was just one final little bump to deal with—the American woman.

Once that was done, everything else would fall right in line and Abu Sayyaf would bring the government of the Philippines to its knees. When it was over, a new power paradigm would rule in its place.

And Agamemnon would be the grand architect of the entire operation.

"You're a good man, Luis. I know we will enjoy success soon," he said.

"Inshallah."

God willing indeed. Agamemnon smiled. In order to gain influence over the men of Abu Sayyaf, Agamemnon had, of course, played on their religious fervor. He knew how it remained one of the most potent methods for controlling the masses. Men stirred into a religious zealotry would do anything if they thought their god demanded it. And radical Islamic fundamentalism seemed a perfect way to accomplish his goals. There were already plenty of examples throughout the Middle East that helped Agamemnon justify certain violent tendencies.

And while he knew true Islam was a religion of peace, Agamemnon had found that any religion could be twisted to the machinations of a man in charge. After all, born-again Christians and fundamentalist Baptists were given to extremes as horrifying as anything al Qaeda had engaged in.

Agamemnon took a breath and then keyed the microphone again. "I have just sent half of my force into the jungle."

"What for?" Luis asked.

"We had an escape."

"The American girl?"

"Yes. She was something more than we expected. Jojo is dead."

There was a pause over the air. Luis had always viewed Jojo as something of a student to be mentored. Agamemnon worried he might take his death hard.

"How?"

"She cut him in half with a sword."

"A sword?"

"I have no idea where she was able to obtain it. One minute she was praying, and the next, she'd cut Jojo in half," Agamemnon said.

"I don't understand where she could have gotten a sword."

"I don't, either. But rest assured when we find her—and the men will find her—I will make her tell me everything."

The radio squawked again. "Agamemnon?"

"Yes?"

"When it is time to kill her, I want to be the one to do it," Luis said.

Agamemnon smiled. Revenge was something that Luis always took as a matter of personal pride. He keyed the microphone. "She will be yours, my friend."

"Excellent. I will inform my men to post additional sentries around our camp, in the event that she happens to wander right into our welcoming arms."

The other camp was situated ten miles away from Agamemnon's location. By splitting their resources and locations, they believed it afforded them better security. And with the American military now actively engaged in hunting down Abu Sayyaf camps, such precautions ruled the day.

"Be careful with your preparations, Luis. Any misstep—"

He heard Luis chuckle through the static. "If there are any

mistakes, I think it will be readily evident to you, Agamemnon. You won't need me to call you on the radio, that's for sure."

"I suppose not."

"I must go now. There's much to be done before we launch this upon the godless infidels."

Agamemnon keyed the microphone a final time. "Good luck to you, Luis. And to the men you choose to go with you."

"I need only the grace of God to help us find our way. Then we will deal them all a blow from which they will never recover."

Agamemnon turned off the radio and leaned back in his chair. Luis would accomplish his mission, no doubt. But there would be casualties when they launched their mission. Such losses were to be expected. In this fight, there was no such thing as a bloodless battle.

The only thing that still bothered him about the operation was the loose thread of Annja Creed. He hadn't had time to think about it until he'd mentioned it to Luis, but where on earth had she gotten the sword?

It was as if the thing had appeared magically in her hands.

Agamemnon frowned. It was my fault for agreeing to uncuff her. I should have had Jojo kill her instead of granting her a moment to be with her god. Then again, not granting her the freedom to pray one final time might have been misconstrued by his people that he saw religion as frivolous.

No, he had done what he had to do. Unfortunately, Jojo paid the price for it.

No bloodless battles, he thought.

One thing was certain, however—when he recaptured Annja Creed, Luis would make sure that all the magic in the world wouldn't be enough to help her. Agamemnon had, after all, witnessed Luis's savagery. It was one of the things that had attracted him to the young man in the first place. Luis had a killer's cold, calculating capacity for extreme violence combined with a reasonably sharp intellect.

He wasn't as smart as Agamemnon, but then, that was the point.

Agamemnon didn't need someone smarter than him around. That would have been foolhardy on his part. He needed men with courage and the ability to kill without regret. He needed women who cared little for the pleas of their victims as they detonated bombs and sprayed bullets in crowded shopping malls.

So far, Agamemnon had been fortunate enough to attract the people he needed.

But losing Jojo would be a blow to morale around the camp.

He sighed. Later on, when the search teams returned with the American woman, Agamemnon would see to it that everyone was properly rewarded. A party of sorts would be in order.

He nodded. He would send some of the women to the nearby village to secure some pigs for roasting. There was nothing like a feast to make his people forget a tragedy.

Combined with the success of their planned operation, Agamemnon felt certain that any lingering sadness over Jojo's death would evaporate in the joyous triumph they would all experience.

Perhaps he would have Luis bring his men over to the party. Luis had a young girl in his camp that Agamemnon hadn't yet taken the time to properly indoctrinate into the more delicate ways of being a revolutionary. After all, the sweet thing would need to understand how the needs of her leader always had to be met in order for the revolution to grow stronger.

He grinned. The island girls were always so much easier to deflower than their counterparts in the big cities. They could be readily persuaded with a bit of extra food and wine.

He felt a swelling in his pants and smiled. Rank, it was very true, had some very distinct privileges.

All I need is for tomorrow to go off well. And for my men to find Annja Creed.

Agamemnon stood and walked out of the hut. Daylight was already starting to fade. Night would soon blanket the camp.

He waved over one of the few men left in camp. "See to it that Jojo's body is prepared for burial. If we leave it too long, he will only attract predators."

The man saluted and ran to find help. Agamemnon watched the flies buzz away from the carcass as a woman approached, waving a broom at the body.

His people, he knew, had learned the lesson.

All around him, people came out of their huts and approached Jojo's body with a degree of reverence. They would see to it that he was buried in the ground beyond the camp.

Later, when the American woman was dragged back into the camp, Agamemnon would allow them to vent their frustrations on her.

Then, and only then, would he allow Luis to kill her.

4

A special-operations commando had once told Annja that the biggest problem in the jungle was disorientation. She now understood why. It was entirely possible to have no sense of direction. Looking out five yards in front of her, Annja couldn't see much. The green-tinged semidarkness surrounded her, giving her a vague sense of claustrophobia.

Already, under the canopy, she felt the jungle's shadowy onslaught starting. Small bugs nibbled at the exposed bits of her skin. The humidity must have soared to over ninety percent. Her clothes were all wet and clung to her like a second skin.

She took a deep breath. Somewhere behind her, she could hear people shouting.

They were looking for her.

Annja knew the direction she'd run into the jungle. She picked out a landmark in front of her roughly fifty feet away. A tall tree arcing up toward the inevitably green sky. Annja maneuvered her way to the tree and stopped when she got there.

She was desperately out of breath, not necessarily due to

the exertion. After all, Annja was in excellent shape. But stalking through the dense undergrowth while breathing air that seemed more like soup than anything else taxed her like nothing she'd done before.

At the tree, Annja picked out another landmark to aim for and then started off toward the clump of vines that stretched high into the treetops.

Behind her, she could hear more noises. The telltale clang as a machete cleaved its way through the greenery.

I need to find a place to hide, Annja thought. And then I need water. Lots of water.

Already she could feel the beginning stages of dehydration coming over her. In the jungle, with her body temperature rising and sweat dripping off of her, she would need a constant supply of water to replace what she was losing. Otherwise, her vision would fade and her body would start to shut down. It already felt as if her skin temperature was higher than the air temperature. Worse, her sweat wasn't evaporating.

She knew she was on a steep downward spiral.

Annja spotted what looked like a red buttress tree farther off in the distance and struck out for that. Scores of thick vines wrapped their way up the trunk like giant snakes. Annja grabbed the vines and pulled herself up the trunk. If she could get off the jungle floor and into the tree, she might be able to wait out her pursuers. With luck, they might walk right past her.

Annja scrambled up the trunk, feeling her feet dig into the vines. Bits of leaves and bark broke off and flittered to the jungle floor beneath her. She hoped it wasn't enough of a sign to indicate to a tracker where she was.

She finally managed to get herself into the nook of the tree where its lower branches forked off in a variety of directions. She found a pile of reasonably dry leaves nestled in the hollow and settled herself down against them, sucking in air.

I need water, she thought.

Annja looked at the round vines wrapping their way up the tree and wondered if they might be tube vines. They were round rather than ribbon flat. That was a good sign.

She closed her eyes and reached for her sword. When she opened her eyes, the blade was in her hands and Annja reached farther up the trunk and cut one of the vines.

Here goes nothing, she thought.

She held the cut vine over her mouth and almost instantly, a stream of water flowed out of the vine. Annja took a mouthful and despite the mossy taste, she thought it was delicious.

She gulped as much as she could. The effect seemed instantaneous. Her vision cleared and she felt better. She took as much water as she could and then slumped back into the hollow.

The sounds of her pursuers grew closer.

She could hear them now, their Tagalog dialect unfamiliar to her, but she could tell by the tone that they meant business. They sounded furious that she had escaped.

Annja risked looking out of her improvised shelter and down on the ground. Several batches of leaves obscured her view, which made her feel somewhat more secure. If she had a hard time seeing them, they would have a hard time seeing her.

Two men in green fatigues and backpacks scoured the ground. A third held back. All three were armed with AK-47s and pistols.

They seemed to be stopping every few feet, checking the ground and then continuing along.

They're looking for ground sign, Annja thought. If she hadn't been careful enough, they would see where she'd left the ground and climbed into the trees. She found herself praying that they weren't used to this jungle any more than she was.

She heard another clang as the lead scout moved away

from her tree, hacking into a fresh batch of jungle. The two other men followed, still chattering away to themselves.

Annja sighed. She was safe.

At least for the time being.

But where was Agamemnon? He didn't seem the type to give up so easily. And Annja knew that he was probably insulted that she had managed to escape. She wasn't sure if Filipino men were like Latin men, who took such things as an affront to their masculinity. They'd pursue Annja even if every bit of reason demanded otherwise.

Annja licked her lips.

More bugs buzzed in her ears. The mosquitoes would be terrible tonight unless she figured out how to ward them off. She wasn't exactly prepared with a good medical kit full of antimalarial medicine.

She scampered around her tree and tried to look off into the distance. If she could get a bearing for some area that was clear and out of the jungle, she'd be on her way back to civilization.

She looked off in all directions, but could see utterly nothing.

Damn.

Annja slumped back into her hiding spot and took stock of her situation. Soon enough, it would be night. She'd need a shelter. In the jungle, there are always two rains a day and she was overdue.

Combined with the heat and the bugs, Annja knew she was in for a rough night if she couldn't find a way to make herself more comfortable.

A fire would keep the bugs away, but it would also alert her pursuers to her presence. She couldn't take a chance that they would track her. If they brought Annja back to the camp, she had no doubt that Agamemnon would give her no quarter. She'd be killed immediately.

Annja made her way out of the nook in the tree and slid

down the vines to the jungle floor. She summoned her sword
and cut two more lengths of vines, this time letting one of
them pour its water into the ground, making it muddy.

Then she knelt and kneaded the dirt into a pasty black mud
that she used to smear all over her skin. She started with her
face and neck and hair, caking on the dirt until she felt sure
she'd covered herself well.

Annja worked her way up and down her arms and legs,
smearing any part of her exposed skin and working the mud
into any areas that might come uncovered. Then she worked
the mud all over her clothes.

When she was done, Annja found a fresh patch of ground
covered in leafy debris. She lay down and rolled back and
forth several times, working all manner of dead leaves, bits
of vines and twigs into her makeshift camouflage.

Annja stood back up and tried to imagine how she looked.
Most likely she probably resembled some bizarre swamp
creature. But if she was going to get out of this situation
alive, she had to ignore her desire to be clean. She had to give
herself over to her primal self, rely on her instincts and keep
one step ahead of her pursuers.

She knelt back by the buttress tree and cut more vines.
Annja drank down as much water as she could. She'd move
on quickly, so she wasn't particularly concerned about leaving
signs. Anyone with half a brain would be able to see that
someone had been active in this immediate area. A few more
cut vines wouldn't compromise her any more than her camou-
flaging activity would.

But now where?

Annja stayed low to the ground. She could follow the men
chasing her; they were leaving enough of a trail to do so. But if
she did that, there was a chance she would walk into an ambush.

Her better option was to strike out on her own, in a direction that took her away from the terrorist camp and away from her pursuers.

Left or right? she wondered.

Annja closed her eyes and checked each direction against her gut instinct. She opened her eyes and frowned. Neither direction had produced the sense of relief that normally told her she was on the right track.

It was going to have to be a pure guess.

Right it is, she decided.

She moved off, keeping herself in a stealthy crouch that she knew would tax her quadriceps but would keep her profile low. The last thing she wanted was to present an easy target someone could take a shot at if she was heard.

With her sword stowed safely away, Annja took her time moving vines and branches out of the way. She ran into scores of thick spiderwebs, each with a very annoyed owner. Annja hadn't read up enough on the tropical varieties of spiders, but didn't want to start thinking about how many poisonous creatures scampered all around her.

Just keep moving, she told herself. Eventually, she would find her way out.

She hoped.

A sudden burst of high-pitched, purring bleeps surrounded her. For a moment, Annja froze, halfway to closing her eyes and calling the sword back out.

Then she smiled with recognition. Her friend from England had called them "basher-out beetles." It was the jungle's way of announcing that it would be nighttime soon enough.

She heard a rumble overhead.

A steady deluge erupted and streamed down through the canopy, soaking her and causing a good deal of her camouflage to drip off. Annja opened her mouth and caught a few mouthfuls of rainwater.

The good thing was that at least her pursuers would have to endure the jungle just as much as she did.

Annja found her way to another tree and maneuvered her way up into the thick branches. As the rain continued to drum down from the heavens, she cut a few vines and sucked them dry. Then she tried weaving them into a makeshift cover for herself.

When she was done, she positioned it over her head.

It wasn't great, she decided, but it did keep some of the rain off her.

Annja nestled herself into the trunk and leaned her head against the wet bark. She could smell more things than she'd ever smelled before. It was as if someone had cranked up her olfactory sense to eleven. She could smell the leaves, the trees, the dirt and the bugs; virtually everything around her had a scent that was at once peculiar and familiar.

The rain stopped as suddenly as it had begun, like someone turning off a faucet.

Already twilight was giving way to pitch darkness.

Annja felt relieved that she was at least off of the ground. Her friend in British special forces had once told her that staying off the floor in the jungle was paramount to surviving. At night, the jungle floor became a superhighway for every insect, rodent, reptile and creature that made its home in the jungle.

If Annja stayed on the ground, she would be bitten by thousands of things that she'd be better off avoiding.

The best shelter she could take was up in the trees.

She wondered if there were pumas in the jungles of the Philippines. She didn't think so. Or, at least, she hoped there weren't.

But what about snakes?

Annja worked her way around until her back was settled comfortably in the crook of the tree. I can't think about that now, she decided. I just have to try to endure this for as long as it takes for me to get out of here alive.

And when she did, she'd make it her business to tell everyone about Agamemnon and his merry band of terrorist scumbags.

5

Annja awoke to gunfire. A single shot at first. Then she counted off a series of semiautomatic shots followed by intermittent automatic gun blasts. From the sound of it, there was a bit of a pitched battle going on some distance away.

Annja peered out into the darkness, which seemed as thick as the air itself. All around her, the jungle croaked, buzzed and whined with the calls of animals out on their nocturnal forays. Annja's muddy mosquito repellent seemed to have done its job at least somewhat. There were still squadrons of buzzing mosquitoes about her head, but they didn't seem able to penetrate the thick cover of her muddy hair.

At least there's a chance I won't get malaria, she thought with a grin.

The gunfire stopped. But the animals of the jungle simply carried on. Annja frowned. They should have quieted as soon as the bullets started flying, but they didn't. That meant they must be used to the violence that sometimes erupted in this part of the Philippines.

Wherever this part was, exactly.

Annja stretched and tried to work a kink out of her back. It was going to be tough finding any degree of comfort in a place like this. She closed her eyes and imagined what it would feel like to sink into a tub of hot steamy bubbles, lounging for hours until every one of her pores had given up the very last remnants of the jungle mud and grime.

She almost moaned but stopped herself. The jungle around her might still contain a few surprises. For all she knew, Agamemnon might have told his men to fire their guns in the hope Annja would run in the opposite direction. Right into his waiting arms.

Fat chance, jack, she thought. She'd been around the block a few times and knew how things worked. And she was most definitely not interested in the prospect of losing her head to some megalomaniac.

She relaxed her breathing and her muscles. She knew she needed a lot of rest if she was going to try to get out of here in the morning. Her plan was simple. She'd get up at first light and cover as much ground as possible.

If she could find a small river, she'd follow it downstream until it merged with a bigger river and then that would eventually run right out to the ocean. It was survival 101. Once she got to the coast, she'd be able to find someone who could help her.

She hoped.

The problem with Abu Sayyaf was that they had a lot of local support in the poorer areas of the Philippines. Many of the local villages and towns would readily give them money and supplies to help their cause.

That meant Annja might find herself being handed right back to Agamemnon.

She'd have to proceed carefully.

Still, her plan seemed sound. Find the water and follow it. Simple and easy. But she wasn't stupid. She knew there was a good chance that Agamemnon would position a lot of his men along the riverbanks in the hopes that Annja would do exactly that.

But what choice do I have? she wondered. There's no way I'll find my way out of here unless I use the water.

With that in mind, she felt herself drift off into a light sleep. She woke every hour or so, shifted position and then dozed off again, only to awaken roughly hours later when it was still quite dark.

"Ugh."

She sighed and shifted position. For some reason, she felt uneasy. More so than she had when she'd first run into the jungle.

She peered over the edge of the tree and searched the darkness. There was little ambient light to use, so Annja couldn't make out very much detail with her eyes, even when she peered at things using her peripheral vision.

But she could sense something moving in the darkness, something that didn't seem so much dangerous as simply out of place with the flow of the jungle around them. The animals seemed to have taken little notice of it and continued buzzing and chirping and clicking their way through the night.

But Annja felt it.

She heard a vague rustle off to her left somewhere. It seemed a microsecond out of the timing of the rest of the noises, as if someone had jumped their cue to move.

She was sure it had to be a person.

But was it one of Agamemnon's men? Or someone else?

Annja frowned. Who would go wandering around the jungle this late at night? Especially one as dangerous as this?

The sound of gunfire would certainly travel for miles, and surely, the local villagers knew enough to stay clear of the jungle if they wanted to stay on Agamemnon's good side.

Another rustle sounded closer to her. Whatever it was, it was definitely moving toward her location.

Annja closed her eyes and saw the sword hovering just in case she needed it. But even as Annja felt the glow of its security, she knew she wouldn't need it for this particular situation.

She had the distinct impression that whoever was moving through the undergrowth below her was friendly.

Or at the very least, an ally.

Annja shifted her position so she could see over the edge of the tree. Her body seemed to know the direction the person must have been taking. Annja leaned farther out of the edge of the tree, her fingers slowly walking toward the last outcropping of branches.

Suddenly she found herself leaning too far, felt her weight shift on the wet vines and her balance vanish as she toppled out of the tree.

Annja tried to pivot in midair, but knew she wasn't high enough to pull off the move. She felt the rush of air—briefly—and then the dull hard thud of impact along her back.

The wind rushed out of her lungs and Annja lay there a moment, stunned.

She tried to sit up, but felt a piece of metal jammed under her chin. A harsh voice broke the night air.

"Don't move."

Annja froze. "I'm no threat to you," she said calmly.

She looked up and saw a vague outline, like a giant blob of leaves and branches, hovering over her. The gun barrel that was aimed at her looked real enough, even in the darkness.

"Who are you?" the man asked.

Annja eased herself up, trying to breathe her way through the pain that shot up and down her spine. She didn't think anything was broken, but she'd be feeling those bruises for a while. Luckily, she seemed to have landed in thick leaf litter.

"My name is Annja Creed. The Abu Sayyaf kidnapped me several days ago. I have no idea where I am."

The gun barrel didn't move. "Kidnapped?"

"That's right."

"I didn't hear anything about a kidnapping."

Annja frowned. "Great. So much for the cavalry coming to my rescue."

The shape shifted. "Doesn't seem like you need them that much right now anyway. You obviously escaped."

"The camp, yeah. But I have no way of getting out of here," she said.

The gun barrel lowered. "You look okay. Seems like you've been getting enough water."

"Tube vines," Annja said.

"Good choice. And your camo looks pretty good. You look like a cousin of Bigfoot."

Annja smirked. "I won't win any beauty contests this way, but it keeps the mosquitoes off of me. At least temporarily."

"Who taught you how to survive in the jungle?"

Annja shrugged. "I've had some friends in the military over the years. I picked up bits and pieces of what they used to talk about."

"Well, it's kept you alive, that's for sure."

Annja looked at the mass before her. "What about you?"

"What about me?"

"You just passing through these parts?"

There was a low chuckle. One of the shape's hands reached up and slid back part of the mess that covered him. Annja could just make out the heavily camouflaged face that emerged from under a thick suit of burlap, grease paint, grass and leaves.

"Gunnery Sergeant Vic Gutierrez, United States Marine Corps. At your service."

Annja pointed at his outfit. "You sure know how to dress for a party, Sergeant."

"This here would be my Ghillie suit, ma'am. And it does a wonder keeping the bad guys from finding me."

Annja looked out into the jungle. "Were you the cause of all that gunfire I heard a short time back?"

"Guilty as charged. They seemed a bit upset that I shot one of their superiors."

"Not a guy named Agamemnon, by any chance, was it?" Annja asked.

The soldier shook his head. "I wish. He's my primary target on this op, but I haven't seen him yet."

"Well, when you do, please be sure to give him my regards, would you?"

"Sure thing. He a friend of yours?"

"Best buddy, actually. So much so he wants to cut my head off."

The soldier shook his head. "Sick bastard. We've had him on the radar for some time now, but only just got the green light to come in and take him out."

"So you're with special operations?" Annja asked.

He nodded. "A couple of us got assigned to do some deep jungle penetrations. Solo ops. No spotters, no backup. Just a man and his rifle alone in the jungle. The belief was no one would ever expect us to go in alone. Hell, I don't even have a radio with me. Just a couple of exfiltration times. I miss one, they come back two more times. I miss those, they presume me dead."

Annja blinked. "That's exactly the kind of assignment I'd expect most men to jump for."

He smiled. "Well, I don't exactly have the kind of workday that most men would pick for themselves. There ain't a lot holding me to this life, if you get my drift. This thing seemed like the perfect chance to get alone with my thoughts while I did some valuable trash removal for the country."

"Interesting euphemism."

"Ma'am?"

"'Trash removal.' And please call me Annja. You keep saying 'ma'am,' and it makes me feel old."

"In that case, just call me Vic."

Annja nodded. "You have any food there, Vic? I'm starving."

He nodded. "Sure do. But first, I want to get us out of here. I have the feeling they might start combing this part of the jungle for me soon. They seemed pretty determined back there."

"How did you get away?"

Vic smiled. "Part of the training, Annja. And with this Ghillie suit, I can slip away into the darkness pretty easily. I'm surprised you heard me coming."

"I didn't so much hear you…"

"Felt it, huh?"

Annja nodded. "Yeah, actually."

Vic grinned. "Don't look so surprised. Sometimes out here, a feeling's all you've got. And plenty of us know that if you don't trust your instincts, you'll end up dead."

Vic held out his hand and Annja grabbed it. He pulled her to her feet. "You okay? That was quite a fall you took out of that tree."

"I'm all right," she said.

Vic looked her up and down. "Yeah, I suppose you are."

Annja smiled. "So, where to now?"

Vic pointed. "I've got a hidey hole two klicks east of here."

"Is it safe?" Annja asked.

Vic looked around. "Well, 'safe' is a bit of a variable around these parts, but it's about as safe as you can get. And once we're there, we can eat, get some more water and then work on how we're going to get you out of here."

Annja smiled. "Now that sounds like a plan."

6

Agamemnon crouched over the radio, listening to the chaos on the other end crackle out through his speakers. His heart hammered in his chest and he felt as if someone had just kicked him square in the crotch.

He keyed the microphone. "Are you absolutely sure?"

"Yes, sir."

"There's nothing that could be done?"

There was a pause and the delay caused Agamemnon to stab the key button again. "Answer me, dammit!"

"I'm sorry, sir. The doctor did the best he could, but the bullet entered his head right between the eyes and just dropped him. There was no exit wound. According to the doctor, the round must have tumbled around inside his head, killing him instantly."

Agamemnon slumped back into the swivel chair. The old rusted springs creaked in protest. Agamemnon felt the air surge out of him, leaving him deflated.

Luis was dead.

I just spoke with him a short time ago, he thought. Everything was set for tomorrow. Everything they'd worked so hard to achieve. Now, it was all evaporating right in front of him.

He leaned forward and keyed the microphone again. "Who did it?"

"We don't know. The shot came from the jungle. Possibly, it was a sniper. That's what we think it was."

"You have men out there now looking for him?"

"No."

Agamemnon frowned. "Why on earth not?"

"It's night, sir. Our men would never find him in the dark. Worse, they might get lost and we'd have to send out more men. Plus, we weren't sure what you would want us to do given the scope of our operation tomorrow."

Agamemnon chewed his lip. "Send out a squad of your best and most experienced men. I want the sniper found. And I want him dead," he ordered.

"And tomorrow?"

"Everything is on hold until we can determine if this killing was due to a leak of our plans to the enemy. If it was, then we'd be fools to go through with it right now. We could be walking into an ambush. And I don't intend to lose the one thing that can level the playing field."

"Yes, sir."

"Report back when you have the sniper's body."

"Very good, sir."

"But before you kill him…"

"Yes?"

"I want him tortured. I want to know who he is and why he was assigned to kill Luis. We need to know the extent of what our enemies know about our plans. If they know anything at all."

"I understand, sir."

Agamemnon was about to disconnect when he thought

better of it and keyed the microphone again. "What's your name?"

"Eduardo, sir."

"Good." He switched off the microphone.

The connection broken, Agamemnon slumped back in the chair again. He supposed being a leader meant somehow managing to keep his people focused even in the face of adversity like this.

But losing Luis was a tough blow. Agamemnon, as much as he manipulated his people for his own purposes, still had a great deal of respect and trust for Luis. He'd kept him close, entrusting him with tomorrow's operation.

Now he would have to find a suitable replacement.

And soon.

A loss, even a small one like Luis, had to be filled or else his people would think Agamemnon had lost his edge, his ability to function in the face of a crushing loss.

We'll see how well Eduardo does with his quest for the sniper. Perhaps if he is successful with that task, then he might make a suitable replacement for Luis. He'd already shown prudence by not sending out his entire force to get the sniper. He had to have something kicking around in his skull. Most people would have panicked and emptied the camp.

Eduardo at the very least seemed to understand the greater good.

He studied the map of this area of Mindanao. The jungle grew thick and impenetrable around these parts, which was why Agamemnon had chosen it as their base of operations. Most of his people had grown up in the area and knew the jungle well.

A thought occurred to him then. Perhaps the sniper was the American woman he'd almost killed earlier.

"That's impossible," he said aloud.

She would have had to kill one of his men and gotten their weapon. And then she would have had to cross the jungle to the other camp, get herself into position and then figure out a good kill shot on Luis.

Agamemnon shook his head. There was no way she could have done that. Annja Creed wanted nothing more than to get out of the jungle and find her way home with her head still intact.

No, the sniper was someone else.

He sighed. He knew that the American military had sent a lot of its special-operations commandos into the Philippines, ostensibly to help an ally, but also to hunt down al Qaeda operatives. And Abu Sayyaf, with its feelers extended to other radical Islamic fundamentalist groups, was a logical target choice for the roving Yankees.

Perhaps one of their famed snipers was on the prowl now in Agamemnon's jungle.

He took a drink of the water in front of him and then replaced his glass. He would have to find out who was causing this disturbance.

The timing couldn't have been worse. Tomorrow was supposed to mark the greatest event in Abu Sayyaf's tortured history. Tomorrow they would have unleashed hell on the government scum that ran the country. The masses would have woken up out of their poverty-induced slumber, risen up and overthrown the fat cats who had their fingers in everything.

No more.

Agamemnon rose from his chair. The pause in the operation would be temporary. Just long enough for Eduardo to find the sniper. Once he did that, Agamemnon had little doubt that his potential Luis-replacement would exact great pain and suffering in his quest to find out all the sniper knew.

Not that Agamemnon expected to learn all that much. He was a realist, after all, at least in some matters. He knew the soldiers in the field generally had little knowledge beyond what their assignments were. If Luis had been the target, then the sniper may not know the reason why, just that he had to be killed.

Still, he would not discourage Eduardo from attempting to find out more than that. Agamemnon knew that Luis had been loved and respected by his men. They would feel his loss hard.

And they'd want revenge.

Agamemnon stabbed his finger into the jungle map. "I hope wherever you are, you are well hidden."

The curtains by the entrance to his hut suddenly parted. One of his men entered the hut, sweat covering his face. Agamemnon could see the dark stains around his uniform. He'd clearly exhausted himself.

"Report."

The man tried to come to attention, but could barely manage it. "Sir."

"Did you find her?"

"No, sir."

Agamemnon frowned. "Did you find anything?"

"Tracks. She'd hidden in a tree. She seems to have a working knowledge of the jungle."

"What in the world does that mean?"

The soldier coughed, but somehow maintained his composure. "We found tube vines. Cut. She knows how to get water."

Agamemnon shrugged. "So she knows how to stay hydrated. That doesn't concern me. And you've hunted enough people in the jungle to know they don't always last that long. Even if they get a promising start."

"Yes, sir."

"Your men have all returned?"

"We needed more supplies, sir. In order to hunt her properly, we had to come back."

Agamemnon quelled his displeasure. The rush to get them into the jungle earlier had been too impulsive. He looked at the soldier and then offered him the remaining water in his glass.

"Drink it, and then go get yourself cleaned up."

The soldier gulped down the water. "Thank you, sir."

"Get your men squared away. Food and baths and then get some sleep. I want you back out there first thing in the morning. And this time, I don't expect you to come back unless you have the body of the American woman with you. Do I make myself perfectly clear?"

"Yes, sir."

"Then go now. Rest well."

The soldier turned and exited the hut. Agamemnon walked to the red plaid recliner he'd had brought into the camp some months ago. The cloth fabric was already beginning to deteriorate in the intense humidity of the jungle air, but Agamemnon loved it anyway. The Americans made the most comfortable furniture.

He kicked his feet up and felt the footstool come up under them.

Today had not gone well.

And certainly, tomorrow was now compromised.

He took a deep breath and calmed himself. He could feel his heart slow as he inhaled and exhaled in slow, steady time.

A slight breeze washed over him and he cracked his eyes. Marta, his personal assistant, stood before him.

"Sir?"

"What is it?"

"You've missed dinner. Would you like me to bring you a plate of something?"

"Is there any adobo left?"

She smiled. Even at her advanced age, Marta could cook

circles around most of the chefs in Manila. "I think I might have saved some for you. Just in case."

Agamemnon closed his eyes. "You're too good to me, Marta. And I sometimes wonder why you choose to stay here. You could live a luxurious life anywhere you wanted with your kitchen skills."

"You are a great man. And I have chosen my place well," she said.

"Very well, then. I would love some of your adobo."

"Yes, sir."

But she didn't leave. Agamemnon opened his eyes again. "Is there something else?"

She smiled. "It's just I thought you might like something after dinner, as well."

"After dinner?"

"Yes, sir."

"What did you have in mind?"

Marta turned and with her withered hands, clapped twice. The curtains parted again as two young girls entered the hut.

Agamemnon could see them trembling. They didn't look much older than sixteen, and their light skin marked them as coming from the north. Perhaps from the cities. He could see a few light bruises from where they'd been roughed up by their handlers.

"Where are they from?"

"Bagiuo."

Agamemnon smiled. "They're a long way from home."

"They are the daughters of a spoiled landowner."

Agamemnon grinned. "Careful, Marta. You betray your past with statements like that."

She bowed her head. "Forgive me, sir."

Agamemnon waved the girls over. They walked tentatively toward him. "They've been trained well," Agamemnon said.

Marta nodded. "They know their place."

"And what is expected of them?"

Marta nodded. "Without question."

Agamemnon smiled and waved Marta out of the hut. "Perhaps I'll have my dessert first tonight."

7

Annja had trouble following Vic through the jungle. He seemed to move like a ghost, intuitively knowing where the biggest tangles of vines were and how to get past them without disturbing anything. And while he carried a fair amount of equipment, he made almost no noise as he moved. In contrast, the night jungle was full of all sorts of animal noises. Annja found herself constantly swatting away the squadrons of mosquitoes that could apparently sense her mud shield was wearing away.

Only after they'd traveled a mile or so from Annja's hiding spot in the tree did Vic signal for a water break. He handed his canteen to Annja, who eagerly gulped down the foul-tasting water.

Vic noticed the look on her face and smiled. "The sterilization tablets still don't do a thing for the taste, but I can't be picky about it. As long as it keeps me hydrated and all."

Annja tried to grin. "I've heard there are better devices on the market now."

"Sure, but you have to take time to use them. I don't have time. So I fill up, drop two tabs into the water, and then my movement alone mixes them up and by the time I stop, I can just go ahead and drink."

"I suppose," Annja said.

He took the canteen and helped himself to a long swig. "In my line of work, the less time spent on the smaller stuff is more time spent on completing my mission."

"What was your mission?" Annja asked.

He wiped his mouth on his sleeve and shook his head. "That's classified."

"You obviously killed someone," she said.

He looked at her. "You think?"

Now it was Annja's turn to grin. "You're a lone sniper in the jungles of the Philippines. And knowing what I now know about this godforsaken area, this is a hotbed of Abu Sayyaf activity."

"I could be out on a training assignment."

"Right," Annja said. "And you accidentally shot someone."

Vic looked off into the jungle. "We should keep moving. It'll be light in another hour or so. I want us bedded down and concealed prior to dawn. That's when they'll come looking for us."

"You really think so?"

He nodded. "They can't find anything right now. Night in the jungle isn't the best time to be out in the bush. No, they're back sleeping now. Resting. Tomorrow, in the full heat of the day, they'll be out. And they'll be hunting us with a gusto."

"Because of who you killed?" she asked.

Vic nodded. "Yes."

He turned and slipped off into the jungle. Annja followed him.

They traveled another mile before Vic slowed and started making frequent stops. He seemed to be checking his bearings quite a bit more than he had earlier. Annja guessed they must be close to his hiding spot.

At last, he cleared away a dense outcropping of twisted

vines and dead tree trunks. Annja heard a rustling that sounded like a thousand tiny jaws eating through wood.

"Ugh."

"What?" she asked.

Vic pointed. "The ants have found my hole."

He brought out a small flashlight outfitted with a red lens and flashed it down into what appeared to be a six-foot wide hole. Annja watched as waves of ants scampered over bags of equipment.

"Great," Annja said.

Vic looked at her. "Cardinal rule in the jungle is don't sleep on the floor. The bugs will get you. Plus, the scorpions and snakes. But sometimes, you've got no choice. And the people hunting you will presume you're off the ground. So they spend a lot of time looking in trees."

"So you did the opposite."

Vic shrugged. "I've got liners that I've used in the past and they've kept me pretty comfortable. I never recommend sleeping on the jungle floor, though."

Annja watched as another wave of ants seemed to crest and then fall all over the contents of the hole. Vic leaned in and hefted one of the bags. Ants by the dozens fell off it.

"Hungry?" he asked.

Annja looked at the ants and then at the bag. "Starving," she said. Vic nodded and reached inside. Annja heard a zipper being drawn down and a second later, Vic handed her a small cardboard box.

"Spaghetti okay?"

Annja tore into the box and then into the plastic bag filled with noodles, sauce and small meatballs. She didn't care that it wasn't served hot. The food tasted amazing.

Vic helped himself to another box and leaned against a tree as he ate. "Make sure you don't leave any bits of that box on the floor. They'll have trackers with them. Any sign and they'll find it."

Annja swallowed and nodded. "How long have you been working in the jungle?" she asked.

Vic shrugged. "My whole life it feels like. I was born in Panama. I grew up around stuff like this. I guess it feels like home to me. I never did enjoy doing stuff in the snow."

"You were in the snow, too?"

He frowned. "Yeah. Winter training. I hated it. I'm a natural in the jungle, but the snow? Forget it. I freeze in that stuff. Doesn't matter how much gear I've got with me."

"How long have you been here?"

"The jungle, a week. I've been in country for about two months. Getting ready for this assignment."

"It's a big one?" she asked.

Vic nodded. "The biggest, I guess you could say."

"Are Abu Sayyaf really so bad that they warrant an American sniper stalking them through the jungle?"

Vic swallowed a gulp of his dinner and washed it down with a swig of water from his canteen. He set his spoon down and looked at Annja. "I don't ask a lot of questions. My job is pretty simple. It suits me. I could never handle a complicated lifestyle, you know? That's just who I am," he said.

"No shame in it," Annja replied.

"Of course not. How many people you know go through their lives trying to be something they're not? Christ, society puts all these labels on everyone, you know? If you're not married with kids by the time you're thirty, you're some kind of failure. My question is, according to who? Do I really give a rat's ass about what the people are doing next door in their four bedroom two-and-a-half-bath Colonial on a half-acre parcel with the minivan and sedan in the garage?"

"Do you?" Annja asked.

"Not one freaking bit." Vic looked up. "This is my home. This is my life. Things get easier once you're honest with yourself about what makes you tick. It's just a matter of being able to look into a mirror and not be terrified at what's staring you back in the face."

Annja sucked another strand of spaghetti into her mouth. "A lot of people, they wouldn't be able to do that."

"Sure. They can't."

"But you can."

"I don't ask questions above my pay grade. I've found that if I just do my job, everyone's happier. Most of all me."

"So you don't know what Abu Sayyaf have planned?"

Vic frowned. "You don't give up very easily, do you?"

"I've been told I'm a bit stubborn," she said.

"That's a fair assessment." Vic ate another bite of his dinner. "So, who are you anyway? There's something about you that seems familiar. But I can't quite place it."

Annja smirked. "I look like Sasquatch right now and you think I'm familiar to you somehow?"

Vic shook his head. "It's not the look. It's the mannerisms."

"I'm a journalist of sorts. I work for a show called *Chasing History's Monsters.*"

"Yeah, okay. I remember that now." He frowned.

Annja held up her hand. "No, I'm not that host."

Vic nodded. "You don't look the type who would lose her top on a televised show."

"I'm not."

"Good. At least that means I'm not being saddled with an idiot," he said.

Annja laughed. "I'll remember that."

Vic finished his dinner and Annja watched him wrap everything up, stuff it back into the cardboard box and then put that into his pack.

Annja did the same and then handed it to Vic. In exchange, he handed her a quart-sized plastic storage bag.

Annja held it up. "What's this for?"

"Number two."

"Excuse me?"

Vic stood up. "Look, I know this isn't exactly going to be your idea of a dream date, but there's a simple rule I live and survive by—leave no sign."

"You mentioned that already," Annja said, realizing where the conversation was going.

Vic nodded. "Yeah, well, it doesn't just apply to dinner. It applies to everything. You have to crap, you do it in that bag I just handed you. Then you tie a knot in it and bring it back to me."

"I never figured you for a collector," Annja said.

Vic sighed. "It goes in the bag along with everything else. We can't leave anything behind. If you take a dump out here, the animals will know about it and the bugs will swarm all over it. A tracker will see and hear all that activity and know he's on the right trail."

"What about if I have to pee?"

"Well, we're a bit short on jerry cans, which is what we'd normally use—"

"You're kidding."

"I'm absolutely serious. On a normal op, we'd patrol in with empties and on the way out, we'd haul our full cans with us."

"Great life you got there, Vic," Annja said with a chuckle.

Vic pointed out into the jungle. "As I was saying, if you have to go, walk out about ten yards—no more or you'll get lost—and find a dead log. Pee under that and then cover it up with the same dead log. It's not a great method, but it will minimize bug activity."

Annja sighed. "All right."

Vic frowned. "There's one more thing."

"Do I want to know?" she asked.

"We don't have any toilet paper."

Annja looked at him. "Are you kidding?"

"Nope."

"How—?"

"If you really need to—"

"If I really need to? What the hell kind of statement is that?"

Vic shook his head. "Like I said, this isn't home, Annja. You'd be surprised what you can do without out here in the bush. If you really need to, use a leaf and make sure you put that in the bag, too."

"A leaf."

"Preferably one that doesn't have bugs or fungus on it. You don't want to deal with that."

"A leaf," Annja said. She was used to primitive life on archaeological digs, but this was pretty extreme.

Vic smiled. "Jungle living isn't too bad, believe it or not. But you do have to make certain sacrifices. Once you do, you'll find it's much easier to get by. You might even grow to like it out here."

"Fat chance of that," Annja muttered.

"Well, it is an acquired taste."

"I don't think I want to acquire it at all. I just want to survive long enough to get the hell out of here and go home."

Vic nodded. "Simple enough request. Let's see if we can make it happen."

Annja sighed. "All right."

Vic waved the flashlight over his hole. "There, now, see the ants have moved on already."

"Where did they go?"

Vic shrugged. "I don't know. Don't really care, either. As long as they're not in the hole with us, that's all that matters."

"We're sleeping in there?"

"'Fraid so."

"But I thought we had to get off the ground. Won't the bugs gets us?"

"Undoubtedly."

"And you don't mind?"

"A few bug bites are always preferable to the other alternative."

"Which is what?"

Vic looked at her. "Being captured and beheaded by your Abu Sayyaf buddies."

8

Annja slept fitfully.

Throughout the night, she had to contend with an airborne
armada of mosquitoes that seemed all too willing to brave the
gauntlet of mosquito repellent that Vic had caked them both
in for a shot at some of Annja's blood. She grew tired of swatting at the incessant buzzers and eventually figured out that
if she tried to remain as motionless as possible under the
cover of the hidey-hole, she was better off.

She glanced over at Vic as the hours passed. He seemed
to be resting quite well in contrast to Annja's situation. She
chalked it up to his being more used to operating in this type
of environment than she was. Plus, he had the advantage of
layers of camo cream and mosquito repellent on his skin.
Any of the bloodsuckers trying to pierce that might end up
with a broken proboscis.

Annja watched his eyelids flutter, indicating he was deeply
asleep. She'd asked earlier if maybe they should take turns
sleeping while the other stood watch, but Vic had disagreed.
According to him, there was little chance they'd be stalked

at night. And in the morning, they had to move at first light if they hoped to stay ahead of their pursuers. Better, he said, to get as much rest as possible and then be ready to go.

Easier said than done, Annja thought. And just who is this guy I'm sleeping in such close proximity to, anyway? He's obviously incredibly dangerous, at least with his rifle. And he's no doubt killed more than his share of people.

Annja grinned. Not exactly new ground I'm traveling here, she thought. She'd been keeping company with the killer elite for more time than she cared to recall.

She knew little about the world of snipers, only that they were a select group of men trained to be able to see their targets up close, watch them through a microscope and then kill them without getting emotionally involved. They had to be able to place a bullet in a kill zone while anticipating movement, predicting windage, figuring out exact ranges and more. And they had to get into and out of position without being detected.

One shot, one kill.

Annja marveled at the picture of composure sleeping next to her. Vic made no noise while he slept. It was as if he'd trained himself not to snore or even draw heavy breaths while he rested. And despite the bugs that landed on him while he slept, Vic showed no signs their presence even registered in his conscious or subconscious mind.

Interesting.

Annja tried to take a cue from him, closing her eyes and placing herself someplace else. She imagined a beach far off in some tropical resort where the crashing waves lulled her to sleep against a backdrop of sugar-white sand as the warm sun's rays toasted her skin.

Her dream was shattered by another wave of buzzing near her ear. Annja swatted at the intruder and felt the bug's body come apart in her hands. She wiped it on her pants and then drifted back off, happy with her small victory.

Vic's hand on her shoulder woke her a minute later.

Annja cracked her eyes and saw that she'd actually managed to sleep for longer than she thought. The canopy had begun to lighten and she could make out a few more details now than when they'd come here during the night.

"You sleep?" he asked.

Annja stretched as much as she could given the confines of the hole. "I guess. Not nearly enough."

Vic poked his head out of the cover and looked around. "Well, some is better than none. Even if it feels like you got nothing, you probably did. And a little bit goes a long way around these parts."

"It'd be nice to sleep in," Annja said.

Vic glanced at her. "You can sleep when you're dead."

She smiled. "Good morning to you, too."

Vic took a swig of water and then handed the canteen to Annja. "That's something an instructor said to me one time. During training, we had to go for extended periods without much sleep. At first, it was a novelty, but eventually you wonder just what the hell you're doing."

"But you did it anyway."

"Had to," Vic said. "I wouldn't have passed the course without going through it. But when you're dead tired, you long to close your eyes more than any other desire. I've been hungry and thirsty like you don't know, but the sleep thing hit me hardest."

Annja helped herself to the canteen again. "How'd you come to terms with it?"

Vic shrugged. "I just did. I know now that I can go a lot further than I thought on precious little rest." He winked at Annja. "I don't recommend it, however. A lack of sleep compromises your immune system, opens you up to sickness and it clouds your ability to make good decisions."

"You didn't seem to have any trouble sleeping last night," she pointed out.

"Yeah, well, that was the next part of the training. We learned how to steal sleep anywhere. Even with artillery shells bursting around us, the ground thundering as they hit. Bullets? No sweat. As long as we were tucked in our holes, we learned how to pass the night in blissful slumber."

Annja handed him the canteen. "So, now that you've told me all about your stint as a tour guide in the Land of Nod, how about telling me where we're heading?"

Vic broke out another cardboard ration box and handed it to Annja. "Forced march. We need to cover six klicks if you want to spend the night someplace a lot more comfortable than another hidey-hole."

Annja tore into the breakfast of ham stew, chewing the dense meal. "Six klicks is a helluva lot of country to cover in thick jungle."

Vic nodded. "Sure is."

"You think I can do it?"

He laughed. "Well, you know, you've got a pretty strong motivational factor going for you."

"I do?"

"Yeah, if you don't hold your own, I'll leave you behind. These woods are about to turn ugly on me, as well. The people I pissed off last night will be out in force looking for yours truly. I'm not hanging around any longer than I have to."

"You'd leave me behind?" Annja asked.

"In a heartbeat, sister. I've got my own agenda to play to. Sorry to break your heart and all."

Annja frowned. "You're not breaking my heart."

Vic smiled. "Let's get moving."

Annja stood and rubbed on some more mosquito repellent. Vic hefted his rifle and then stopped. "Here."

Annja turned. Vic held out a small-caliber pistol. "You know how to use one?"

Annja took the gun, dropped the magazine and racked the slide. As the bullet in the chamber spun out, she caught it in her hand. Then she topped off the magazine, rammed it home and racked the slide again.

"Yeah, I think I can handle it," she said.

Vic pursed his lips. "You're not exactly a damsel in distress, are you?"

Annja pointed out ahead of them into the dense jungle. "Just set the pace and don't worry about me."

Vic turned and broke down the hidey-hole, scattering the framework that concealed the hole and then filling in everything with deadfall, leaves and bits of dirt.

"As it gets hotter, the heat will help conceal our presence," he said.

Annja slid the pistol into her belt. "You sure they won't know we were here?"

"Oh, they'll know. These people know this jungle like the backs of their hands. It's only a matter of time."

"You don't seem worried," she said.

Vic shrugged. "I'm a little new to the whole teamwork concept. Like I said, I normally come out here alone. I've been in plenty of tough spots before. I guess I'm not used to showing my fear on my face."

"How long do we have?"

Vic checked his watch. "It's 0500 now. I'll give us maybe a forty-minute head start."

"That's it?"

"Hey, I let you sleep in."

"What?"

Vic chuckled. "If it was up to me, we'd already be done with the first mile. But you spent so much of last night swatting mozzies, I figured you needed the extra time."

"Just what time did you wake up?"

"Probably right after you finally fell asleep."

Annja frowned. "Great."

Vic strapped down his pack and unslung his rifle. "We move as fast as possible, but carefully. You follow my lead. And watch for any hand signals. If I motion to stop, freeze. And always keep your eyes peeled for the next bit of cover and concealment. Got it?"

"Aye, aye, captain."

Vic aimed a finger at her. "Hey, look, I didn't ask for this. As far as I'm concerned, you're a bit of an unwelcome guest. I'm watching out for numero uno on this jaunt. I suggest you do the same."

"Sorry," Annja said.

"Forget it. It's just the exfiltration is always the toughest part of any assignment. And—no offense—having you along has just complicated things tremendously."

"I'll hold my own, Vic. Just set the pace and let's get hustling."

Vic looked at her for another moment and then nodded. "All right. Any last-minute trips to the toilet before we go?"

Annja checked herself. Her stomach seemed to have clenched up. Vic must have noticed because he started chuckling again.

"What's so funny?" she asked.

"That look."

"What look?"

Vic pointed at her stomach. "The MRE look. The rations we carry are so dense that they almost block you up, if you get my drift."

"You mean—?"

He nodded. "Yeah, you'll be constipated for a few days, I'd expect."

"Great."

"It's no biggie. Happens to everyone who eats those things. Best cure is some fresh food. Maybe a chocolate bar and a cup of coffee. That'll clear you out once you get back to civilization."

"This is some amazing lifestyle you've got for yourself here, Vic."

"Ain't it, though?"

Annja frowned again. "I was being sarcastic."

"I wasn't," he said with a grin.

"You really like it?"

Vic nodded. "Yep. I'm my own boss out here. As long as I complete my assignments, no one hassles me. I'm working in nature, having a ball and loving life. Not too many other people can say the same."

"You're killing people."

Vic shook his head. "I'm killing monsters who kill innocent people. Far as I'm concerned, it's justifiable. Even necessary."

Annja shifted the pistol on her belt. "I guess it would be futile to argue with you."

Vic leveled a finger at her. "Are you telling me you've never killed anyone before? I find that hard to believe."

"Why?" Annja asked, shocked by the question.

"Because you've got the look," he said.

"There's a look?"

Vic shrugged. "I think so. People who have been close to death or even dealt some of their own have a certain expression that creeps over their face from time to time."

"And you see it on my face?" she asked.

Vic smirked. "Well, not right now."

"Why?"

"Because you're filthy from all that mud you caked on yourself."

Annja sighed. "You're no prize yourself."

Vic nodded. "Yeah, but I clean up real well."

"I'll bet."

Vic pointed out to the jungle. "Let's get moving."

"Okay."

"One more thing."

Annja stopped. "What is it?"

"We go out in the bush, we don't say a word. Sound travels out here, even with the thick canopy all around us. The last thing we want to do is make it easy for them to find us."

"Understood."

Vic looked at her for a final moment and then turned. Slowly, they began making their way back into the jungle.

9

Eduardo Archibald Gomez could not believe his luck.

Their great leader Agamemnon had radioed him and informed him that he was being tasked with the search for the mysterious sniper who had killed Luis in the night.

"I am placing great faith in your abilities, Eduardo," Agamemnon had said.

Eduardo could barely contain his excitement. To be given this great a responsibility after only a year in the service of Abu Sayyaf was truly an incredible event. And it was one Eduardo took extremely seriously.

He had bowed toward the radio a moment before keying the microphone. "I swear to bring him back. Or I will not return."

Then he had assembled the best men he knew in the camp. All of them wanted a piece of the action. Luis had been a kind and remarkable leader for their group. He had personally taken Eduardo under his wing and taught him the finer points of ambushes, shirtsleeve explosive formulas, improvised munitions and much more. To see him cut down with a single shot to the head last night had scared and infuriated Eduardo.

He looked toward the jungle. Somewhere out there was the man who had killed Luis. And he would prove a very competent quarry. Eduardo would need to be careful; otherwise the sniper would sense them coming and kill them all.

Eduardo had no intention of letting that happen.

He called forth a withered old man with a long, wispy, white beard. The old man was clothed only in the scantiest of rags, but apparently cared little about his state of dress.

"Are you sure?" he asked.

The old man nodded. "Leave me be for now. I will find the trail before long." His voice sounded like a rock being scraped against moldy bark, and he smelled of a thousand layers of dirt, but Eduardo knew he was the best tracker in these parts. The old man had grown up in these jungles and knew every one of their secrets. Even around the campfire he spun odd tales of strange serpents and people who wandered into the deepest parts of the jungle never to return.

Eduardo and many of the others considered the old man strange. He'd simply shown up one day as they were building the camp. They hadn't been able to get rid of him. Death threats didn't sway him. He insisted he could be useful.

Eduardo nodded. "Very well, but you will need to report back to me within the hour or we will lose any time we might have gained with this early start."

The old man bowed once and then seemed to slide right between two clusters of dense shrubs at the periphery of the camp. In another second, he had disappeared completely.

"He is a strange one," the man behind Eduardo said.

Eduardo smiled. "How many times have I heard you say that, Miki?"

"Probably too many times. But I am not comfortable with the idea that this old man is responsible for leading us around the jungle. We have many other competent trackers that could do the same job."

Eduardo shook his head. "No, there's only one who knows the jungle as well as we need in order to fulfill our mission. And it's that man."

"So you say, Eduardo. But do you trust him yourself? He's not really one of us, after all."

"He has shown himself willing to lead us around the jungle in our search for the sniper. He saw the death last night, as well. Perhaps he knows it could have just as easily have been him that was felled by that single bullet."

Miki frowned. "I don't presume to understand his motivations for helping us. It is too dangerous to do so, I believe."

"Be that as it may, Agamemnon has ordered us to find the sniper and bring him to justice—our justice. I intend to succeed in that mission. Only when we have the sniper will we be free to undertake the mission that Luis intended to launch."

Miki sighed. Eduardo looked at him. They had been fast friends for many months now, their skills complementing each other on kidnapping missions and extortion runs. Eduardo felt a certain kinship with Miki and they both held the same rank, although with Agamemnon's blessing, Eduardo was currently the man in charge of the camp.

Still, he wouldn't let the rank go to his head. And he valued Miki's opinion, even if it differed from his own.

"Don't worry, my friend. The old man will not let us down. He knows what will happen to him if he does."

"I don't think he cares," Miki said.

Eduardo waved his hand. "Regardless, how is the rest of the team? Are they prepared?"

Miki pointed at the four other men sitting on their haunches nearby. "They are anxious to go out."

"As we all are."

"But only four? Surely, that will not be enough to capture the gunman," Miki said.

"I think it will, actually."

"The others in camp are restless. They want to be involved in the capture just as much as everyone else. I think some of them feel left out by your decision to only use a small unit."

Eduardo nodded. "I do not doubt their commitment or their willingness to participate in the mission."

"So why not take them along?"

"Because the man we are tracking is not an ordinary person, Miki. A sniper is a specialized breed of soldier. If we were going out looking for a band of civilians, then yes, the more men we employed in that regard, the better."

"But the sniper is different?" Miki asked.

"Yes. Extremely so. A man like this is used to operating alone. He knows how to move, how to use the jungle to evade and confuse us—even though we might know it better—so that he is able to take advantage of the situation."

"But he is only one man."

"One well-trained man. And he is motivated to escape us, surely knowing what we will do to him when we find him. No, by going out with a large force, we will simply make larger targets of ourselves. A small force of highly trained men is exactly what we need."

"Well, the four you had me assemble are the best we have here."

"And along with the old man tracking for us, I fully expect that we will have the sniper in our possession before nightfall," Eduardo said.

Miki glanced out at the jungle. "There are many ways to get out of the jungle without seeing another person."

"The old man will plot our path and then we will take steps to set an ambush."

Eduardo reached down and hefted the AK-47 he carried. The gun was heavy but its reliability in the jungle was superb. And the rounds it fired could take an arm off at distance.

"While I'm gone, you will be in charge of the camp," Eduardo said.

"Me?"

Eduardo looked at him. "It only makes sense, don't you think? We are the same rank, but Agamemnon has given me this assignment to carry out prior to our real mission. In the event I don't come back, the people here need someone to lead them, someone who can be trusted. That person is you."

"I don't know if it will even be necessary—"

Eduardo shook his head. "I've already spoken to Agamemnon about it. He agrees you are the most logical choice to assume command if I am killed."

Miki frowned. "I don't like the way you are talking."

Eduardo smiled. "Don't get sentimental on me, my friend. You know as well as I do that the path to heaven lies before us. One way or another we must persevere on our mission to rid the planet of the infidels. Only then will we find ourselves in the graces of God."

"You are right, Eduardo. I just hope that it is you who comes back to lead us. I am not so sure we are cut from the same cloth of leadership."

Eduardo laid a hand on his friend's shoulder. "The greatest leaders are sometimes the ones who least expected themselves capable of handling such a mantle."

"I'm going to get a seminar on leadership from you now, you old bum?"

Eduardo laughed and then smiled. "I think it might be too late for you, but I still have to try."

Miki gestured to the men. "Shall I have them come over now?"

"Yes."

Miki waved the team over. As they approached, Eduardo could sense their desire to race into the canopy and find the sniper. Luis had engendered an amazing amount of respect and love from his men simply by leading by example. Now that he was dead, that task fell to Eduardo. If he made a mistake, the men might doubt his ability to lead them. And Agamemnon would certainly make sure he never made a mistake again.

"We will wait here while the old man finds the trail the sniper took once he killed our leader."

"Then we will kill him?" one of the men asked.

"When we find the sniper, we must bring him back here. Agamemnon has demanded that we use every technique at our disposal to get information out of him."

"I don't think he has any," another man said. "They are just here to kill us all."

Eduardo nodded. "That may be true. But we cannot assume to know his mission. And since Agamemnon wants to make absolutely sure that our real mission is not in jeopardy, we must take steps to ensure the sniper is not too badly wounded to answer our questions."

"And once we are done with the questions?"

Eduardo smiled. "At that point, I believe we will be able to do with him as we wish. And I suggest that whatever it is be both painful and prolonged. The memory of our leader Luis deserves no less."

The men nodded and grinned among themselves. Eduardo could see their approval. He took a breath. One step down, many more to go.

"And what then?"

Eduardo looked at the last man who had spoken. "Once the sniper is dead, then we will be free to carry out our initial mission. And we will strike a deadly blow into the hearts and minds of the infidel elite. No longer will they be able to deny us or our existence. No longer will they think we are merely pesky annoyances they can swat away like flies. They will be forced to treat us with respect, or they will feel our wrath again and again. And as their dead lay in the streets, and their buildings crumble in ruin, they will come to us on their knees, begging our forgiveness."

He paused, looking into the eyes of each of the men seated before him. "But we will only laugh in their faces as we kill them."

The men screamed their approval and others in the camp hurried over to ask more questions. As Eduardo answered them all in turn, he saw Miki on the periphery of the group, still watching the jungle.

He's worried, Eduardo thought. I don't blame him. The mission before him was not an easy one. But then again, Eduardo didn't want it to be.

All he wanted now was to prove his worth and find the sniper.

Then Agamemnon would reward him in kind, perhaps with command of his own cell. Surely then he would rise even further in the ranks.

Miki turned and smiled at Eduardo. "It was a very good speech, my friend."

Eduardo smiled back.

One of the men suddenly turned and pointed at the jungle. Eduardo could see a ripple of movement coming down the nearest hill. It broke intermittently, like a wave trying to crest on a beach.

"What is that?" Miki asked.

Some of the men gathered their guns and began to point them at the ripple. Eduardo shook his head. "Hold your fire."

"What if it is the sniper?"

"It's not."

"You can be so sure?"

Eduardo looked at them, forcing himself to put on a calm demeanor. "Trust me, I would never downplay risk."

The men lowered their rifles and watched as the motion grew closer. They could hear nothing, only see the ripple as it proceeded down the hill toward their camp.

Miki came close to Eduardo. "You know what it is?"

"I think I do, yes."

The ripple came closer. Finally, in the last few feet before the jungle became the camp, the foliage suddenly parted and Eduardo smiled when the old man's bearded face broke into the sunlight.

"Have you found it?"

The old man nodded. "Yes. It is hidden but clear even to my old fragile eyes. I can show it to you."

"You'll do more than that," Eduardo said. "You will show us and then lead the hunt for the sniper."

10

Annja maneuvered her way through the thick jungle foliage. Her clothes, which she'd been wearing for almost a week, were utterly glued to her by the sweat pouring out of her. Even if she hadn't been sweating, the pea-soup-like humidity under the jungle canopy ensured she would stay soaking wet. It was a horrible feeling.

Vic wound his way through obstacle after obstacle without ever breaking stride. If he was exhausted, he showed no sign of it. Even during the frequent stops they made to collect water from the streams and rivers they crossed, Vic seemed totally in his element.

Annja was jealous.

She'd been in strange situations before, but there seemed to be something about this particular jungle that was worse than any of the others she'd been in. Something about how the buttress trees leaned in close, about how the tube vines snaked their way up from the ground, wrapping themselves around everything in sight.

It all seemed so...ancient.

Annja actually shivered once or twice as they passed through a particularly claustrophobic part of the jungle. She'd heard that people could get the willies in the tight confines of a jungle when the sun or sky wasn't even visible above due to the dense growth of plants and trees.

Around them, the daytime birds gave up an endless cacophony of sound. Annja could imagine their bright plumage on display as they hopped from branch to branch somewhere high above them on the hunt for a meal or a mate.

The barrel of Vic's gun nosed through the jungle ahead of him. Often, he would pause on bent knee and check the compass Annja noticed he'd taped to the buttstock of his gun. He would check it against a small folded and laminated map he carried in his uniform. Only after taking another bearing would he rise and resume his path.

Annja had absolutely no idea where they were headed. At varying times during their march, she thought they were traveling north, but then they switched directions and Annja thought perhaps they were now moving in a more easterly fashion.

But after the third direction switch, she gave up trying to figure it out.

Vic checked back on her every few minutes. He'd warned her what would happen if she didn't keep up and from the grim expression on his face, Annja had little doubt that he would do what he said—leave her behind if she couldn't keep up.

About two hours after they started, Vic called a halt by raising a clenched fist. He turned and put a finger to his lips, warning Annja that the no-talking rule was still in effect.

He took out an MRE for each of them and Annja tore into it, devouring the macaroni and cheese as if it was the last meal she'd be having. She washed it down with what felt like a gallon of water. Vic refilled the canteen from the nearby stream, and Annja found that the sterilization tabs didn't taste that bad if you were thirsty enough.

Vic put his mouth up close to her ear and in a very quiet whisper said, "Make sure you pee."

Annja nearly coughed. "What?" she whispered.

Vic frowned. "Pee. And check it. If it's dark yellow and smelly, you need to get more water into your system. If it's clear, you're okay."

Annja plopped a forkful of macaroni into her mouth and nodded.

Vic moved off and began eating his own food. Annja watched him and then, when she was done, moved over to where he sat. "How far have we gone?" she whispered.

He smirked. "About a mile and a half."

"That's it?"

Vic looked at her. "We're not traveling in a straight line."

She nodded. "I noticed. But why not?"

Vic pulled out his map. He pointed with a small twig he found on the ground. "This is where we started earlier. This is where we need to get to."

"Okay."

"And this," Vic said, pointing at a spot marked with a bright red X on the map, "is the location of the camp where I completed my assignment last night."

"Uh, okay."

"You see anything special about that?"

"Not really."

Vic pointed. "The enemy camp is located at a point where they can intersect our path if we aren't careful."

"That wouldn't be good," Annja said.

Vic frowned. "Genius."

Annja sighed. "You don't have to be sarcastic about it. I was only making a small joke."

"Damned small." Vic pointed again. "Our path will take us around their search line. Or at least what I hope their search line will be."

"And then we make our escape?" she asked.

"Hopefully."

"What's that supposed to mean?"

Vic smiled. "We have another group to contend with—the folks you left behind when you escaped from the other camp. I imagine they'll be very interested in locating you. We have to assume they're out looking for us, as well."

Annja took a swig of water. "This is a royal pain in the ass."

"Escape and evasion is never easy," Vic said. "Especially in a place like this."

Annja looked at him. Something about his expression made her frown. "Something bothering you, Vic?"

"No."

"Liar."

Vic looked at her. "What do you mean by that?"

Annja shrugged. "Your face. It looks more serious than before. Like you know something but you're not sharing it."

"No sense sharing it." He shook his head. "It's nothing."

"So you keep saying."

He looked at her and then grinned. "Fine, but don't say I didn't warn you."

"Okay."

Vic pointed at the jungle. "You been feeling a little claustrophobic lately?"

"Yeah. I have," she admitted.

He nodded. "Me, too. And that's rare for me. I'm usually at home in any jungle. But this one, I don't know. It feels a little too…closed in."

"Is that it?"

Vic brought his rifle up into his lap. "The last time I was

on leave, I spent some time a little south of here in a small village. The locals are always great at making you feel at home. Anyway, one night after too much food, I fell in talking with one of the town elders. Guy was so old he looked like a wrinkled prune. But his eyes, I mean if you saw them, you'd swear they were on fire."

"I've known people like that," Annja said.

"This old guy, he starts telling me about this jungle. This particular stretch. About how it holds a lot of secrets."

Annja smiled. "Secrets?"

"I know, right, you think the same thing I thought—the old guy's had too much stale beer. But he tells me then that my next mission will take me straight into a place I've never known before. A place I've never thought existed."

"Weird."

"Yep."

"And you think this is that place?" Annja asked.

Vic frowned. "Not really. But the old man's words have been ringing in my head today. Ever since we started out. Like I've got this feeling I can't place."

"What kind of feeling?"

"Like someone's keeping an eye on us," he said.

Annja glanced around. "The search teams?"

"No. Someone else. But it's like they stay on the periphery just enough for me to think I might be imagining things."

"Like they know how to flirt with your subconscious enough to make you question your gut," Annja said, knowing how he felt.

"Exactly."

"Those would have to be some pretty skilled people. I don't imagine you're the kind of guy who has survived as long as he has without trusting your gut," she said.

Vic smirked. "I suppose so."

Annja looked out into the jungle. She hadn't felt much today, but then again, she'd been concentrating almost exclusively on trying to keep pace with Vic. Her attention had been so focused on that that perhaps she'd lost sight of her natural ability to detect danger.

Now, though, as she glanced around her, she could feel something, too. It seemed to gnaw at her just a tiny bit.

"Well, I'm real anxious to go pee now," she said.

Vic finished his MRE and packed it away along with Annja's trash. "I'll stand watch. Do your business over there and cover it with the log when you're done," he whispered.

Annja headed toward the log. She glanced back at Vic and was amazed that despite being only a few yards away, he was already difficult to notice in the jungle. His camouflage was so effective, he seemed to merge with the trees and plants around him.

Now I know how he can get so close to his targets before he kills them, she thought.

She turned the log over and lowered her pants. She heard an instant buzzing frenzy as mosquitoes dive-bombed her backside.

Great, she thought, this just keeps getting better. It's a good thing I'm not overly concerned about looking dignified.

She stood and flipped the log back over onto the moist ground. As she pulled her pants up, she crushed a few flying bugs between her backside and the cloth of her pants.

Vic turned when she came back through the jungle. "All set?"

Annja nodded, making sure the pistol she wore was still secure.

Vic led them on, pausing at the next large tree to take a bearing. Annja knew a little about orienteering, but Vic seemed to know right where he was heading.

Annja looked around the jungle. How people could find

their way through this maze was surprising enough. It all seemed to utterly infinite. Trees, plants, animals, birds, snakes, insects, wet humid air and…rain.

She heard it before she felt it. Overhead, the sudden eruption of millions of pellets of water pelting the large leaves reaching up to the sun. The drops splattered against leaf after leaf, making their way down to the floor below in a way that reminded Annja of the *pachinko* parlors in Tokyo.

In a short time, the rain reached them, soaking them even more. Annja let some of the water run into her mouth, grateful that it didn't taste like sterilization tablets. Vic was moving up ahead, but he stopped and pointed at the ground.

Annja looked down and understood why. The dirt was turning into thick, gooey mud. With every step the earth seemed to suck at her feet, making progress slow and exhausting.

Worse, they were leaving a very distinct set of tracks through the jungle. Anyone following them would know they went this way.

That fact didn't make Annja feel very good.

But Vic seemed to be taking that into account. Annja noticed they were traveling now more to the right side, almost as if they were making a very large circle.

What the hell was he up to?

Annja didn't quite understand why they would switch directions again after so much work getting to this point. Wasn't there an easier way to do this? Couldn't they just run for the edge of the jungle?

She smirked. Like so many times before, Annja knew that she was in the company of a professional. Vic knew what he was doing. All she had to do was shut up and keep pace. He would take care of her.

She supposed that was the problem.

Annja didn't like knowing someone else was responsible for her safety. She much preferred being in charge of her own welfare.

But then again, she hadn't planned on being kidnapped, either, and then escaping into the jungle equipped with absolutely nothing but her legendary sword.

Vic stopped suddenly and held up his clenched fist.

Annja froze.

Vic turned abruptly, took three big steps to the left and then gestured for Annja to do the same. She did and came over to squat next to Vic.

"What's the matter?"

Vic pointed at about eleven o'clock to their position. "Out there."

"What?"

Vic brought his rifle up into his shoulder and sighted through the scope. He pulled back and nodded for Annja to look through it.

Annja closed one of her eyes and peered through the scope. Instantly, she saw movement. It was muddled at first from the rain streaking the scope, but then she saw it.

An old man with a long white beard.

Behind him, five men with rifles.

Vic's mouth brushed Annja's ear. "They've found us."

11

The old man, whom Eduardo had nicknamed Balut due to his proclivity for eating the black aged duck eggs as he tracked, turned and held up his hand. He spotted Eduardo and called him forward.

Eduardo approached. "What is it?"

Balut shushed him. Eduardo frowned and then took a breath before whispering, "What?"

Balut sniffed the air. "Can you smell it?"

Eduardo sniffed. "Smell what?"

Balut continued scenting the air as if he were some type of bloodhound. "A woman. I can smell her."

Eduardo frowned. Agamemnon had mentioned that an American woman had escaped from his camp. Was it possible they had stumbled on her trail?

"She's nearby?"

Balut sniffed the air again. Then he moved off the trail and poked his way through the dense undergrowth. Eduardo watched as he poked his nose here and there before settling on a log on the ground close by. He turned the log over, got down on all fours and proceeded to stick his nose right into the ground.

When he came back up, he wore a smile. "This is fresh."

"What is?"

"She has pissed here recently."

Eduardo rolled his eyes in disgust. "You just stuck your nose into her waste?"

Balut came back toward him plucking another black duck egg from the pouch he wore, peeling the shell and popping it into his mouth. "A good tracker knows the surest way to find his prey is to study their waste."

He chewed slowly, letting bits of eggs fall around his mouth. Eduardo felt repulsed. Not only did he hate *balut* as an edible substance, but the manner in which the old man devoured the eggs was sickening.

Still, if the American woman was close by…

"What about the sniper?" he asked.

Balut frowned. "He will, no doubt, be tougher to track."

Eduardo looked overhead. The rain continued to sluice down through the trees. The mud all around them was thick and mucky. Eduardo was amazed Balut was able to smell anything over the strong scent of fresh rain.

Eduardo waved his men forward. When they were around him, he smiled through the rain pouring down his face. "Nice day for a walk, eh?"

The men grinned. Eduardo knew he had their confidence. All he had to do now was get the woman and then the sniper.

"The old man here says there is a woman close by. Agamemnon told me about an American woman he had kidnapped for ransom. She escaped yesterday. And it is very possible we have stumbled onto her trail. She is close by, according to the old man who has…smelled her effluents."

Balut cracked a smile. "She smells lovely."

Eduardo sighed. "Be that as it may, you are to fan out from here and we will attempt to catch her. Agamemnon wants her taken alive, as well. She is unarmed and should be relatively simple to catch. Alone out here, she is probably very weak."

Balut frowned. "I doubt that."

Eduardo ignored him. "We will form a line with each of us four yards apart and then proceed. She will not be able to escape the line and we will catch her. Be sure to take your time and check everywhere. If she knows we are close, then she will try her best to elude us."

Eduardo turned back to Balut. "Can you give us a bearing of which way she went?"

Balut turned and walked farther away. He came back and pointed. "Perhaps ten minutes before we arrived here."

"That's it?"

Balut nodded. "You ask, I show."

Eduardo checked the safety on his gun. His men fanned out and they waited for his signal. When he saw they were all in position, he waved them forward as one.

The fact that they had come across the woman's trail surprised him. He would have thought that they would come across the sniper's trail first, but then again, as Balut had said, he would no doubt be tougher to track.

And much tougher to corner.

"Eduardo!"

One of his men from the left waved him over. Eduardo pushed his way through a tangle of vines and then looked at the ground where the man pointed. "Do you see it?"

Eduardo nodded. There on the ground were what appeared to be two sets of tracks.

Balut appeared next to them and knelt in the mud, feeling the tracks with his hand. He glanced up. "They are fresh. But the rain is washing them away. In this weather, they were probably recently made. I believe they are close."

"The woman?"

Balut nodded. "And the one we sought originally."

Eduardo breathed. "The sniper."

"Yes."

Eduardo waved for the men to fan out again. If the sniper was close, that meant things were a lot more dangerous than if they'd just been after the woman. The sniper could turn the tables on them if he thought they had found his trail.

He grabbed Balut. "Be extra careful from here on out. If he sees us, he will kill you first."

Balut smiled. "He would have to be able to see me."

"Maybe he already has."

Balut shrugged. "I'm an old man. I've had a good life."

Eduardo shoved him away. "Find the trail and keep us on it. If you think they are close, then signal and we will take over."

Balut nodded and stalked off.

Eduardo readied his AK-47 and then moved on. In his peripheral vision, he could see his men moving ahead with him. Their distance was still such that they could keep visual range.

Balut disappeared from view ten yards ahead of them. Eduardo frowned. Figures, he thought. I tell him to stay close and he goes and does what he wants. Well, just so long as he gets results. That was all that mattered.

Out of the corner of his eye, Eduardo saw the man farthest away to the left suddenly vanish.

He stopped.

The man closer to him on the left saw Eduardo stop. "Sir?"

"Where did he go? The one on the other side of you?" Eduardo asked.

"I don't know. He was there a second ago."

"Go and find him!"

The man turned and ran off into the jungle. Eduardo frowned. He didn't like this. Not one bit.

Balut still hadn't returned. Eduardo called a halt to the advance. Had the sniper picked off the man on the far left?

No, it couldn't be. They would have heard the shot. Unless, of course, he had a sound suppressor on his rifle. Eduardo frowned. It was possible, but did it make sense? Suppressors could affect the accuracy of the bullets, he had once heard.

Whether it was true or not was another matter.

He called his men in close to him. He knelt on the ground and tried to figure out how to best approach the situation. The man on the left came back from the jungle shaking his head.

And only one man came from the right.

"Where is the other one?" Eduardo asked.

The man from the right turned. "He was behind me as we came in. I heard him walking behind me."

Eduardo swept the area with his rifle, ready to fire. The two men with him looked scared. Eduardo had seen them both in action enough in the cities to know they didn't frighten easily.

"What's going on, sir?" one of the men asked.

Eduardo shook his head. "I don't know."

"We have to find them."

Eduardo nodded. "All right, we'll go together. But slowly and stay close. I don't want either of you disappearing."

"What about the old man?"

"Leave him," Eduardo said. "He can find his way around these parts. He doesn't need our help."

They rose and moved toward where Eduardo had seen the first man vanish. As they crept through the jungle, all of them kept their rifles up at their shoulders. It was a drill they'd been taught over and over again. With the rifle stock in their shoulder it was much easier to bring the gun to bear on an enemy.

Eduardo saw it before the men with him. "No."

A smear of fresh blood coated the trunk of a buttress tree. Eduardo felt the sticky blood and knew that one of his men had been hurt.

But where was the body?

The area around the blood showed little sign that anyone had been there. Eduardo could see evidence of his man's presence, but beyond that, nothing.

If the sniper had shot him, then there would be a body. There was no way the sniper would have exposed himself just to come and get the body. Was there?

He thought about what to do. "We'll move to the other side and check for the other one," he said.

Again they rose and crossed back over the area they'd trekked through. On the right flank, they found another smear of blood but nothing else.

Where were his men? And where was Balut?

The old man had vanished just like the men on either side. Eduardo frowned. Was it possible that Balut had led them into some kind of trap? Was he working with the Americans?

Rage flooded Eduardo's veins. "If the old man has betrayed us, we will kill him, as well," he said.

Both of the men with him huddled close by, ready to shoot at anything that moved. One of them turned to Eduardo. "Now what, sir?"

Eduardo felt his heart hammering in his chest. "We go forward."

"Sir?"

"We need to find out who is doing this."

The other man frowned. "Whoever it is, they are able to kill without making any noise. That means they are accomplished and skilled. Very dangerous."

Eduardo took a hand off of his rifle and laid it on the man's shoulder. "You, too, are also accomplished and skilled. And you, too, are dangerous. We will go forth and find the people who did this. And we will kill them."

Both men looked unsure but rose with Eduardo. He nodded at them both. "Let's go."

But as he took his next step, he heard what sounded like two big breaths swishing past his ear. Instinct took over and he dropped to the ground, squeezing off a burst from his heavy AK-47 as he did so. The relative silence of the jungle exploded as the rounds tore into the undergrowth.

Eduardo lay there breathing hard. He could see the man on his right also lying flat. Eduardo crawled over to him.

"Did you see anything?"

He got no response.

Eduardo nudged the man with the butt of his gun. The body shifted and then separated from the head. The head turned over and Eduardo was face-to-face with the dead man's stare.

Blood pumped out of the body into the ground. Eduardo covered his mouth and choked back the rising tide in his throat.

He crawled away from the corpse and moved to his left. He heard the angry buzz of insects before he got close enough to know that the man on the left was dead, too.

Decapitated.

Eduardo huddled in the vines with his rifle. What could possibly have taken their heads off? He knew of no bullet in the world that could do such a thing.

It was as if their heads had been cut with a very sharp blade.

But who had done the cutting? And had the blade been thrown?

Eduardo knew that he would be the next to die unless he acted. With a rush of adrenaline, he got to his feet and screamed as he pulled the trigger on the AK-47. Shells tumbled out of the ejector port as his bullets tore into the jungle. Bits of leaves, branches and bark exploded as the bullets found their marks.

Eduardo raked from side to side until at last, the magazine was empty.

Click-click-click.

He breathed long and hard. Sweat had soaked him through.

And when he heard the next sound, it was almost too late for it to register before Eduardo felt something bite into him.

And he saw nothing but blackness.

12

"Where'd they go?"

Vic's voice remained nothing more than a whisper. But Annja could detect a sense of something else—fear.

She peered out from the undergrowth. "What do you mean?"

"I mean they're gone."

"How is that possible?"

Vic shook his head but kept himself glued to his scope. "I don't know. After that last burst of fire, I fully expected them to come storming through the jungle straight for us."

"Was he aiming at us?"

"Tough to tell. It looked like they were shooting ahead of them, but we're still about half a klick away. They could have seen something else, I suppose, but I don't know what."

Vic slid down next to her. "I don't know what's going on here."

"And you don't like it," she said.

"No."

Annja smiled. "Welcome to my world."

He ignored her. "I'm used to being a ghost, Annja. People

don't know I move in and out of their world. I take my time, I move on the periphery of their awareness, make my shots and then vanish right back where I like to be." He frowned. "But this, this is something else. And it just feels…weird."

"Weird."

"Yeah."

Annja lay on her back looking up at the green above her and all around her. Tube vines, trees, palms and some of the tall grasses seemed to arc above her like a greenhouse of skyscrapers. Scattered raindrops still worked their way down from far above, splattering her face and clothes. But Annja was beyond caring about her comfort at this point. Somehow she'd managed to tune out the physical discomforts of jungle living and she concentrated now on the most important aspect of it all—survival.

She closed her eyes and breathed slowly. Her gut was needling her with concern. Somewhere out there was something dangerous.

But what? An animal? Could there be some type of deadly jungle predator that had attacked the search team? It didn't add up.

Human? Were there people out here that neither the terrorists nor Vic knew about?

Annja opened her eyes.

"Bingo."

Vic looked at her. "What?"

Annja rolled over and looked through the plants back at where the search team had gone down. "Tell me again about the stories you heard about this place."

"We don't really have time for that right now, Annja."

She frowned. "I think there's someone else out there tracking us. And I think that's what we've been feeling today."

"Not the search teams?" Vic looked skeptical.

Annja shook her head. "No. I don't think they even knew what hit them."

Vic got behind his rifle again, peering into the scope. "They'd have to be extremely adept if they could escape notice like that."

"You've heard rumors about them?"

"Not really. Just what I told you earlier. That a lot of people used to come into this part of the jungle. Inevitably, they went missing."

"But you came in here."

Vic grinned. "Orders, ma'am. Just following my orders."

Annja sighed and closed her eyes. Hovering in her mind's eye, she could see her sword ready to pull out the moment it seemed she was in danger. Of course, there was no telling how Vic would respond when he saw the blade.

But she'd have to risk it.

"Vic."

"Yeah?"

"If something happens…"

He glanced at her. "Use the pistol. You said you knew how."

Annja nodded. "I do. It's just that something might happen and I don't want you to be shocked."

Vic looked away from the scope. "What the hell are you talking about?"

"Just remember I said that, okay? Don't be shocked."

He smirked. "Uh, yeah, okay. Whatever." He went back to peering through his scope.

Annja felt for the pistol. She knew it was ready to fire, but she slid the safety off anyway. Somehow, having the gun didn't make her feel nearly as safe as when she'd had her sword in her hands.

Vic shifted. "I thought I just caught a glimpse of something."

Annja rolled over. "Where?"

"One o'clock to our position."

Annja swept her eyes over the point just to their northeast. She ran her eyes back and forth, preferring not to try to focus, but instead let her peripheral vision pick up the motion.

"I don't see any—"

Her words were cut off by the sudden explosion from Vic's rifle. As quick as could be, Vic slid the bolt back, caught the ejected shell casing, and then slammed the bolt back forward again.

His voice seemed almost robotic, and Annja knew he had switched on to the part of himself that ran on automatic during such situations. "Movement. Moving now to one-thirty," he said.

He fired again and Annja winced as the deafening roar echoed into the jungle. Birds overhead that hadn't moved during the first shot suddenly erupted from the trees, scattering like bits of ripped paper into the winds.

Vic repeated his shot and then waited before firing again.

"Did you get him?" Annja asked.

"I don't know."

Annja frowned. This situation was rapidly becoming extremely uncomfortable. She didn't like waiting for the enemy to come to her. She much preferred to go on the offensive. She'd found it worked more times than not.

But this waiting…

Vic brought himself up into a kneeling position, sweeping his arcs from left to right and back again.

Annja's sense of danger continued to grow. The intensity of it increased and she knew that Vic had not scored a hit on his target.

"You missed," she said.

But Vic didn't even look at her now. "How do you know?"

"Gut feeling," she said.

He sniffed. "I'm one of the best, Annja. That's not bravado, either. If I shoot at something, I hit it."

"Not this time."

"How can you be so certain?"

Annja sighed. "The same way you knew there was something else out there today watching us. The same way you know there's something out there right now that wasn't even scratched by your shots."

Vic stopped moving. "You got a suggestion? I'm all ears."

Annja shook her head. "I don't know."

"In that case, I'll keep shooting if I see something. One of these times, I'm going to get the bastards."

He swung left at the moment. "Get down!"

The rifle spit a round just as Annja ducked down into the leaf litter. Vic chambered another bullet and waited. "How the hell did they get to the other side without us seeing them?" he said.

Annja looked down at the pistol in her hands. There was no way it was going to be of help in this situation. Bullets didn't seem to matter one whit to whatever it was that was stalking them.

I want my sword, she thought.

Vic's rifle suddenly dropped.

Annja blocked it from striking her on the head. "Hey!"

Beside her, Vic's body crumpled to the ground.

"Vic!"

Annja searched for any obvious wounds, but found nothing. She rolled him over and saw something bright and flashy jutting out of the side of his neck. It was a small piece of wood tipped with bright feathers.

A blow dart?

Annja closed her eyes and summoned her sword. When she opened her eyes, her hands were wrapped around the hilt. She took a breath, feeling the energy from the sword wash over her, seeping into her system and energizing her in ways she hadn't felt since the last time she'd used it.

Annja frowned. Forget the pistol. This is how I'll deal with this, she thought.

She got to her feet and felt a wave of energy build inside her, and in the next moment, she opened her mouth and let loose a roar of challenge.

She sensed movement all around her.

My God, she thought. It's not just one, after all.

There were almost twenty of them.

As they stepped from the undergrowth, Annja knew why they hadn't been easy to spot. They wore very little in terms of clothing, but their brown skin was carefully painted with greens and browns in a mesmerizing pattern that made them blend in completely with their surroundings.

They stood roughly five feet tall, but their small stature did little to diminish the looks of absolute ferocity simmering in their eyes.

Annja held her sword out in front of her.

They seemed to consider her something strange. A few of the men glanced at each other as if surprised by the appearance of a woman wielding a sword in the middle of a jungle in the Philippines.

That makes two of us, thought Annja with a wry grin.

I'd much rather be home.

Three of the tribesmen wielded small bows and arrows. Annja wasn't concerned about them. She knew the sword would be able to cleave any airborne missiles out of the air without much effort.

The other tribesmen held wicked-looking small scythelike objects, however. Annja could see the glint of metal, and the edges of those weapons looked positively lethal. Several others held up long tubes. Blow guns.

Annja knew she'd have a tougher time fighting those off. The small darts would be hard to deflect.

But she would have to try.

Vic's body lay behind her and Annja had no way of knowing if he was dead or simply unconscious. The dart could have been tipped with a sedative or a poison.

She couldn't risk getting nailed by one of them.

Annja spun the sword in her hands, its blade flashing back and forth in the jungle air, whistling as it did so. The tribesmen seemed to almost smile. Two of the men wielding the scythes did their own maneuver with their weapons as if answering Annja's unspoken challenge.

Annja almost grinned. Maybe they respect the fact that I'm not using a gun, she thought.

She leaped into the air and did a four crosscut with the sword before landing softly on the jungle floor again.

This time the men whooped once before launching into their own complicated acrobatic stunts.

Annja found herself smiling now. Common ground, she figured. If they respected her as a warrior, there might be hope for some kind of détente.

Maybe.

"Excuse me."

Annja's mind whirled. She turned and in the next instant felt two things.

The first was that something small and sharp pricked her flesh on her throat. The second was that her sword was plucked from her hands as if she hadn't even been holding it.

As she started to topple to the ground on her back, the last image she saw was the curious face of an old man with a long, wispy white beard.

And the wide smile that blazed across his ancient face.

13

"Annja!"

She heard the voice but it buzzed in her head like the annoying mosquitoes that surrounded her in the jungle. She tried to ignore it, focusing instead on how lovely it felt to be sleeping in the pitch darkness of her mind.

"Annja!"

And just like the mosquitoes, the voice was not going away. Annja moaned and opened her eyes, squinting as she did so to ward off the possibility of bright light greeting her.

But she wasn't in sunshine at all. And it was only a little bit lighter now than when she'd been asleep.

Asleep?

Annja's mind swam as she tried to remember exactly what had happened. She was in the jungle. Running away from terrorists. And then...Vic? She'd fallen out of a tree.

Annja glanced around. For some reason, her arms felt weird. She looked overhead and saw that they were stretched out akimbo. At least five feet separated them from each other. And she was suspended off the ground somehow.

"What happened?" she asked.

"Annja, wake up and pay attention."

She turned her head. Vic was strung up in a similar fashion. All of his equipment was gone. He wore only his camouflage clothing and boots.

Next to Vic was another man who looked Filipino.

"Who's that?" she asked.

Vic shrugged. "Would you believe one of the bad guys?"

Annja saw a swirl of images coming at her as her memories returned. "I thought I saw him in the jungle. Right before…"

Vic nodded. "Yeah. Right before we were taken down by the blowguns. Nice, huh? Whoever said high-tech wins wars never went to battle." He frowned. "Anyway, we're here now, although I have no idea where here is."

"Why is it dark? Is it nighttime?"

"I don't know. I only woke up a few minutes ago." Vic struggled to move but his binds had been fastened tight and he could barely arch his back, let alone do anything else.

"Where is the rest of that guy's party? I saw several more of them," Annja said.

"I think it's safe to assume they're dead. I've only seen us since I woke up. And no one has been by to check up on us. I think if any of his guys were still around, they'd be here with us. They're not, which probably means—"

"They're dead."

Annja watched as the Filipino lifted his head and looked at them both. He coughed once and licked his lips. "They're dead. Their heads were severed from their bodies as we were taken. For some reason, they only knocked me out. I don't know why."

"They were decapitated?" Vic asked.

Annja nodded. "I remember seeing some of the guys who got us armed with something that looked like scythes or razor blades or something. Whatever it was, they looked pretty nasty."

The Filipino smiled. "Cut right through the neck and didn't even topple the head. That's how sharp those things must be. It was impressive, to say the least."

"Lucky you," Vic said. "You get stuck here with us."

The Filipino spit. "I will not ally myself with you."

"I wasn't asking," Vic said.

"You don't have much choice," Annja said. "Given the condition we're in right now, I hardly think they intend to become best friends with us."

Vic smirked. "Maybe invite us over for tea later?"

"Exactly."

Annja looked at her hands again. Unless she could bring them together, she wouldn't be able to conjure the sword, and even if she could she probably wouldn't be able to use it for anything. She closed her eyes for a split second to check on the sword. It hovered right in the space it always did, and just seeing it made Annja feel better.

When she opened her eyes again, Vic was looking at her. "Everything okay?"

"Yep."

He nodded. "Good. Whatever the hell that means."

Annja looked at the Filipino guy again. "What's your name?"

He eyed her for a second, seeming to fluctuate between hating her and realizing that they were in a bit of a jam here. "Eduardo."

"You were sent to find me?"

Eduardo shook his head. "No, I was sent to find him." He spit in Vic's direction, but it failed to carry the distance and fell between them with a dull flop.

"Seems personal," Vic said.

"You killed our leader."

"Did I?"

Eduardo nodded. "He was a good man. Luis didn't deserve to die with a bullet between his eyes."

Vic sighed. "Let me tell you something. If he was a good man, he wouldn't have been in my sights. Dig? Your pal Luis was some bad stuff. And he was one of the guys who had to go."

"My men will find us and when they do, you will die a very painful slow death," Eduardo said.

Vic sighed. "Yeah, like I haven't heard that before. Good luck carrying it out. I don't know where the hell we are and I doubt very much that your friends will find us, either."

"We know this jungle."

"Yeah, well, something tells me the guys who took us know it even better than both of us put together. And I don't think they'll let themselves be found unless they want someone finding them." Vic leaned back as much as he could. "May as well make peace with the fact that you're stuck here like the rest of us."

Annja looked at Eduardo. "Did you know about me?"

Eduardo frowned. "I heard you escaped."

"They were going to kill me," she said.

Eduardo shook his head. "What do I care about the life of one American? Your country inserts itself where it is not needed or wanted. Your leaders seem to think they have some God-given right to act as judge and jury for the world's affairs. They do not. What they propose to accomplish in the name of goodness is merely a front for the fact that they are all motivated by only one thing—money. If there is no money to be made, America will ignore you. Look at the situation in the Sudan. Did America get involved? Of course not. No money to be gained. But if you threaten oil or an ally in a region that has other resources, look out."

Annja looked at Vic. "He makes a convincing argument," she said.

Vic smiled. "I think it's illegal for me to have this conversation."

"Right."

"No, really. I think the Uniform Code of Military Justice prohibits me from saying anything disparaging about my country or its leaders."

Annja's eyes narrowed. "You're being serious?"

Vic nodded and closed his eyes. "My lips are sealed."

Annja heard something and turned her head in time to see the last face she'd seen as she was being knocked out. The old man with the white beard walked toward her.

"Awake now?" he said.

"Apparently," Annja replied.

"You traitor," Eduardo said.

The old man grinned. "What do I care what you think? You are all alike. You would destroy the jungle and its beauty for the sake of your little wars. That's not something I can allow to happen."

Eduardo struggled against his bonds. "You will be killed when my men find me."

The old man kept smiling. "And you think they will find you?"

"Yes."

"Then you are a fool. And they will only die in the process. And your little scheme will fail, as well."

Vic's eyes opened. "What little scheme?"

The old man regarded him. "Didn't you know? I assumed that is why you were sent to kill Luis."

Vic frowned. "Luis was part of an overall mission profile to eliminate the leaders of Abu Sayyaf factions operating in this area."

The old man nodded. "Ah, well, then why should I be the one to spoil the surprise?"

"Because it will piss Eduardo off if you do?" Vic said.

The old man laughed. "I like your sense of humor." He

walked closer to Eduardo. "What do you think of that? Should I tell him about your little suitcase nuclear device? The one you intend on detonating in the Makati district of Manila?"

Annja caught her breath. "You'll kill thousands of people," she said.

Eduardo looked at her. "So what? They are all living off the fat of the people. The wealthy deserve to die. The masses are clamoring for it, even if they don't realize they want the change."

"But so many innocent lives. What about the children?" she pleaded.

"The cost of war." Eduardo glanced at Vic. "Surely you understand collateral damage."

Vic shook his head. "I don't operate that way. In my line of work, we kill who is supposed to die and don't accept anything else. Indiscriminate killing is one of the reasons I've been assigned to hunt you assholes down."

The old man shook his head. "It's a good thing you're all tied up. I fear you might kill each other if I let you."

Annja looked at him. "Where are we?"

"You are in a cavern located far beneath the surface of the jungle. Surely you've noticed the change in temperature?"

Annja took in a breath. He was right. The humidity was far less than what it had been in the jungle. The air was cooler here. And she wasn't wet anymore.

"We're underground?" Vic said.

The old man nodded. "There is a network of tunnels all over this part of the island. It's how we're able to move as stealthily as we do."

"'We?'" Annja asked.

"My tribe."

Annja frowned. "So I did see other members of your tribe."

"Of course. It was necessary for you to see them in order

for me to sneak up on you, distract you and then enable my fellow hunters to knock you out."

"Great."

Eduardo struggled against his bonds again. The old man shook his head. "You're wasting your time. The cord we tied you with shrinks as it dries and the knots become almost unbreakable. You would need to be a lot stronger than you are in order to break free."

Eduardo glared at him. "I will break free, just wait. And once I do, I will kill you for betraying us all."

Vic sighed. "Hey, Einstein, you might want to lay off the threats."

"Don't tell me what to do."

"You keep threatening him and he's liable to just kill you now and be done with it. You ever think of that?"

Eduardo fell silent. Vic sighed again.

Annja looked at the old man. "What do we call you?"

"My name is Hector. Whatever you call me matters little to me. Your fates have already been sealed the moment you were chosen by me and my men."

"What's that supposed to mean?" Annja asked.

Hector started walking away. "You are to be sacrificed to our gods at sunset tomorrow."

"What?"

Hector stopped. "It has been ordered by the spirits. Your deaths will help pave the way for an era of peace on the island. And your petty squabbles will end as your lives will."

He walked away leaving Annja, Vic and Eduardo to ponder his words.

14

As the sun began to set, Agamemnon sat in front of the radio and waited for Eduardo to send him a report. Agamemnon had little doubt that his newly appointed leader would do his utmost to ensure success in his given task.

Now I just have to wait for the good news, he thought.

But as the minutes ticked by and Eduardo failed to meet the check-in time for radio communication, Agamemnon grew anxious.

Already today, his other search team had returned with nothing to show for their efforts. As far as they could tell, the American woman had simply vanished into the jungle. They had initially managed to find where she'd hidden in a tree and then followed the trail for a little while, but then it had gone utterly cold.

The search team leader had suggested that perhaps the American woman was dead. "After all, sir, she had no equipment."

"You're willing to stake your life on that theory?"

"I think so."

That made Agamemnon even more displeased.

His thoughts were interrupted by intermittent screams coming from outside the hut. He sighed. It always took them so long to die when they were buried in the earth and honey was poured over their heads. The ants weren't exactly the fastest eaters, but they were thorough. And Agamemnon had little doubt that by the time the army ants were done with the search team leader's head, they would move on, leaving very little behind.

He sighed again. He needed more men to take care of these loose ends that plagued him. The American woman was still alive. He felt sure of that. And the presence of the sniper did little to allay his fears that at any moment, a bullet could come biting through the air with his name on it.

No, things were not good at all.

The one thing that had managed to save him from descending even deeper into a funk was the anticipation of Eduardo's communication. Surely the new leader of the second camp would have good things to report.

Agamemnon checked the clock on the wall and then the wristwatch he wore. Thirty minutes late now.

He leaned forward and keyed the microphone. "Eduardo? Come in. Eduardo."

He released the microphone key and heard static greet him as the radio crackled and sizzled as if it had been plopped on an open grill.

"Sir?" a voice came through the static.

Agamemnon jumped forward. "Eduardo?"

"No, sir. This is Miki."

"Miki. Who are you?"

"Eduardo's comrade. He is my best friend, sir."

"You did not go out with him today?"

"No, sir. He insisted I stay behind in case of a problem."

Agamemnon nodded. Good thinking. Eduardo was a fine replacement for Luis. He would no doubt step right into those vacant shoes and possibly do even better than Luis had. Agamemnon keyed the microphone again.

"Where is Eduardo?"

"I don't know, sir."

"You don't know?"

"We haven't heard from them since they left early this morning."

"No one has returned?"

"No, sir."

Agamemnon steepled his fingers and tried to imagine what was going on in his jungle. He didn't like the fact that people seemed to be disappearing with startling regularity.

"How many were in his party?" he asked.

"Four, plus Eduardo and his guide."

"Guide?"

"Yes, sir. The old man was here when Luis established the base camp. He's helped us ever since and we've sort of adopted him."

Agamemnon frowned. He didn't like hearing about outsiders being involved in his group's activities. That was a security risk. And he thought that was understood by everyone. The fact that Luis had permitted this man to be in camp at all angered him.

"Tell me about the old man."

"Not much to tell, sir. He's very old. Ancient, almost. He wears a long white beard that comes down almost to his chest. He is extremely skilled at tracking, also."

"Is he?"

"Yes, sir. This morning, Eduardo sent him out to find the sniper's trail. He came back shortly and said he knew how to track him. That was when Eduardo and his team left."

"And that was the last you heard from them—is that right?"

"Yes, sir."

And now it was nightfall. "Would they be able to set up a camp in the jungle with this old guide?"

"I believe so, sir. Yes."

Agamemnon chewed his lip. He didn't like it. If people he didn't know were leading his men around, no good could come of it. Experienced tracker or not, the old man was an unknown variable and Agamemnon hated leaving things like that to chance.

"Sir?" Miki asked.

"Yes?"

"Do you think there's a problem?"

Agamemnon hesitated a moment before replying. "Possibly."

"The old man?"

"Yes."

Miki seemed to hesitate now before keying his microphone. "I can have another team ready to go in one hour, sir."

"No."

"No, sir?"

"You stay where you are, Miki. Eduardo was right to leave you behind. I want you to take command of the project that Eduardo would have told you about. Do you know what I'm referring to?"

"Yes, sir."

"Good. I want you to carry on getting ready to carry that plan out. I will form another search team and we will find our missing comrades. In the meantime, I need to know that things are being handled on your end. Do what you need to do to get the package ready to move into Manila within a day. Can you do that?"

"Yes, sir."

"Excellent. I will leave first thing tomorrow and find Eduardo and his men. I want you ready to leave by tomorrow afternoon. With luck, we'll have everything accomplished within the next twenty-four hours. And then we will have much to celebrate."

"I understand, sir."

Agamemnon switched off the radio and leaned back in his seat. Eduardo and his men were missing. A strange old man was leading them around in the jungle. A sniper and an American woman were loose in his turf. All were things that annoyed Agamemnon to no end. And now he would have to take care of it all himself.

But not right away.

He walked outside of the hut. Off at the edge of the campsite was the dying search team leader. Even as the sun's rays vanished and darkness started to bleed across the sky, Agamemnon could see the undulating carpet of ants crawling all over the man's head.

He screamed less now. His cries had diminished to mere whimpers that floated only a few feet in the tepid jungle air.

As Agamemnon moved closer, he could hear the ants chattering, their mandibles no doubt slicing and biting into the soft tissue of the man's face. His eyes would be bloody sockets full of ooze. The ants would have invaded his sinus cavities, crawling down into his trachea and esophagus. From there, they would eat away at him from the inside out.

Other ants would have marched into his ears and gained access to his sinuses from that direction, or else started gnawing on his eardrum as they made their way to the soft brain tissue farther in.

Agamemnon lit a cigar and sucked on it, the bright red tip glowing in the evening air. Truly, the man was dying in horrible fashion, he thought with satisfaction.

As he approached, some of the ants reacted to the sudden intrusion. Agamemnon stomped on a few that ventured over to investigate his presence.

"You won't get anything from me," he said, blowing out a stream of smoke at the ants, who quickly retreated.

The search team leader's head turned slightly toward Agamemnon. He tried to speak, but he coughed and spit out bits of ants instead, retching as more of the tiny bodies filled his mouth and lungs.

Whatever he had hoped to say to Agamemnon was lost amid the feasting army.

But Agamemnon knew what he would be trying to say to him. He knew because he'd seen men die like this before. And after a man reached the point of no return, there was only one thing they wanted more than anything else.

Agamemnon unholstered his pistol and chambered a round. He puffed on his cigar and blew more smoke out into the night air. Amid the chattering ants, Agamemnon heard the first pellets of rain starting to fall. Tonight, it would storm. Already in the distance, peals of thunder sounded.

The ants would probably retreat under the deluge. But in the morning, when the sun came out and started to cook the jungle, they would return, drawn by the smell of baking flesh.

Agamemnon considered the man in front of him. He wasn't really such a bad guy. He'd simply failed to live up to what Agamemnon expected of him.

And that, unfortunately for him, was not tolerated. Not when they were so close to unveiling their masterpiece.

"You could have gone so far," Agamemnon said. "I trusted you to do your best and you let me down."

The man didn't respond. He couldn't anymore. His head lolled from side to side, but only tiny sounds escaped him.

Agamemnon's pistol barked once in the night air.

Agamemnon chomped on his cigar and then slid his pistol back into its holster. He blew another stream of smoke into the jungle air and turned to walk away.

Marta stood behind him. "You are hungry now?"

He smiled. "How long have you been standing there?"

She bowed. "You are most merciful. You did that man a great service by ending his life."

"He was already dead."

"Dying, master. And still suffering."

Agamemnon shrugged. "What good are they to me if they cannot fulfill my expectations?"

"No good at all, sir."

"Indeed."

Marta looked at him. "You will need to eat before you leave tomorrow."

Agamemnon smiled. "Now, who told you I was going somewhere?"

"It seemed obvious. If no one else is able to find the woman, then you must assume leadership yourself."

"As much as it pains me to do so," he said.

"Yes, sir."

Agamemnon took another drag on his cigar. "I will eat."

"And after that?"

He smiled. "Tell the men to get ready. We leave at first light to look for the people who have gone missing. We will find them ourselves and then, if all things go to plan, we will have much to rejoice in when Miki at the other camp carries out his assignment."

15

Annja spent the night trying to sleep despite the constant pain in her body. She could no longer feel her hands; they'd gone numb sometime after the fourth hour of being positioned above her. But her back ached and her legs now joined in the party, sending muscle spasms that ended just short of her abdomen.

She figured she had gotten maybe twenty minutes in total when Vic stirred next to her. He had somehow managed to sleep despite being in the same position as Annja.

He looked over at her and grinned. "Already awake, I see."

Annja shrugged. "Guess I'm not as skilled as you are at being able to sleep in the strangest positions ever known to man."

Vic glanced overhead. "This? Oh, this isn't the worst. Not by a long shot. There was this one time I was in Botswana and we had to find our way into this warlord's lair by trekking through the most inhospitable swamp—"

"Would you kindly shut up."

Vic turned. Eduardo had woken up.

Annja smiled. "Guess who woke up on the wrong side of the bed."

Eduardo frowned. "I didn't sleep."

"No?"

"No. I can't get comfortable."

"Join the club," she said.

Eduardo eyed Vic. "You don't seem to suffer from that problem."

"I was trying to tell Annja before you so rudely interrupted that I've actually been in worse positions than this."

"I don't care."

Vic sighed. "Apparently."

Eduardo looked around. "How are we going to escape?"

Vic scowled. *"We?"*

"Yes. None of us will be able to do this on their own. Our best bet is to…join forces, at least temporarily. Until we get out of here and find our way back to the surface, we should consider ourselves allies."

"And what guarantee do we have that you'll keep your word?" Annja asked.

"No more guarantee than I have that you won't kill me as soon as you get the chance."

Vic nodded. "He has a point."

Annja tried moving her fingers, but she couldn't tell if they responded or not. Without fresh blood reaching them, she was worried the tissue might start dying. She couldn't stay here any longer, and escape was the only option. Trying to dodge an execution at the last second might have worked once, but Annja wasn't too keen on gambling that way again.

"So how do we get out of here?" she asked, thinking aloud.

Annja took a look around the area. Torches illuminated the cavern, and the light flickered and made shadows dance in every corner. It wasn't as spooky as Annja would have thought, but it did make her uncomfortable knowing they were some-where underground. Even if they were able to escape, what promise was there that they could find their way back up to the surface?

She frowned. Promise or not, they had to at least try.

Vic seemed to be doing something with his left arm. Annja watched as he wriggled his left shoulder forward and then back again.

"What are you doing?" she asked.

Vic winked. "Probably something that is going to cause me an inordinate amount of pain. But then again, desperate times and all that jazz."

Annja heard a sudden vague pop. Vic groaned but gritted his teeth.

"Good lord, did you just dislocate your shoulder?" she asked.

Sweat ran down Vic's face as his body lurched to one side. "Yeah."

Eduardo shook his head. "You are insane."

Vic ignored them both and continued to use his body weight to generate momentum. "If I can get enough motion going, it might break that knot."

Eduardo sighed. "Didn't you hear Hector? He said the knots are virtually unbreakable. There's no way you'll be able to do that. It simply won't work. You're a fool for trying it."

Vic eyed him. "You're a real up person, aren't you?"

"Excuse me?"

Annja cleared her throat. "Will it work?"

Vic shook his head. "I don't know. But we seemed out of other options. I can feel the knot tensing and releasing as I swing back and forth. Maybe if my body weight doesn't work I can get some friction going against the backboards and that might gnaw at the knots enough to break them."

"And once you're down?" she asked.

"I can pop it back in, don't worry," Vic said with a grimace.

Annja grinned in spite of herself. Vic hung at an odd angle since one of his arms seemed longer than the other. "How in the hell did you ever learn to do something like that?" she asked.

"High-school wrestling."

"What?"

He smirked. "I always wanted to be on the team, you know?" He grunted and continued swinging. "But for some reason I never did well. Turns out that this shoulder of mine just won't stay in place. So every time I had to muscle someone over or try to get a takedown, the damned thing would just sort of pop out. Or even worse, if they got to me first, my arm would jump out of the socket and the ref would call the match. Sucked at the time, but it's had its benefits since then."

"Such as?" Annja asked.

Vic smiled. "Excluding possibly saving our lives? It's a great pickup line."

Annja almost laughed. "You use that to pick up women?"

"Sure. There's nothing like the shock-and-awe effect."

"And yet, somehow I can't see any women flipping out over an arm suddenly going slack. It's actually kind of gross."

Vic swung back again. "Yeah, well, it's not a foolproof bedding-down kind of thing. I have to work it just right and then spring it on them. There's a fine art to it. Like everything else. You have to be patient."

"Right. Are you really moving all that much with your other arm still tied like that?" she asked.

Vic nodded. "There's enough motion to get most of me moving. But I'm not swinging like a pendulum here. Wish I was."

"This is taking far too long," Eduardo said. "We need to think of something else. Something more effective than this."

Annja frowned. "We're all ears if you've got a better idea. Vic's the only one I see being productive."

"You're not doing anything," Eduardo complained.

"I'm also not whining about ridiculous things like you are," Annja retorted.

Eduardo glanced around and then up at his binds. "I had a knife in my shirt but they took it."

"And you wouldn't be able to use it anyway," Annja said. "Look, I'm not exactly enjoying the sight of Vic's dislocated shoulder here, but at least he seems to be doing something. Let's give him some time to see if it works."

Eduardo frowned. "Every moment we wait is another step closer to our deaths."

Vic shook his head. "Isn't that what you people groove on anyway? I thought you loved the thought of dying. Don't you get all those virgins and shit when you go?"

"I can accomplish more by being alive," Eduardo said.

"Uh-oh," Vic said.

Annja looked at him alarmed. "What?"

"Looks like we've got an unfaithful one over here."

Eduardo spit at Vic. "What do you know about faith? You think your Western ideals will serve you well when you die?"

Vic sniffed. "I'm not presumptuous enough to even begin to imagine what will and won't help me when I cross over. But I'm also not dumb enough to follow someone who thinks that killing innocent people is the right thing to do."

"Your leaders are no different."

Annja sighed. "Didn't we cover this already? Last night at some point? Or am I already imagining things."

Vic grimaced again as he moved some more. "Yeah, you're right. What's the point anyway? I've known enough fanatics to understand they won't give a contradictory thought a chance if it butts heads with their belief system."

"Not all Muslims are fanatics," Eduardo said.

"Did I mention Muslims? I said 'fanatics.' That means

anyone, pal, regardless of religion. In case you haven't noticed, the United States has more than its fair share of nut jobs. It's not like any country or religion has a monopoly on them."

Annja looked up at Vic's bonds. "How are you making out?" she asked.

"I think I might be getting somewhere."

Eduardo peered closer. "Really?"

"Yeah, keep pissing me off. I think it helps."

"Cut it out, Vic," Annja said.

"I'm being serious. I think I made the most progress when our new friend there started bitching and moaning."

"You would equate me with a woman?" Eduardo sneered. "I am no such thing."

"Uh, did I miss the part where you suddenly let us all know you were a misogynist?" Annja frowned. "Because, you know, really that's not the best way to get on my good side."

"I don't care about getting on your good side," Eduardo said. "I care only about escaping this place. Once we are back on the surface, all bets are off and we go our separate ways."

Vic started humming.

Annja looked at him. "What are you doing?"

Vic stopped. "Sorry. I had a flashback to a Journey concert I went to when I was younger."

"Aren't you in pain?" Annja asked.

Vic nodded. "Oh yeah. Definitely."

"You've got a funny way of showing it."

"Well, I'm a bit more used to it than I would be if I just did this for the first time. After a while, it gets a bit easier. I'll be sore as hell for a few days, though."

"I'm thinking you only do this if the woman happens to be someone you really want to get with, huh?"

Vic nodded. "You got that right. The ol' dislocation trick only makes its appearance if the chick is a hot babe."

"And if you need to escape crazed tribesmen in far-off jungles."

Vic looked at her. "Nah, only if I want to impress a babe."

Annja stared at him. "You aren't seriously attempting to flirt right now, are you?"

Vic chuckled. "Let's just say that I have a lot of faith in what a shower and a fresh set of clothes would do for you."

Annja grinned in spite of herself. "This is definitely a first for me."

"What, you don't think mud is sexy?"

"And jungle grime? Not a chance."

Eduardo sighed. "If you two are quite through, could we refocus on the task at hand?"

"Party pooper," Vic said. He shifted and twisted slightly as he moved. "Piss me off again and I think I may just kill you."

"Unless I have your word, the moment you get down from there, I will scream and draw attention to you." Eduardo scowled. "You two will be dead before you get twenty feet from here."

"You'll die, too," Annja said.

"Ah, yes, but I'm the mindless fanatic, remember?" Eduardo nodded at Vic. "He said as much."

Vic shook his head. "Why bother arguing?"

"Don't," Annja said. "Just get it done."

Vic shifted again and Annja heard something. "Was that it?" she asked.

Vic gritted his teeth. "Hang on…"

Eduardo cleared his throat. "Do I have your word?"

Annja looked at him. "We have a truce, yes. Now keep quiet."

Vic took a deep breath and shifted hard to his right. Annja heard a snap. And then in the next moment, Vic's left arm came free, flopping down to his side.

"Ugh." Annja blanched. "That looks really bad."

Vic smiled. "Putting it back in is even more fun."

Annja closed her eyes. "Just get it done and get us out of here."

16

Even before the sun had a chance to send its rays across the horizon, Agamemnon was awake and getting his troops ready to move out. He thought briefly about Miki and how the fate of their cause rested in his hands. To delegate such authority surprised even him. But necessity dictated he go out and find his missing men, the woman and the sniper. Only then would he be able to return to his objectives.

He had ten men with him at the edge of the camp. Eight of them were from the camp itself and two were specialists he'd brought in for just this task. After thinking about it long and hard, he'd radioed in for some experienced trackers. They'd appeared before dawn and both of them looked lethal and capable—the kind of men Agamemnon preferred.

They paused by the head of the search team leader. His skull showed in places as the ants carried on their gruesome task of devouring the flesh. There seemed no end to the trail of them leading to their nest in the jungle. Twin lines of the tiny workers moved to and fro, some returning to the head and others ferrying bits back to the queen and her brood.

"If only I had men who worked this hard," Agamemnon said, "we would have already toppled the government."

One of the men waiting nearby vomited his breakfast on the side of the trail. The sight of his friend proved too much for him. Agamemnon frowned. If he hadn't needed him, he might have shot him for being so easily upset.

Agamemnon wrinkled his nose in disgust. "Well, since there seems little point in basking in that ungodly stench, I suppose we'll be off now," he said.

The two trackers moved out. Each of them carried only a pistol and a long machete on his belt. Agamemnon himself plotted their course on the map. They would pick up where the search team had left off yesterday, but first they would have to find that point on the map. Every few hundred yards they would have to stop and reassess their position. Agamemnon had no intention of getting lost or vanishing amid the jungle vines.

After about a mile, one of his men waved him over. Agamemnon stopped by the trunk of a huge buttress tree. "What is it?"

The man pointed at the ground. "Here. Tracks, sir."

"Whose?"

"The search team from yesterday. And before that, a woman."

Agamemnon looked at the landmarks on his map and sent two more of his men off to find higher points to the east and west to confirm their position. They returned and told him the points were where he said they should be.

He marked their position on the map and then called over the second tracker. "See if what he says is true. The woman's tracks start here?"

The second tracker knelt and studied the earth. After a minute he glanced up. "Yes. Her tracks are still evident. But there is another set, as well."

"More tracks?"

"A man."

"You're sure it's not a member of the search team from yesterday?"

The second tracker studied the ground for another two minutes and then looked back up. "Tough to tell, but the aging on them is different. The tracks I'm looking at are older than the search team's. The age seems to match the tracks of the woman."

"Who could he be?"

"The tracks correspond with the boots worn by members of the military, sir."

"Filipino military or American?"

The tracker shrugged. "Impossible to say, sir. I can only tell you that the man who made the tracks stands about six feet tall and weighs about 175 pounds."

"So it could be the American sniper."

"It's possible. Yes, sir."

Agamemnon called for a water break and then turned back to his trackers. "According to the search team leader, they followed the woman's tracks for about a mile before they vanished. Your job is to find them even if it appears they go missing. Can you do that?"

They both nodded.

"Then go."

Without a sound, both trackers melted into the undergrowth. Within a few seconds, Agamemnon could no longer make them out. Their dark green clothing, mottled with bits of fabric and muddy brown splashes, helped break up their lines and better blend them to the jungle's environment. Neither of them wore boots, but seemed to prefer soft-soled cloth shoes that resembled moccasins.

As long as they find the trail, Agamemnon thought, we will take care of the rest of the equation.

He looked back at the eight men he'd brought with him. Each one was armed with either an AK-47 or an AR-15. Both weapons were excellent in the jungle and required little care in order to keep operating.

But the jungle expedition was taxing. And his men weren't necessarily used to trekking long distances through the dense canopy. Their clothes were already soaked with sweat and humidity.

Agamemnon himself felt the unbearable thickness of the air surrounding him. He twisted the cap off of his canteen and tilted it toward his mouth. The rush of tepid water refreshed him but only until he stopped drinking. As soon as he swallowed the last gulp, the heaviness of the jungle returned.

The sooner we get this finished, the better, he decided.

If the American woman and the sniper were together, so much the better. They would be able to deal with both of them at the same time. One of his men carried a video camera in his rucksack for just such an event. Capturing two beheadings on tape would help their cause.

Agamemnon smiled. This could turn out to be a good day after all.

The two trackers returned. While both of them were breathing heavily, they at least seemed better conditioned and used to the jungle than the rest of his men.

"The trail continues, sir," one said.

"How far up?"

"Very close. The man tried to conceal their tracks as much as possible by choosing difficult ground to cover."

"Meaning?"

The second tracker cleared his throat. "If they walked over the dirt and mud, it would be easy to find them. But their path goes over rocks and lot of dead leaf fall. It also twists and turns in unpredictable ways, making it difficult for us to follow. In places, their tracks seem to disappear so we have to cast around for them and then pick up the trail farther on."

"But you can find them. That's what you're telling me, right?"

"Yes. We can find them."

Agamemnon replaced his canteen. "Good. Take a quick water break and we'll get going."

"We're all set, sir."

Agamemnon frowned. "Don't be ridiculous. You need water. Make sure you hydrate."

"We've already had our drink, sir. We cut some tube vines farther down the path as we tracked. If we can keep moving, we'll be able to find them by nightfall, we expect."

Agamemnon raised his eyebrows. "Is that so?"

The other tracker nodded. "Absolutely."

Agamemnon spread his hands. "Well, then, lead on. I look forward to watching you both work."

The trackers bowed and then waited as the rest of Agamemnon's men got themselves ready to move. Agamemnon watched them glance at the trackers with a mixture of fear and distrust. He smiled. His troops disliked outsiders. Especially outsiders who made them look like fools.

He knew the memory of the team leader's death was still fresh in their minds. Failure was unacceptable and Agamemnon had made that abundantly clear in his final judgment. But now here were two outsiders who showed an ease, both with the jungle and the task of tracking the woman and sniper, that unsettled his men.

"Come on, now, get yourselves up and moving. We're not out here to waste any time. The sooner we get this done, the sooner we can get back to camp and enjoy the evening," he said.

Agamemnon's thoughts moved to Miki again. If everything was going well, the young man would be preparing to move the device from the safety of the camp to the posh section of Manila.

When he'd thought about where the bomb should be placed, Agamemnon had considered Roosevelt Park, an area lined with exclusive housing compounds. But then he figured that exploding the bomb in Makati, where a number of powerful banks and businesses were based, would be a more crippling blow. Not only would he destroy the businesses, but also the people who worked there.

Instead of killing a bunch of lazy residents, he could destroy the backbone of the country. The government would be powerless to respond.

Agamemnon grinned. Traffic was a nightmare in the Philippines, and if the government couldn't even get that under control, there was no way they'd be able to respond adequately to a nuclear incident.

His men passed him down the trail. Agamemnon felt good and clapped each on the back as he walked by. He offered words of encouragement.

"Doing okay?"

They would smile and nod and say, "Yes, sir."

"Good. Keep going, men. Keep going. We're going to get these infidels and then kill them for all the misery they've caused."

"Yes, sir."

"You're with me?"

More men grinned. "Yes, sir!"

Agamemnon nodded. "That's what I like to hear."

They made their way through the jungle, and the men, unconcerned with leaving a trail, used their machetes to hack into the thick vines and move through them.

Yards ahead, the trackers worked in perfect time to each other. One tracked ahead of the other, and they would change roles frequently so neither tired too much. Agamemnon marveled at how easily they moved through the jungle. Neither of them hacked through the vines the way his men did.

They simply melted through them.

Agamemnon called a break to get his men watered and to apply more mosquito repellent. As he lathered the stuff on his skin, he noticed the harsh scent and frowned. It would take a good long bath to get truly clean after this outing.

His men all breathed heavily, their lungs heaving from the increased humidity. As the sun grew higher in the unseen sky overhead, the heat increased, as well. Soon enough, they would run out of the water they carried.

Agamemnon called the trackers over.

"We will need to stop and replenish our water supplies soon."

The first tracker pointed at a nearby tree. "We are surrounded by tube vines. Your men can cut into them with their machetes and then bleed the water off into their canteens."

"Will it be enough to sustain us?"

"For the rest of the day, yes. If we are forced to spend the night out here, we will find an alternative source of water."

Agamemnon frowned. "You told me you'd find the trail and we'd be done with this by nightfall."

"We will be, sir. But we also plan for contingencies. Just in case."

"Very well."

Agamemnon took another sip of his water and felt his canteen was growing light already. He wasn't used to long treks any more than his men, but to keep up appearances, he had to minimize any discomfort he felt.

If his men thought he was slacking, they would lose respect for him. And even threats of death by ants would not rouse them if they believed him to be weak.

He waved his men on. "Let's go. We have people to find

and kill." He glanced overhead and wondered how much hotter it could actually get under the canopy. Surely the woman couldn't survive in this heat.

He frowned again and hurried on. If she was still alive, once he caught up with her, she'd wish she wasn't.

17

Annja watched as Vic struggled with the knots binding his second wrist. "No luck?" she asked.

Vic yanked on the knot one more time and then slumped, gasping for breath. Sweat rolled down his face, staining his camouflage even darker than before. "I can't get enough purchase to loosen the knots."

"He said we wouldn't be able to."

Annja glared at Eduardo. "I don't see you doing anything to help the situation any."

"I'm listening for anyone's approach. We don't want them to see us doing this, after all."

"Way to take one for the team," Annja said. She looked at Vic, who was clearly angry with himself for not being able to break the binding. "Don't sweat it, we'll figure out another way out of this," she said.

He smirked. "Will we?"

Annja nodded. "We can't give up now. We've got all day to figure it out."

Vic sighed and hung there with one arm free. "We don't.

I've got to finish this or they're apt to wander by and see me hanging like this. Besides, my other arm is killing me now. It's taking all the weight."

"What about the shoulder you dislocated?"

"I'm used to it."

Annja looked around the small clearing. The torches, which had burned throughout the night, looked as though they might go out at any moment. She knew the cavern would sink into darkness when they did. It would be the perfect time to try to make their escape.

Otherwise, if they stayed there, Hector or his men would come through, light the torches and check on them. Once they saw Vic hanging there askew, they'd fix him up and undoubtedly tie him even tighter than they had before.

Annja closed her eyes. The sword still hung where it usually did. Annja could see it so tantalizingly close. If she could only release it, she could cut herself down and then free Vic.

And Eduardo, too, she supposed.

But how could she grasp the sword without both of her hands wrapped around the hilt?

She watched it hover, vaguely moving in her mind's eye. She studied how it hung there, almost as if it was surrounded by some type of force field or aura. Annja tried to fathom how the entire process worked. She wondered if the sword was in purgatory or limbo or just on another plane. And if it was on another plane of existence, then how was she alone able to access it?

In the past, all she'd ever done was reach in with both hands and grasp it. Then she'd retreated and the sword was hers.

She heard a sudden shout and thud. She opened her eyes and saw Vic was flat on his face on the ground. "Vic!" she said. "Are you okay?"

"Maybe," was Vic's muffled reply.

Eduardo shifted. "The idiot broke free. Are you just going to lay there? Do you plan to get us out of here or not?"

Annja frowned. "You aren't much for being patient, are you?"

"Not when my life is on the line, no."

Annja ignored him. She looked at Vic. "Can you reach my foot with your free hand?"

Vic frowned. "Yeah, I think so." He twisted and then stretched toward her foot.

Annja felt his fingers close around her toes and then her ankle. She nodded. "Good."

Vic struggled. "I don't think I can cut your binds loose if that's what you're thinking."

"You have to," she said. "I know you can do it. Chew through them if you have to."

Vic worked on her ankle bindings and eventually he did resort to chewing them. It worked and Annja was able to stand. As soon as she did so, the bindings around her wrists slackened slightly. She worked her right wrist until it was raw and bleeding, but suddenly her hand slipped free.

Vic was still working on his ankle bindings and Eduardo was still doing nothing.

Annja looked at Eduardo and Vic. "I need to ask you both a favor."

"Anything," Vic said.

Annja smiled. "I need you both to turn your heads away from me and close your eyes."

Eduardo frowned. "I can assure you there's nothing I haven't seen before. I have been with many women."

Annja smiled. "Wonderful for you. But I need to do something and I need privacy to do it. When it's over, we'll all be free."

Vic shrugged. "Okay, whatever. As long as it works."

Eduardo frowned. "Very well, but I warn you not to betray me. I have a very long memory."

"Don't worry, lover boy," Annja said.

Eduardo turned his head and closed his eyes. Annja looked at Vic, who winked at her once and then did the same.

Annja took a breath, closed her eyes and reached for the sword.

When she opened them, the sword was in her hand.

Annja cut her left arm loose, carefully moving it until she had checked it out. It seemed okay, perhaps a little sore for right now. But Annja suspected it would be fine in short order. Her whole body ached.

She looked at the sword, feeling strength run through her body. It felt great holding it again.

She looked at Vic and Eduardo. She could tell they were desperate to know what she was doing.

Annja smiled and then cut them both loose.

They needed to get out of there.

18

Agamemnon watched his men work their way through the jungle. He could hear them struggle to breathe. They were tired and even the frequent stops he ordered did little to assuage the growing fatigue that was evident on their sweaty, grime-covered faces.

His two trackers were still out in front of the rest of the group, picking their way through the vines and over tree trunks. Even they were beginning to show signs of exhaustion. And still the trail seemed to move them ever forward through the steamy undergrowth.

Agamemnon spotted one of the trackers coming back toward him. Agamemnon held up his hand, and his men seemed to breathe a collective sigh of relief when he did so.

The tracker came up to him. "Sir." His breathing was labored and Agamemnon was at least glad that he was also tired.

"What's the matter? Why have we stopped?" he asked.

"We've picked up another trail, sir. More men. And they were following the people we seek."

Agamemnon frowned. "Can you tell how many?"

"Five in boots. One in bare feet."

"Bare feet?"

The tracker nodded. "He seems to be out in front of the others. It's curious but we think it was the search team's tracker."

Agamemnon pulled out the map of the jungle and traced his finger along the path they had taken. He then looked at the location of his second camp and drew an intersecting line. Yes, it was entirely possible that Eduardo had intercepted the trail and set off after the American woman and the sniper. He smiled. Good for Eduardo.

But where were they?

He glanced back at the tracker. "You can follow them easily enough?"

"Yes, sir. They have made no effort to conceal their path. And it helps us, actually, since they were tracking the people we seek. And those tracks are older now, tougher to distinguish amid the litter on the jungle floor."

Agamemnon helped himself to some more water, drinking deeply before nodding. "Very well, you can proceed."

The tracker turned and hurried back down the trail. Agamemnon watched him go and then looked at his men. Each of them seemed lost in his own thoughts. Agamemnon had seen the look before on men going into battle. A hard struggle had its own way of tunneling minds. It was almost as if each man had to find his own way to handle the never-ending physical punishment of trekking through the jungle.

Ordinarily, Agamemnon would have chosen a much more leisurely pace. Jungle travel exerted a tremendous amount of strain on people. And traveling more than a mile or so per day could easily kill a squad of men.

But time wasn't a luxury they had. Not with the American woman and the dreaded sniper somewhere out in the jungle.

If they got to safety, then all of his plans would be for nothing.

Plus, he wanted revenge.

He grinned. He knew he could never admit that. But he did want it, because of what the woman had done to him. She'd embarrassed him. And then the sniper had killed his best man.

Both of them would perish for their misdeed. And Agamemnon would enjoy watching them die.

He pushed himself off the trunk of the tree he leaned against and urged his men up. "Time to move, men. Come on, now."

None of them groaned. That would have been too obvious a sign of their growing frustration. But Agamemnon could sense that they wanted nothing more than to quit and hunker down for the night.

Night was a long way off yet. And so was the idea of stopping.

A burst of motion up in front of him caused Agamemnon to pull his rifle up into his shoulder. But then he saw that it was only the tracker coming back to him again.

Agamemnon frowned. Now what?

As the tracker came closer, Agamemnon could see the expression on the man's face. It didn't look as if he was happy.

"What is it?" he asked.

"Blood."

"Excuse me?"

"Farther up the trail. There is evidence of…something."

"Something?"

The tracker shrugged. "We're not sure. But it looks like several men were killed in the clearing."

Agamemnon felt his gut tighten. "Show me."

The tracker led him down the trail. As he passed his men, Agamemnon fanned his hand. "Take up defensive positions. Just in case."

His men spread out to form a defensive arc around their area. Each one faced out into the jungle, his gun ready to fire.

"The blood is old," the tracker said. "And the insects have had their share of it already."

"But you're sure it is blood?" Agamemnon asked.

"Yes, sir. Very sure."

Agamemnon crawled over a downed log and felt his legs slip on something. He glanced down expecting to find a body, but it was only a carpet of moist moss. He took a calming breath and continued on.

Ahead, he could see the first tracker, who knelt in the tall grass of a clearing. As they approached the man looked up and nodded at Agamemnon. "Sir."

"Show me."

The first tracker parted the grass and Agamemnon could see the slick darkness standing in contrast to the brilliant green. Ants swarmed over the site and there was a buzzing of flies, as well.

But there was no body.

"Is this it?"

The tracker shook his head and pointed. "Isolated patches there, there and there, as well. It looks like four men were killed here."

Four men. Agamemnon's thoughts raced. That was most of Eduardo's team. And there was no telling if Eduardo had been among the men who had apparently been killed.

"But no bodies?" he asked.

Both trackers shook their heads. "We've looked. But the corpses, which we presume there were due to the volume of blood spilled, seem to have just disappeared into the jungle."

"Disappeared?"

"Yes, sir."

"And they left no trail?"

"None we could follow for more than a few yards. The bodies appear to have been dragged somewhat and then they vanished."

"You realize that sounds impossible, right?"

The first tracker nodded. "We've checked the trees, sir. We couldn't find a single body or evidence they were even taken up."

Agamemnon sighed. This wasn't good news. If Eduardo's team had been killed somehow by the sniper and the American woman, there would be evidence of some fashion aside from spurts of blood on the ground. There was no way two people would have been able to hide four bodies and not leave some evidence behind.

That left the possibility of something else. And it was something Agamemnon wasn't at all pleased to admit to himself.

"It's possible there are others out here, then?" he asked.

Both trackers nodded. "We were thinking the same thing, sir."

"They would have to be good," Agamemnon said. "To be able to ambush a group of trained soldiers like Eduardo and his men. To do that means they are not amateurs."

"And to not leave a trail," the second tracker said, "means they are adept at moving through the jungle. Possibly in ways that even we are not."

Agamemnon chewed his lip. How much worse could his current situation get? He sighed and brushed at the flies that had begun investigating him. "We'll need to move on very carefully. If there's a chance that some other group is operating out here, I don't want us falling victim to them the way Eduardo's team apparently did."

"There's still the question of what happened to the other two members of Eduardo's team, sir."

Agamemnon nodded. "Two would seem to be still alive, yes?"

"Yes."

"Then we need to find them. And save them if they are in trouble."

The trackers stood. One of them slid out his knife. Agamemnon could tell that it was a handmade *balisong* with a dangerous blade on it.

"You sure you wouldn't rather use a gun?" he asked.

The tracker shook his head. "I don't think a gun will do any good against people who have the skill to do what they did here, sir."

Agamemnon frowned. "Do you know something you're not telling me?"

The trackers eyed each other and then the second one cleared his throat. "Just legends, sir. Nothing more."

"But given the situation," the first said, "we just don't know anymore."

"Tell me," Agamemnon ordered.

The second tracker leaned against the tree behind him. "This jungle is supposed to be haunted by the spirits of a once powerful tribe of Moros warriors who controlled this area."

"Moros? The tribe who used to fight off armed conquerors with knives?"

"Yes, sir. But they were all nearly hunted to extinction, it is said. Except for the ones who live in these jungles. Somehow, they managed to survive and eke out a living here. For years, this jungle was avoided by all the local people who live on the coast of the island. Tourists who used to venture in here were never heard from again. The locals refused to step foot in here."

"But now," the first tracker continued, "people have forgotten about the old legends. Everyone wants more from the islands, and a lot of them are being eaten away by developers."

"Or people like me," Agamemnon said.

The first tracker nodded. "Obviously, this is the perfect

place to use as a base for your operations. The army has a hard time tracking in this type of environment. But the legends are still whispered about."

Agamemnon wrinkled his nose as a bug attempted to fly into his nostril. He exhaled sharply and blew it out. "You think we are being hunted?"

Both trackers shook their heads.

"But," the second tracker said, "someone most definitely tracked the first team and apparently killed some of their men."

"And you've got no trail to follow now."

"That's correct."

Agamemnon shook his head. "Trails just don't disappear. There's simply no way to erase a presence from the jungle. There's got to be something we're not seeing yet."

"We've searched up ahead about ten yards."

Agamemnon took a deep breath. "Expand your search. I want to know exactly what happened here beyond the four deaths. I want to know how these trails can simply disappear."

"Very well, sir."

Agamemnon started back to his men and then stopped. He turned around and looked at the trackers. "These legends, did they say what happened to the people who disappeared?"

The first tracker shook his head. "No, sir. But no one who disappeared was ever heard from again. The logical assumption was they died here in the jungle."

"No remains were ever found?"

"No, sir. It was like the jungle just swallowed them up. Bones and all."

Agamemnon nodded. "Keep looking. I want answers."

He turned and headed back down the path. Already he could hear the murmurings among his men. Four dead. Spirits. Legends. Trapped in the jungle. They were tired, scared and whispering among themselves.

"Get up!" Agamemnon moved faster, urging the men to rouse themselves. "Forget the legends. We're armed and skilled and whatever is out there is no match for us."

He glanced back down the trail and prayed he was right.

19

Agamemnon's trackers had moved a hundred yards farther down the trail when they waved their tired leader over to them again. Agamemnon was now thoroughly exhausted and only just able to keep his face from showing the strain of traipsing through the jungle undergrowth all day long.

"What is it now?" he asked.

The first tracker pointed at the depressions in the ground. "This is where two people lay."

"Two people?"

"A man and a woman. They are the people, I think, you are looking for?"

Agamemnon looked around. He could clearly make out where the tall grass had been crumpled under the weight of two distinct bodies. But he saw little else.

"Is there any sign there was a battle here?"

"There's no blood, if that's what you're asking," the second tracker said. "We don't think whoever was here was killed."

"Or even wounded," the other said. "But there are signs

they were somehow incapacitated. See over there? It would appear they were dragged away."

"Like the others," Agamemnon said.

"Yes."

"And how much farther along is it before they vanish like the others?"

The first tracker frowned. "Twenty yards."

Agamemnon shook his head and then checked his watch. If things were going as they should have been, Miki would be well on his way to getting the device on its journey to Manila. He estimated it would take him the better part of two days to reach the city and get the device secreted away.

In the meantime, Agamemnon needed to know if anyone else knew of his plans. He needed to get his hands on the sniper.

He looked back at the trackers. "There has to be a clue. Somewhere. You need to find it. I don't care if we search all night."

The first tracker gestured overhead. "We're running out of light."

Agamemnon shook his head. "I don't care. Keep looking."

The second tracker frowned. "As the sun goes down, we'll be greatly limited in what we can see. It's dark enough during the day under the canopy. But doing this at night could mean we make mistakes."

Agamemnon rubbed the top of his rifle. "I suggest you don't make any mistakes. That wouldn't bode well for your future."

The trackers nodded and turned away from Agamemnon. He cursed. He didn't care if they liked him or not. All they had to do was follow his orders. They had to find the clue that would point them in the right direction to finding the sniper, the woman and possibly Eduardo.

Agamemnon returned to the rest of his men. They were completely worn-out. Agamemnon knew he was on dangerous ground here. He knew that if he pushed them too far, they would stumble and be completely ineffective in the event of a firefight.

But a little fear might help nudge them along.

He waved them over. "Men, we're going to keep following this trail a little while longer. I know we're all tired. But I think you'll agree we should keep going."

"Why so, sir?" one of his men asked.

Agamemnon looked at the exhausted face of the young recruit. "Because something else out here is hunting us."

The men murmured among themselves. Agamemnon nodded. "It's true. The trackers have found evidence that we are not alone. And they've discovered that the search team from the other camp was quite possibly ambushed."

"Were they all killed, sir?"

"It looks like four of them were, yes. But there were survivors."

"Where are they, sir?"

Agamemnon shook his head. "I don't know. Their trail seems to vanish after they were dragged for several yards. That's what the trackers are looking for right now. We need to find out where they went."

"What about the American woman?"

Agamemnon nodded. "It appears that she is still alive. Although she and the sniper that we're also searching for appear to have been taken by force, as well."

Another recruit spoke up. "What do you think we're dealing with here, sir?"

"I don't know. The trackers tell me there are legends about this jungle. Rumors mostly, but supposedly the spirits of an old tribe still inhabit this land."

"Do you believe them, sir?"

Agamemnon didn't believe in spirits, but he knew many of his men did. And perhaps a little hint of the supernatural would help propel them further. "Well, I don't really know.

My own experience with the spirit world has been limited. But the men tracking for us are convinced the spirits are active. And they are not happy that we've come into their territory. Our best bet now is to make our way through as quickly as possible and get out of here. Once we find the woman and the sniper, we will return to our camp and await the news of our plan in Manila."

"Will they succeed, sir?"

Agamemnon nodded. "I believe they will, yes. And once our gift to the aristocrats is received, we will be able to bring the rest of the country to their knees. In time, we will assume control of the government."

The men nodded. Agamemnon could see the looks on their faces turning from exhaustion to determination. He stood. "A few more hours and we should be able to get out of here. We'll have what we came for."

The men stood, as well. Some of them seemed to have new energy. Others struggled but made the effort.

Agamemnon helped some of them up. "We can do this, men. I know we can. Each of you was chosen by me because I believe in you all. We can and will do this!"

As he walked among them, they smiled and drank from their canteens.

Agamemnon nodded. "Fill up on the water. Cut the tube vines if you need more. The trackers tell me we must keep moving, so we won't be stopping at any rivers unless we absolutely have to."

Agamemnon turned and headed back down the trail. In the bush ahead, he could see the trackers working together. They seemed to be moving slowly.

Damn them, he thought. I need them moving faster than that.

But even he had to admit that the fading sunlight was making it difficult to see even a few feet in front of him. The sun was dipping toward the horizon. Ordinarily, it would have been prudent to simply set up camp.

But prudence wasn't what Agamemnon wanted now.

He pushed through a stand of tall grass. Around him, his men chopped at the jungle with their machetes, their clanking swishes biting through the dense undergrowth. The mosquitoes, already a nuisance during the day, began stirring in the evening air. The air buzzed with their drones. Agamemnon swatted one that landed on his face and his hand came away bloody, the scent of copper staining the air.

More bugs swarmed. He could hear his men complaining about them. A nice fire would keep them at bay, but they had to keep moving.

A few minutes farther down the trail, one of the trackers retreated. Agamemnon could see the pain in his face.

"What?" he asked.

"We need to stop, sir."

"Why?"

The second tracker gestured overhead. "It's simply too dark. We can't keep on stalking them under these conditions. Feel tracking, which is what we'd have to do when it gets dark, is a tough skill to perfect over good ground. Doing it in the jungle at night is impossible. I beg you to consider stopping."

"We have an agenda to keep to. Stopping isn't part of the equation."

The tracker shook his head. "We won't be able to continue. In the darkness, your men could easily wander away from the trail and get lost. Your manpower would suffer in the event that we come under attack."

"And if we set up a camp, aren't we just inviting whatever is out here to come and get us?"

"We could post sentries, sir."

"My men are worried. They are scared. And tired. Stopping now will allow the uncertainties that exist out here to fester in their minds. They will become even more frightened. And then they will be completely useless to me."

"And if we keep going, some of them may die."

Agamemnon took a breath. "Your partner, does he agree?"

The second tracker nodded. "He does. The only reason he has not come back to protest is because he needs to mark the trail so we can find it again in the morning."

Agamemnon looked overhead. In the short time they'd been talking, daylight had shrunk even further. The night was coming down fast. Shadows grew longer off the trail.

A fire would be a welcome thing. So would a decent meal.

Part of him wanted to go on, to push his men past their breaking point in order to show them what they were truly capable of. But a bigger part of him knew the trackers were correct. They had to stop.

"Very well," he said.

The second tracker looked at him. "You're sure, sir?"

"You just said we needed to stop. That it's too dangerous to continue. I value the lives of my men. I'm not a fool, after all."

The second tracker nodded. "It's the right decision, sir. Tomorrow, we will find them. I swear it."

Agamemnon raised his hand and turned to address his men. "We'll stop here for the night."

"Sir?"

Agamemnon nodded. "You heard me. It's too dark to go on. Set up the shelters and get some fires going. I want sentries posted first. Rotate the men so everyone gets a good rest. We'll get some food and water and rest here. At first light, we will continue."

As tired as his men were, some of them had been so roused by Agamemnon's speech that they didn't want to stop. He had to place his hands on them and urge them to sit down.

"It's okay, men. We've worked hard today."

"What about the spirits, sir?"

Agamemnon shook his head. "I doubt very much they'll trouble us tonight. Spirits need to rest, too."

They all laughed. Agamemnon allowed himself to lean against the trunk of a spindly tree, and then slid all the way to the ground. Even the dive-bombing mosquitoes did little to annoy him as fatigue washed over his entire body.

I could sleep here, he thought with a small grin.

"Sir?"

He glanced up. The second tracker stood in front of him. "Good God, man, we've stopped already. What more could you possibly want now?"

The tracker grinned. He held out a canteen. "Fresh water from the tube vines nearby, sir. You look as though you could do with a drink."

Agamemnon nodded and accepted the canteen. "Thank you."

The tracker squatted next to him. "We'll get them first thing in the morning, sir."

"How can you be so sure?"

"It's a feeling."

"You've hunted men before?"

"Yes, many times. We were hired to do this over in Laos a few times."

Agamemnon nodded. "I was impressed with your experience when I called for you to join us."

"My brother and I—"

"The other tracker is your brother?"

"Yes, sir."

"Incredible."

"We were trained by the very best. When we were much younger we used to live out in the jungle for weeks at a time."

Agamemnon nodded. "Well, go and get your brother.

Tonight, we rest and maybe you can entertain us with some stories of your more memorable trackings, huh?"

"Very well, sir. I'll go get him."

Agamemnon sipped the water, feeling the tepid liquid slide down his throat. It tasted only vaguely of dirt and he was grateful for the chance to rest.

But his reprieve was short-lived. Moments after he left, the second tracker was back.

When Agamemnon saw the look on his face, all peace fled his body. "What's the matter?"

The second tracker shook his head. "My brother...he's vanished."

20

Vic eyed Eduardo and Eduardo returned the stare as Annja began to look around. From what she could make out in the dark environment, the cavern they were in was part of a much larger series of interconnected caves. Elaborate cave paintings decorated the walls. She could see some type of script but couldn't make out what lingual family it might have belonged to, if any that she even knew of.

Farther off in the caves, she could make out a few ambient noises that seemed man-made. But for the moment, at least, they seemed to be in no danger of being discovered.

But what time was it? Annja frowned. She'd never known how much a watch meant to her until she didn't have one. But even then, being aboveground usually gave her a fair indication of the approximate time of day. Being underground, however, was akin to a form of sensory deprivation. She had no idea what time it was.

"I think we're okay. For now," she said.

Vic nodded but didn't take his eyes off Eduardo. Eduardo didn't blink, either.

Annja sighed. "Guys, maybe you should just kill each other now and get it over with."

Vic shook his head. "It would cause too much commotion. And that wouldn't be good for any of us."

"He's right," Eduardo said. "As much as it would give me pleasure to kill you both, it would be like committing suicide. And since I wouldn't be taking out a lot of high-value targets with me, it would be a waste."

"Well, when you put it like that," Annja said, "maybe we should just try to get along and find a way out of here, yeah?"

Vic glanced at Annja. "Did you find something?"

"No. But it seems pretty quiet out there, too. I'm not sure if everyone's asleep or not. I have no idea what time it might be."

"It can't be night again. They would have come for us by now. Even if we don't know what time it is, I'm sure they know," Vic pointed out.

"Yes," Eduardo said. "And Hector seemed very sure of himself that we would be killed at sunset."

Annja smiled. "Which is exactly why we should make ourselves scarce now. Let's get moving."

Vic eyed her. "You're armed, right?"

Annja simply smiled.

Vic nodded. "At some point, you're going to tell us exactly how you managed to cut the bindings, right?"

Annja smirked. "Not likely."

"Obviously, you have a blade hidden somewhere on you. Is it secreted in some dark nether place that you can't show me?"

Annja smacked him on the shoulder. "I'll let your imagination run away with that one for a while. But don't press me on the issue, okay?"

"Okay."

Eduardo stood nearby. "We should have an order of travel. Someone will need to take point."

Vic looked at Annja. "You want me to do it?"

Annja shrugged. "You've got the most experience creeping through the jungle, so maybe."

"This isn't the jungle. This is under the jungle. I have no idea what we might encounter," Vic said.

"You're still tops for the job in my book," Annja replied.

"Yes," Eduardo said. "You do have the skill to be stealthy. I will grant you that at least."

"Lucky me."

Annja pointed at Eduardo. "You'll go next."

"Next? I was going to suggest I bring up the rear."

"I'll take the rear," Annja said.

Eduardo smiled. "You don't trust me."

"Not one little bit."

He leaned closer to her and Annja could smell the foul breath caressing her face. "And what will you do if I suddenly kill Vic here? How will you stop me then, woman?"

Annja grinned. "You don't want to know what I'm capable of, Eduardo. So don't push me."

"What you're capable of?" Eduardo laughed. "What an utterly ridiculous statement."

"Hey," Vic said. "She survived out in the jungle with nothing but the clothes on her back. That says plenty to me."

"She survived because she ran into you."

"Not right away she didn't."

Eduardo started to say something else but thought better of it. He clamped his mouth shut and then just nodded.

"We should go," Annja said.

Vic led the way out of the small entrance to their cavern. Annja followed behind Eduardo and cast a final glimpse back at their prison. It would have been nice to bring a torch along, but they couldn't risk the light giving them away as they made their way through the cave complex.

They'd have to do it all in the darkness.

Fortunately, Annja didn't think that whoever else was down there with Hector would be able to maneuver without a torch. That meant they'd have a pretty good warning of someone approaching them. It might just give them enough time to hide.

She hoped.

Vic eased his way down the path. Annja found it hard following along until she relaxed and sank deeper into her subconsciously aware state. Instead of relying on her conscious mind to guide her via her five senses, Annja allowed her instincts to take over.

As soon as she did so, she could feel Eduardo's presence in front of her and beyond him, Vic. Moving in this fashion, she knew how fast to travel and when to slow down. Vic didn't keep his pace constant, but would sometimes slow down if he needed to check up ahead.

Vic was nervous. She could sense it in the way he moved. Here and there, he made small noises that she knew he wouldn't have made if he'd been totally comfortable in his environment.

But if Vic was nervous, Eduardo was utterly terrified. And Annja didn't think his fear stemmed solely from their predicament. He seemed to be scared of the darkness itself.

That worried Annja. His fear could give them away if he didn't do something to control himself.

Annja sensed Vic stopping. She heard Eduardo whisper a message back to her. "He's checking something out."

Annja nodded. "Are you all right?"

The fear in Eduardo's voice vanished. "I'm fine."

"You're not. You're terrified. I can tell," she said.

"How can you tell?" His voice was a harsh whisper now,

and Annja felt anger and wounded pride beginning to color his timbre.

"I just can. Don't worry about it so much. None of us can see."

"Vic doesn't seem to have a problem."

"Only because he's used to operating in near darkness. But even he's nervous. Trust me."

Eduardo paused. "Who are you?"

Annja smiled. "No one special. Just take some deep breaths and you'll feel better about all of this. Vic will get us back up top and then we'll be fine."

"You really think so?"

"Sure."

Eduardo sighed. Perhaps he wasn't so evil after all, Annja thought. She frowned. No. She wouldn't let herself think that. She'd been too optimistic about humanity in the past and knew that people were capable of concealing their true nature if they thought it would help their cause.

If I was in Eduardo's position, she thought, I'd be doing exactly the same thing. He needs a friend right now. Otherwise, Vic will most likely kill him once we get out of here. But if he befriends me, he'll think I might intervene long enough for him to either escape or kill us both.

She knew she'd have to watch him carefully.

Eduardo's voice came back to her again. "Thank you," he said.

"You're welcome." But Annja wasn't sure what to make of him. She sensed Vic returning and then they started moving again.

Annja's hands passed over cave walls that felt incredibly smooth, almost as if water had worn down all the nooks and crannies over the years until the stone felt like cool marble.

Had an underground river carved this network out of the jungle?

Annja wished she had a light source to see what they were passing. No doubt, it would have made for a great story on *Chasing History's Monsters*. If only the threat of being sacrificed to some unknown deity hadn't figured so prominently into it. Annja didn't relish losing her life for the sake of good television. There were plenty of other saps who would aspire to that.

They moved slowly for the better part of fifteen minutes. Annja felt sweat break out along her brow, even though the air here felt much less humid than it had aboveground.

It's the pace, she thought. Plus, the stress of not being able to make noise. Together, it would make anyone sweat.

Well, she thought. Maybe not Vic.

She sensed him getting more comfortable as he led them on past more tunnels and caves. Twice, they had come to an intersection, a choice where they could have gone either left or right. Both times, Annja checked the direction against her instincts and both times she felt Vic had chosen wisely.

But there was only one way to find out, she decided. And that was to keep on going in the direction they were headed.

Scattered bits of noise reached her ears now. Was there something going on up ahead of them?

Annja assumed they'd only traveled a few hundred yards in total, so they still weren't that far away from their prison cavern. Was it possible that they were coming into a more populated area?

Perhaps Hector was rousing his tribe and getting them ready for the sacrifice.

Vic stopped moving suddenly.

"Someone's coming," Eduardo said. "Hide."

Annja shrank back against the rock, trying to find a way to press herself into some kind of niche. But the rock was as smooth as what they had been passing so far.

"There's no place to hide," she whispered.

She sensed more movement. Vic's voice appeared in her ear. "Three men are coming with torches. If they pass by us, they will see us. We need to hide."

"Where? We can't see," she said.

"I know. I was hoping you might have an idea."

"Me?" Annja frowned. "How would I—?"

"I don't know," Vic said with an edge in his voice. "But you'd better figure something out. I'm all out of ideas and those guys are coming closer."

Annja leaned closer to Vic. "Okay. Follow me."

21

"What do you mean he's vanished?"

The second tracker, whom Agamemnon had learned was called Joey, shook his head. "When I went back to get him as you ordered, he was nowhere to be found. I searched the area close by but he's gone."

Agamemnon frowned. This was not good. Losing one of his trackers, especially Joey's brother, was a horrible event. It would surely lead to a further loss of morale, something Agamemnon could not afford. With his men already worried about the nature of what they might be fighting and the possibility of spirits stalking them, another mysterious event could push them over the edge.

Agamemnon summoned his patrol leader. When the exhausted soldier squatted next to him, Agamemnon pushed himself up. "Joey is going to show me the lay of the land for our search tomorrow. Take care of getting the men squared away. I want small fires only, nothing too large. There's no sense advertising our presence if we can avoid it. Get them fed and to sleep. We'll be back shortly."

The patrol leader nodded and moved away, pushing the men into action. Agamemnon watched him for a few seconds and then turned to Joey and spoke in a low voice. "Let's go."

Joey led him out of the small clearing and down the trail. Agamemnon watched the tracker carefully pick his way through the thick brush. Agamemnon kept a hand on his pistol, just in case.

After fifty yards, Joey stopped and pointed to the ground. "This is where his last track is."

Agamemnon frowned. "I can't see anything."

Joey took his hand and placed it on the ground. "Touch lightly here."

Agamemnon did so and felt a shallow depression. "Ah."

"You feel the rounded parts?"

"Yes."

"From the ball of his foot. He pushed off here. But his trail ends and I have cast around for the next one but can't find a thing."

"You say he pushed off?"

"Yes."

Agamemnon nodded. "So that's good, right?"

Joey frowned. "I don't follow, sir."

"Well, if he was taken captive or killed, he wouldn't necessarily be pushing off, would he? He'd be dragged somewhere."

"That's true, I suppose."

"And since his track shows no sign that he was incapacitated, there's a good chance he's fine and has just wandered off, right?"

Joey shrugged. "Well, I suppose so, but it's odd that his trail ends. No matter where he'd gone, I'd be able to follow him."

"Are you sure?"

Joey grinned. "We were trained together. We each know

every one of the tricks the other uses to throw people off our trail. God knows we've had plenty of occasions to use them. When we were training to be trackers, we learned how to find each other regardless of what we tried to do to disguise our trail."

"But you can't find him now."

"No."

Agamemnon glanced back over his shoulder. He could see small fires springing up. He couldn't be out here much longer if he hoped to avoid his men growing suspicious. "Well, what do you suggest we do?"

"Look for him," Joey said.

"Now?"

"He could be in trouble."

Agamemnon frowned. "Look, we stopped because you and your brother told me it was too dangerous to go poking around here at night. Now you want me to forsake that very order and go off looking for your brother who may, in fact, be fine."

"He's not fine," Joey said.

"It's downright dangerous." Agamemnon pointed over his shoulder. "Look, I've got a patrol of hungry, tired men who are already jumpy about our predicament here. Thanks to the rumors about spirits, they're thinking nasty thoughts. If I go back there and tell them your brother has gone missing, it's liable to make them run for parts unknown. Imagine how bad it will look knowing one of the trackers—one of the very people who are supposed to be helping us—has disappeared. I'll have a mutiny on my hands."

Joey looked away. "I can't leave him out there."

"I'm afraid you're going to have to," Agamemnon said.

When Joey looked back at him, he found himself staring into the muzzle of Agamemnon's pistol.

"You should know that I will shoot you dead unless you

come back with me right now and pretend that everything is fine. I need you and your skill," Agamemnon said.

"He's my brother—the only family I have left."

"These men are my family. And I have a responsibility to keep them together, focused on what needs to be done. You going off on your own will not allow me to do that."

Joey's eyes flashed and for a moment Agamemnon was worried he might indeed have to shoot him. But then Joey seemed to relax. "All right. You win. We'll look for him tomorrow."

"Good."

Joey put his hand on Agamemnon's arm. "But if anything happens to him between now and then—"

Agamemnon pulled away. "Don't threaten me, Joey. Don't be that foolish. I've killed men, women and children for far less. And I've enjoyed doing so."

They made their way back to the improvised camp. As they approached, Agamemnon could hear a few stray laughs percolating in the darkness. That was good, he thought. They still had the capacity for humor.

His patrol leader looked up as they came in. "Where is the other one?"

Agamemnon glanced at Joey, who took his cue and cleared his throat. "My brother likes to make sure we aren't surprised and has opted to spend the night out beyond the periphery of the camp."

"Alone?" the patrol leader asked.

"Yes," Joey replied.

The patrol commander frowned. "He's crazy."

Joey smiled. "We're a bit unorthodox, yes."

"Isn't he worried?"

"About what?" Joey's smile looked genuine enough.

The patrol commander started to say something, seemed

to think better of it and then just shrugged. "I thought he'd at least join us for dinner."

Joey shook his head. "We're skilled at finding food without the need for fires and the like. He's probably got himself in a tree, enjoying the solitude. He is a bit of a loner."

Agamemnon clapped his hands together. "Well, then, let's get some dinner, shall we?"

The patrol commander handed him a plate of rice and chicken. Agamemnon took a forkful and chewed it, marveling at how suddenly ravenous he felt. He tore through the food and then got himself a second helping.

Joey ate little. Agamemnon could tell he was still thinking about the safety of his brother. That was fine, he reasoned. Provided he didn't do anything stupid. And as long as no one else noticed his concern and got suspicious.

The patrol commander passed around a canteen. Agamemnon washed down his meal with several long swallows. He passed it to Joey, who took a long drag on it before handing it back.

"Thanks."

Agamemnon nodded. "You mentioned something about being in Laos a little while ago."

"Yes."

"Why?"

Joey shrugged. "We hired ourselves out to the local warlords in the Golden Triangle. They had someone who'd gone off with a suitcase full of money. Apparently the person took off into the jungle and the warlord wanted someone who could track them."

"They didn't have anyone local who could do that?"

Joey shrugged. "There's a difference between knowing the jungle and being able to track. A local guide is good, but you still need the skill to be able to follow a man. That's where Michael and I came in."

"So they paired you up with a guide?"

Joey shook his head. "Nah. We just went in and did our thing. As long as we have a trail to follow, why bother with a guide? It's not like we needed to know where we were going. We only needed to know where our quarry was headed. The evidence was the only map we needed."

Good, Agamemnon thought. I just need to keep him talking about this and I'm sure he'll forget all about the need to go off and find his brother. "Was it a difficult task to find the man?" he asked.

Joey grinned. "Wasn't a man."

"No?"

"A woman. A clever one at that."

Agamemnon smiled. "They sometimes are." Just like the American woman I'm trying to find, he mused.

"She'd apparently been one of the warlord's favored concubines. I guess she had finally had enough and thought she deserved some severance pay for her troubles. She ran off with over a hundred thousand dollars in U.S. currency."

"That would make for a heavy suitcase, wouldn't it?" Agamemnon asked.

Joey shrugged. "She had it in a rucksack, actually. It was probably a good deal of weight, but she kept it squared on her back pretty well. It showed in her tracks, though."

The patrol commander spoke up. "So you can really tell how much the person weighs by their track?"

Joey nodded. "Absolutely. More weight means the tracks sink deeper or register more on different types of terrain. You can tell where the weight is situated by how they push off—it will show on the toes or the heel."

"It's fascinating stuff," Agamemnon said truthfully.

"We could tell that she had it on her back. And that she was in great shape. This wasn't a sedentary woman. She knew how to walk and run, probably because she was a local. She'd grown up in the jungle until the warlord decided she'd make a good concubine."

Agamemnon smiled. Joey could certainly sell himself when he needed to. Agamemnon had almost forgotten about his missing brother.

The patrol commander leaned forward. "So, what happened?"

"We tracked her toward the base of a giant waterfall. You hear about these things, but finding one untouched in the mountains is truly an amazing thing in and of itself."

"Yeah?"

"She'd climbed the waterfall. She was trying to use the water to conceal her path, make her almost vanish, as it were."

"Remarkable."

"It was, yes," Joey said. "Until she fell."

"She fell?" Agamemnon asked.

"Blew open her skull when she bounced off the boulders at the bottom of the falls." Joey shook his head. "What a waste. She was a beautiful woman, too. Obviously very headstrong, but you have to admire an independent spirit like that. She took a risk and it didn't pay off for her. But you still had to respect her decision to risk it all. She knew what would have happened if we'd caught up with her."

"You would have killed her, right?" the patrol leader asked.

Joey shook his head. "Not us. Our job was to bring the money back. But we would have brought her back, as well. And I don't think the warlord we worked for would have been very kind to her. We'd seen his handiwork before."

Agamemnon smiled. "What did he do?"

Joey faced him. "He liked to gouge out eyeballs and pour acid into the sockets, listening to his victims scream as the acid ate into their brains."

That's one I haven't considered, Agamemnon thought. He grinned. "So, you brought the money back."

"And got paid and we left," Joey said. He stretched. "And on that note, I think I'll retire. We've got an early morning ahead of us."

Agamemnon nodded. "Wise words. Everyone get to bed." He stretched and then got to his feet. The patrol commander pointed to a hammock a few feet away.

"Your hammock is all set, sir."

"Thank you." Agamemnon rolled into the hammock and pulled his mosquito netting over him. Instantly, he felt a blanket of sleep settle over him. He could hear the whine of mosquitoes trying to get at him but stymied by the netting. Their discordant lullaby filled his mind and he fell asleep.

The next thing he knew, the patrol commander was shaking him. Agamemnon's hand went right to his pistol. "What is it?"

"Sorry to wake you, sir."

"What time is it?"

"Almost midnight."

"Why are you waking me?"

The patrol commander shook his head. "It's the tracker. Joey."

Agamemnon sat up. "What about him?"

"I just went to check on the troops. They're fine. But he's gone."

Agamemnon gritted his teeth. Dammit. He looked out into the darkness. God help you, he thought. When I get my hands on you, I just might pour some acid into your eyeballs.

22

Annja huddled against the wall of the cavern, feeling the cool rock under her skin. Close by, Vic and Eduardo tried to tuck themselves into the various crannies the rock wall afforded them. They'd raced back to the spot Annja had remembered passing earlier. It was their only hope.

The sounds of the approaching party grew louder. Annja could make out two distinct voices but couldn't understand the language. It sounded similar to Tagalog, but it was a dialect she couldn't place.

She saw the faint glow of light coming closer and getting stronger. They do have torches, she thought.

Will they see us? she wondered.

Annja tried to work out a way out of this mess. As soon as the people walked by, they'd have to get out of there. Their disappearance would be known as soon as the group reached the prison cavern and saw they weren't tied up any longer.

But where could they go?

The underground network seemed to be a maze of twists and turns. Heading one way or the other without a real sense of direction could just as easily get them killed as it could show them the way out.

The voices grew louder. Annja ducked her head lower.

She saw the sudden firelight of the torch.

She held her breath and waited.

As they approached, Annja steeled herself to leap into action if they were spotted. She could feel the adrenaline seeping into her bloodstream. Her muscles felt galvanized. She was ready. She visualized her sword.

The voices continued past her.

The glow from the torches faded.

Annja looked. The coast was clear.

"Now," she said, "let's get the hell out of here."

Vic and Eduardo unfolded themselves from the rock wall. Eduardo limped away, nursing several bruises.

"You okay?" she whispered.

"I'll be fine," he replied.

Vic tugged on Annja's sleeve. "We have to go. Now."

"I know. But which way?"

Vic looked at her. "You figured out where to hide us. Why don't you take point?"

Annja shook her head. "Stealth's not my thing."

Vic smiled. "Stealth isn't going to mean squat in about three minutes. Once they see we're not back there, they're going to start screaming bloody hell. And then we're going to have the rest of those goons coming down on top of us. I suggest we forget trying to go undetected and just go for it."

Annja glanced at Eduardo. "And you?"

Eduardo frowned. "As much as it pains me to do so, I agree with him. We need to get out of here and now."

"You trust me to lead?" she asked.

"It seems I have little choice."

Annja smirked. "And with that vote of confidence…" She

turned back to the corridor and closed her eyes. Which way, she wondered, right or left? It was time for a leap of faith. Her instincts told her right seemed to be the correct way to go.

She opened her eyes and glanced at Vic. "All right, let's go."

Without any light, it was still almost impossible to move fast. But at least they could go faster than they had been before. Annja found that by relaxing herself, she could feel ahead of her, almost as if she was projecting some invisible sensory awareness.

Twice she'd ducked and missed banging her head into a stalactite. Vic seemed as attuned as she was, but every once in a while, Eduardo would mutter a curse as he hit something else in the darkness.

They'd gone about a hundred yards when they heard the sudden commotion behind them. Shouts filled the caverns.

"That's it," Vic said. "I think that's our cue to get the hell out of Dodge."

"They're coming," Eduardo said.

Annja glanced behind them. The caves were lighting up with the dim glow of torches. "How many?"

"Probably the two guys from earlier," Vic said. "They've got to come back this way to warn the others."

Annja nodded. "You and Eduardo keep going. I'll handle these guys."

"Are you nuts? They're armed. I saw they had awful-looking knives with them. They'll kill you, Annja."

Annja shook her head. "I'll be fine."

Eduardo cleared his throat and pushed past Vic. "I think she has a good suggestion. We should keep moving."

Vic glared at him. "You're only out to save yourself."

Annja pushed Vic after Eduardo. "Keep going. I'll find my own way out. And hopefully, this won't take that long."

Vic squeezed her arm. "Are you sure?"

"Go!"

"We could take them together," he said.

She smiled, sure he couldn't see it. "I can handle them. And it's better this way, if you know what I mean."

"I have no idea what you mean, but I suppose that's really your point, isn't it?" he asked.

"Something like that."

"Be careful," he said.

"I will."

And then Vic and Eduardo were gone. Annja glanced after them in the dark. No time to get all wistful, she supposed. She turned back toward the cave. The light was growing brighter.

They'll be here any minute, she thought. Time to get ready.

Annja closed her eyes and summoned her sword. When she opened her eyes, the sword was in her hands. She reached around with it to determine what she could about the area.

The cavern measured roughly ten feet by twelve feet, and the roof was about seven feet high. Not a lot of room, she figured, but enough to make short work of the people coming at her.

She dropped to her knees and took several deep breaths, feeling the rush of oxygen flood her system. Just holding the sword made her feel empowered again.

The shouts grew louder.

Annja looked up.

Three torches broke through into her stretch of tunnel. She saw three muscular dark-skinned men covered in elaborate symbols painted on their bodies. Their eyes burned as they saw her.

But they didn't look surprised. Or scared.

Annja braced herself.

One of the warriors took the other torches and stepped

back as the first two men unsheathed long thin blades from
their loincloths. Annja watched as their lean sinewy arms
gripped the blades.

Both men moved in a carefully choreographed fashion.
They obviously knew how to fight.

Annja racked her brain, trying to remember everything she
could about the indigenous warriors of the Philippines. She
knew the Moros were mighty warriors who had very nearly
beaten the Spanish conquerors a few hundred years back.
Were these possibly descendants of that tribe?

If they were, it meant Annja was going to face some
tough opponents.

She assumed a defensive posture. The sword seemed cum-
bersome in the confined space of the cavern. Both of the
warriors seemed to sense this, and their blades, while longer
than an average chef's knife, were nonetheless well suited to
fighting in tighter quarters.

Annja kept her feet close together and her knees bent.

The two warriors split apart and took opposite sides of the
cavern. Annja knew they were feeling her out, trying to
fathom what her strategy might be for this encounter.

One of them threw a half-hearted feint that Annja ignored.
No sense lunging for something that wasn't there. And she
had no doubt that if she did, the other warrior would gut her
in no time.

No, the better option was to wait for the committed strike.
She would respond to that attack.

The torches being held by the third warrior flickered as
they all circled one another, breathing in and out. Annja could
feel the tension growing.

They'll have to move sooner than later, she thought. There's
no way they can let this go on much longer.

And even as she thought that, the warrior on her right side

suddenly launched himself, cutting at her throat as he brought his blade diagonally down from his opposite shoulder.

Annja pivoted and struck out at him as his blade sliced through the air. But he sensed her counterattack and spun himself out of range, retreating just beyond the effective arc of her sword.

She could see the eyes of the second warrior flare. But there was something else in them, as well. Perhaps they were curious about her. Maybe they didn't expect to face someone like Annja.

The second warrior dropped low and stabbed straight in at Annja's midsection, trying to gut her.

Annja dropped her blade down, trying to cut the arm, but again, the second warrior yanked it out of the way just in time to miss having it cut off.

Annja took a breath and felt the perspiration dripping down her face.

Two moves and she was already getting winded.

The first warrior cut in at her again, but as Annja went to parry the stab, he jerked it back, pushed past the inside of her parry and cut down on top of her forearm. Annja whirled, feeling the bite of the blade through her skin.

She caught the scent of blood in the air. The cut wasn't very deep, but it hurt like hell, and worse, Annja knew they now understood how to neutralize the effectiveness of her sword. A feint would draw her out and they'd use her movement to bridge the gap.

Once they were inside, they could destroy her.

I wish this thing was shorter, she thought. With a knife the same size as what the warriors wielded, she'd have a better chance of handling them.

The second warrior cried out and threw himself at Annja. His stab came from high overhead and was the last thing

Annja expected him to try since it seemed so utterly suicidal. All she had to do was drop down and bring her blade up and he would impale himself.

She started to do just that, but then stopped, whirled and stuck her sword out to the side.

The first warrior screamed as Annja's blade slid into his midsection.

They'd tried to bait her and she'd almost fallen for it.

Annja yanked her sword out and spun, cutting down. Her blade hit the first warrior. Blood spouted from his neck and his body slumped to one side, unmoving against the side of the cavern.

Annja spun to face the second warrior.

He eyed her carefully now. The plan hadn't worked.

But there were still two very potent men facing her. Annja couldn't let herself get sloppy. Not now. And not with Vic's safety resting on her shoulders. She had to buy them more time.

The second warrior circled her. The third warrior was searching for a place to rest the torches.

Annja could see that he'd found a torch holder in the rock. She heard a thunk as the torch slid home.

Great.

Now instead of just one, she had two to face again.

And this time, she knew they would change their tactics.

Both men suddenly came at her simultaneously. Annja parried the first horizontal slash, keeping her sword up as she stepped between them. It was a foolish move and one she paid for.

She felt the bite of another cut in her lower back. Only the fact that she had been moving forward meant the difference between a shallow cut and a mortal stab to her kidney.

I've got to finish this, she thought. I'm running out of time.

One more misstep and she'd be dead.

23

Agamemnon rolled out of his hammock and instantly felt the dive-bomb assault of the mosquitoes as they descended to rob him of his blood. He swatted a few of them and followed his patrol commander out past the ring of fires.

Agamemnon sighed. "I wondered if he would do this."

"Do what, sir?"

"Go after his brother."

The patrol commander frowned. "I thought his brother was asleep out past the periphery of the camp."

"His brother went missing as we were settling in. He wanted to go after him then, but I wouldn't allow it."

"Why?"

"Because the men would get scared. Losing one of our trackers is cause for concern, don't you think?"

The commander shrugged. "I think losing one is better than losing two, sir, which is what we've got on our hands right now."

Agamemnon cursed. "You are right."

"So, what now?"

Agamemnon glanced back at the camp. "Are the men asleep?"

"Yes, sir. Today was a hard one on them. I think they'll all be appreciative in the morning if they get some solid rest."

"Good. Get me a rifle."

"Sir?"

"I want a rifle. I'm only carrying a pistol."

The commander hesitated. "What for, sir?"

"I'm going to find our trackers."

"Alone, sir?"

"Yes."

The commander left him alone in the jungle night. Agamemnon looked out into the darkness. He could hear the animals moving through the undergrowth. The jungle came alive at night, it seemed to him. Usually, he liked to pass the time asleep.

The commander returned and handed him an AK-47. "It's fully loaded, sir. I brought you an extra magazine, as well."

Agamemnon accepted it. "Thank you."

"I'll come along with you, sir. It's not safe out there for a man all alone. Especially given the nature of our situation."

Agamemnon shook his head. "I'll go alone. There's less chance of me getting attacked if I'm alone. I think it's more dangerous being in a group at this point. Besides, the men need their rest."

"What good will that rest be if you are killed?"

Agamemnon shrugged. "I don't believe I'm going to be killed." He racked the slide on the assault rifle. "I need to do this, anyway."

"As you wish, sir."

Agamemnon slid the extra magazine into the pouch on his belt and then checked to make sure he still had his pistol and knife. "Here's the plan. I'll go out and see if I can find our missing trackers. If I can, I'll bring them back. If you hear gunshots, that means I'm in trouble."

"Try to keep firing and we'll find you, sir."

Agamemnon nodded and tightened his straps. The less noise he made as he worked through the undergrowth, the better. "Tell me, do you know anything about the Moros?"

"Only what we've all learned in history class. That they were comprised of several splinter groups that resisted foreign attempts at control. First with the Spanish and later with the Americans."

"In those ways, they're a lot like us," Agamemnon said. "Interesting, isn't it? The similarities, I mean."

"I doubt they were ever as well organized as we are, sir."

"Still," Agamemnon said, "they were able to keep the Spaniards from making any real punitive missions to the interior of Mindanao and other islands. The best the Spanish could do was to garrison the coasts. The Moros owned the interior."

"Dangerous fighters, it is said," the man said.

Agamemnon nodded. "I think they owe that reputation to the fact they were so ferocious in combat. They were extremely skilled knife fighters, if I recall."

"The kris knife was one of their specialties."

"Indeed."

The commander coughed. "Do you think we're up against them now, sir?"

"I don't really know what to think. All this talk of vengeful spirits doesn't sit well with me. I don't like thinking that our lives are so fickle as to be influenced to that extent by the afterlife."

"But the men—"

"Are superstitious, yes. I'm well aware of their beliefs. If nothing else, that makes them susceptible to events like we face now. At other times, it makes them easier to instill courage in. It's a trade-off for any commander, as I'm sure you're aware. We learn to deal with it the best we can."

"Yes, sir."

Agamemnon nodded. "I'm ready."

"Be careful, sir."

"Thank you."

The commander turned and walked back toward the camp. Agamemnon watched him go and then turned to face the jungle.

Now, he thought, now we'll see what is truly going on out here.

But where would he start his search?

It seemed to make the most sense to begin with the track that Joey had shown him. Agamemnon felt certain that Joey would have started his search there. And if nothing else, it gave Agamemnon a place to plan.

As he walked through the tall grass toward the spot he remembered, Agamemnon listened to the jungle. Somewhere far off in the night he could hear the various growls, chirps and caterwauls of the creatures that preferred the night to the day.

What else lurks out there? he wondered.

He found his way back to the track and pressed his hand down. His fingers brushed the depressions. A few short hours had helped wear it away even more, but he could still make out the markings.

Agamemnon looked up. Where would Joey go from here? Where would he look for another track?

He tried to imagine himself as an expert tracker. What did they look for aside from footprints? Most likely, it seemed they would try to pick out places where nature had been disturbed. Breaks in the plants or vines that might suggest someone had passed through them as they walked. They'd look for overturned leaves that hadn't been exposed to the sunlight.

But at night, he couldn't read that kind of sign.

Agamemnon stood and chose a direction, picking his way through the undergrowth. Several downed logs barred his path and he had to clamber over them. The AK-47 felt heavy in his hands, and as much as he hated doing so, he had to rest the weapon on the other side of the downed buttress trees.

I'm not as young as I used to be, he thought. And here I am out all alone in the night in the jungle searching for skilled trackers, a sniper and an American woman who shamed me in front of my men. Meanwhile, I have a nuclear device on its way to Manila.

He almost laughed at the thought of trying to write a biography of his life. Who would have thought it would get to this point?

A spiderweb stuck to his face, and Agamemnon jumped back in shock. He felt something scramble through his hair and clawed at it, feeling the large hairy body flit through his fingertips.

He bent and threw it to the ground, praying it didn't bite him in the process. There were plenty of poisonous things in the jungle. The last thing he needed was to be bitten by a spider. He saw it start to run away and ground it under his boot. Dirty thing, he thought. That was the last web he'd ever spin.

He scratched his head again, feeling as if there were bugs all over him now. He was sweating profusely and stopped to take a long drink from his canteen.

He thought about the men in camp. In the morning they'd be well rested and ready to resume their search. Let them sleep, he thought. It's important for me to do this, anyway.

Agamemnon kept moving. He kept his eyes almost permanently fixed to the ground, looking for any indication that Joey had come this way. But he found nothing for his trouble.

Fortunately, the moon had broken out from behind the clouds. The canopy shielded most of its light, but even still, some found its way down to the jungle floor. Agamemnon could make out some details, and it helped guide him several yards.

After a half an hour, he stopped to lean against a tree.

This isn't getting me anywhere, but lost, he thought.

He frowned and took another drink. What is it that I'm not seeing? What am I missing?

A thought occurred to him and he moved back the way he'd come. It was only a matter of fifty yards, but he found even doing that was confusing. He marveled at how utterly simple it would be to become completely lost in the jungle, especially at night.

And yet, a lot of his men had either been killed or captured by people who knew this land like the back of their hands.

Agamemnon looked for the place he'd started his search. He walked back and knelt in the tall grass. The track was still there.

What if the problem is everyone has been looking at this like a tracker? What if it's not supposed to be that simple?

He sighed. He had no idea what made sense anymore.

The closest point to the track was a stand of trees off to the right. They were closely bunched together.

There's no way anyone would go over there, he thought.

He stopped. That was logic speaking to him. Forget the logic, he told himself. Let's try it anyway.

Agamemnon rose and walked over to the clump of trees. Their trunks reached up toward the sky and they must have easily been several hundred years old.

Perhaps they were here back when the Moros were fighting the Spanish, he thought.

He appreciated the sense of history it gave him.

He looked around the base of the trunks. Tube vines wrapped around the trunks as they did throughout the jungle. Tall grass obscured parts of the roots. Agamemnon could find no tracks.

He looked higher.

He squinted. Was that a gouge on the bark just above his eye level?

He ran his fingers over it. There was definitely a break in the tree bark, just shy of where a vine covered part of it. Agamemnon moved the vine and saw the scrape was larger than he'd originally thought.

He looked further up and saw that the trunks parted, each one branching off in a different direction. He took another look around. He didn't feel like he was being watched. But even still, it never hurt to be prepared.

He tried standing on tiptoes to see what the crook of the tree looked like where the trunks diverged. But it was too high up to see that far. He'd have to climb.

Agamemnon slid the strap of the AK-47 over his shoulder and then grasped part of the tube vine closest to him. It seemed thick enough to support his weight.

Here goes, he thought.

He grunted once and then pulled himself up. He struggled to get his legs up and over part of the trunk. The vine felt as if it was coming away from the bark and he started to fall back until he got his hands around a thicker part of the branches closest to him.

With a final grunt, he hauled himself up and into the thicker trunk area.

He looked down and saw darkness.

He dropped his hand down and felt something smooth. He frowned. His fingers closed over something that didn't feel natural. He recognized it almost immediately—a handle.

Agamemnon looked back toward the camp. Should he go and wake them all?

No.

Instead, he pulled on the handle and felt it lift. From what

he could just barely make out, the opening led down into a
space between the trunks that could not be seen when looking
at the trees from down on the ground.

A secret tunnel?

Agamemnon slid the AK-47 off of his shoulder and aimed
it down into the hole.

I guess I know where I'm going next.

24

Annja whirled, facing the two remaining Moro warriors. Each of them held the wicked-looking kris knife that Annja had read about. The curvy blade had more than enough cutting power to end her life. And the two cuts she now endured were sign enough that she had to finish things off as quickly as possible.

She concentrated on the first warrior, who wanted to edge his way around to her left. Annja used her lead foot to keep it in line with his centerline. By dipping the tip of her blade just a bit, she could keep him from getting to that side.

The second warrior also was starting to edge his way to her right.

Annja frowned.

They wanted to flank her at the same time. By splitting her attention, they'd be able to get a kill shot in on her.

Not this time, she thought.

Annja waited for the first warrior to make another move and, as soon as he did, she rolled and cut horizontally at his legs. She felt the edge of her sword bite into the front of his shins.

He cried out and leaped away from her, knocking into the cavern wall.

Annja got to her feet and instantly pointed at the second warrior in order to keep him at bay. She feinted with a stab at his heart and he dodged it. Annja flicked the blade up and cut him on the back of his hand. The cut wasn't enough to make him cry out, but Annja had delivered her message.

She wouldn't be that easy to kill.

The first warrior's legs were a mess of blood, but Annja doubted the wound was serious enough to cause him to make another mistake. But they'd treat her with a bit more respect now, and besides, Annja felt better that she'd gotten a couple of good shots in on them.

She wondered briefly if the amount of blood was enough to make the ground beneath them slick.

Annja's breath came faster now and she was soaked through with sweat. Something about the close confines of the cavern made it tougher to get her air back. She felt a bit more exhausted than usual.

She found that was strange.

Ordinarily, using the sword made her feel more powerful. She could feel its power still coursing through her veins, but somehow, it felt muted.

Annja frowned. Was it another new discovery about the sword she hadn't known before? Or had the psychological advantage the sword usually gave her worn off now that she was so accustomed to using it? She realized this was not the ideal thought process to follow given the circumstances.

The first warrior circled toward her front. The second tried edging his way to her right again. Annja frowned. They seemed to be moving slower now.

Her head swam.

She took a deep breath, struggling for more oxygen. She

blinked twice and then saw the first warrior coming straight at her.

Annja spun, bending back just as the blade of his knife streaked in at her heart. Annja knocked it away and then righted herself, thrusting with the sword straight at him.

She felt the blade cut into the side of his neck. More blood spurted as she severed his carotid artery. He clamped a hand on the wound, but the blood ran too fast for him to alleviate the spraying artery. He took a halfhearted stab at her and Annja danced out of range, still wary of the other warrior.

The first warrior slumped to the ground.

The final warrior risked one glance at his fallen comrade and then glared at Annja. He screamed something at her in the language he spoke, but Annja just shrugged.

"I don't have a clue what you said."

Her head ached. Her lungs heaved and she was literally dripping with sweat. It seemed harder than ever to keep moving. Somehow she had to kill this guy and get out of here.

Perhaps there was some sort of natural gas in the cavern that was making her so woozy? She didn't know, but she had to get out of there.

And fast.

The warrior rolled on the ground and grabbed the other man's knife. When he came to his feet, he wielded a blade in each hand.

Great, Annja thought. Now he's got two.

She feinted a thrust at his heart, and he parried it while simultaneously slashing down at her. The way he moved reminded Annja of some of the more talented *escrimadors* she'd seen practicing.

They had used twin rattan sticks, but Annja knew the sticks represented machetes. Real *escrima* was an exceptional art, provided you could find someone who actually knew how to teach it properly. Like a lot of other martial arts, it could be difficult locating a really good teacher.

It was obvious this guy knew what he was doing.

Annja backed up and he recalibrated himself. He whirled the two blades and moved into another fighting posture.

Annja's head swam. He seemed to be moving even more slowly.

Or was she moving slower?

The wound on her back throbbed. She could feel it pulse erratically, as if it was already infected. But it was too soon, wasn't it?

With a sinking feeling in her gut, Annja recognized the possibility that they had somehow poisoned her. Maybe their blades had been coated with a topical poison of some sort. She had little doubt they knew any number of potent toxins in the indigenous jungle plants.

And she'd been lucky enough to get the business end of some of them.

She took a deep breath. If she didn't end this fight soon, she'd be dead. She needed to kill him and figure out how to neutralize the toxin probably coursing through her veins.

That must be why she felt weaker even with the sword. If she put the blade away, she would probably already be dead.

She thrust out at her opponent and he again parried the attack. Annja heaved a breath into her lungs.

I'm running out of time. But how can I deal with this guy?

She held the blade and faced him. She could see the rage burning in his eyes. His skin had a dull sheen of sweat on it. But a poison wasn't causing it. He's just angry I've killed two of his pals, Annja thought.

He stabbed in with one of his blades and cut down diagonally with the other, retracted it and turned it into a stab. The rapid-fire three strikes came at her faster than she expected. It was all she could do to parry and dodge them one after another.

He broke off the attack and Annja retreated even farther. She sensed the wall behind her.

I'm losing it, she thought.

He attacked again, another round of three attacks coming at her almost too fast to handle.

Annja breathed heavily, trying to get more air into her lungs. Come on!

He ducked low and tried to attack her legs, flashing the blades, striking like a cobra. He darted this way and that, probing her defenses, keeping her moving, always on edge.

Annja kept evading him, and the more she did, the more tired she got.

He's wearing me out deliberately, she thought. The faster I tire, the easier it is for the toxin to take effect.

She'd played right into his hands.

I'm not going down that easily, she decided.

She eyed him as he continued to circle her. The tip of her blade kept him at bay, but as he continued to dance around her periphery like a hungry shark, Annja let the tip of her sword wobble a bit.

Her eyes grew watery. Her sinuses seemed to be running, as well.

The toxin was starting to shut her down.

She could feel the hammering of her heart as the wound to her back continued to throb mercilessly. If that cut had gone deeper, she thought, I'd be dead already and wouldn't need to worry about poisons.

The warrior pressed her again, attacking her hard this time. He cut down, slashed horizontally and then up at an oblique angle before rebounding and immediately launching another series of attacks.

Annja parried, dodged and leaped to avoid being cut. Each movement seemed to grow more painful than the last.

What poison is this? she wondered. Her muscles felt as if they were seizing. As if they'd lost all their natural flexibility and elasticity.

The warrior must have sensed it. He smiled now at Annja and said something else to her. She couldn't understand it, but it sounded as if he was taunting her.

"Shut the hell up," she murmured. She gritted her teeth.

The tip of her sword wobbled even more and she had trouble keeping it in line with his eyes. It faltered and then she allowed it to drop even more until it pointed toward the floor.

He must have been waiting for that because as soon as her sword lowered, he charged right in at her, his arms starting to knock the sword blade down and away from him. If he could just bridge the gap and get inside her defenses, he'd be able to kill her.

Annja stepped to one side and dropped to her knee, flicking the blade up and inside the man's arcing arms as they came down. The blade caught him on the inside of his forearms, slicing into his skin. It continued to travel as his momentum pitched him forward and then slid right into his sternum, bisecting his heart.

Annja heard a sharp gasp of breath and then the unmistakable sound of bones giving way to the steel blade of her sword.

Annja withdrew the sword and he toppled to the ground.

She used the blade to push herself back up to a standing position. She took two steps and then had to lean against the wall for support.

Her vision blurred. The flickering torches didn't help.

Got to reach the exit, she thought.

Got to make it. For Vic.

Her heart rate seemed to be slowing. Even her injured back seemed less annoying now. She took a breath and realized she was losing sensation in her limbs.

Paralysis?

Whatever the poison was, it was extremely potent. She decided it had to be something that attacked her nervous system, gradually shutting down all of her systems until she was dead.

And if her heart stopped, that would be it.

"Vic—"

Annja tried to call out, but even her voice seemed faraway and removed from her.

She took another step and dropped to the floor of the cavern.

She could vaguely smell the blood on the floor from the men she'd killed.

Was she going to die here, as well?

She gripped her sword in one hand and tried to pull herself along the floor with the other. But her legs didn't seem to want to obey her commands. And she couldn't tell if her brain was even functioning enough to deliver the neurological impulses.

Annja licked her lips. Her mouth tasted like a sweaty sock.

She looked at the sword and the dull gray light it cast off.

Is this my last battle?

She tried to crawl again, but only managed to get a mouthful of dirt and stone for her weak efforts.

Annja took a breath. It was shallow and she felt as if her heart rattled against the inside of her chest.

The sword.

Annja had to put it away before someone else found it. If she was going to die, then the secret of its existence had to die with her.

She took one last breath and closed her eyes.

Darkness reached for her.

25

Agamemnon dropped into the hole. Six feet down, he stopped. The opening was barely large enough to accommodate him. He squinted in the dark, trying his best to make out whatever he could possibly see, which wasn't a whole lot.

He turned and squatted, feeling with his hands. There was another opening in front of him. He moved forward slowly, not wanting to suddenly plunge down some unseen hole to his death.

He shook his head. Who would have ever imagined that a secret tunnel would be carved right into a series of tree trunks? Certainly not him. And yet, here he was, already neck deep in it.

Literally.

He moved ahead and the tunnel seemed to slope down at a gradual angle. Agamemnon reached up overhead, but still found the opening not quite large enough to stand up in.

Strange.

He frowned. If his other men had been taken by force, how had their captors managed to get them into this tunnel? He had a hard enough time navigating it himself. Trying to get people in here under duress would have proved very difficult.

Unless there were other openings scattered throughout this section of jungle. It was possible, he supposed. After all, he'd found this one.

He kept crawling forward, the AK-47 dragging along the ground, causing an occasional scraping sound. Agamemnon picked it up and got off his knees. He could sense better airflow coming at him and surmised that the ceiling was growing in height the deeper he went.

He stood and didn't bang his head on the ceiling, although he felt long tendrils reaching down for him. He almost cried out. He brushed them away and realized they were roots from the jungle floor that was now above him.

He was headed deeper underground and marveled at how elaborate the structure would have to be to not cause cave-ins where the tunnels ran underground. In any other structure, they would need some system of joists or supports to keep the ceiling intact. But by running his hands overhead, he could feel the thick underside of old roots woven into a patchwork of supports.

Incredible.

Agamemnon wondered how long something like this could have been in existence, but then remembered hearing stories of the Moros being able to vanish in the blink of an eye.

Now he knew why they could. With hideouts like these throughout the jungle, they could disappear and reappear at will. No wonder their reputation as deadly and cunning foes was so well established.

The root ceiling gave way to solid stone and the air cooled considerably. Agamemnon felt his sweaty uniform starting to dry. He stopped and took a drink from his canteen before continuing on his way.

Twenty yards farther on, the slope seemed to level off. All around him was solid stone. The floor had also gone to stone instead of dirt. There was still some dust on it, but the tunnels now seemed carved right from bedrock.

He brought the muzzle of the AK-47 out in front of him now, however, suddenly realizing that he was very much in unknown territory. No sense letting himself get surprised and taken if he could help it.

He came to a fork with one tunnel leading left and one to the right. Agamemnon paused and strained to hear or see anything down either side. He was amazed at how much he'd been able to make out in almost total darkness.

It seemed that instead of seeing, he was more sensing things with regards to dimensions. He was also using his hands quite a bit more, trying to get an image of where he was.

He found himself amazed at how extensive things were. He'd read about the tunnels used by the Vietcong in the Vietnam War, but he doubted if they were anything even remotely as sophisticated as this system appeared to be.

He'd seen a documentary about how cramped the VC tunnels were. But these felt spacious and cool. Surely the people who had constructed them were engineering geniuses.

But which way to go now?

He paused and considered his options. At some point he was going to have to find his way back out to the jungle. He had to make sure he remembered exactly how he had come. He glanced back instinctively before realizing he wouldn't be able to see much.

He could have marked the wall perhaps, but what good would it really do?

Right or left?

He paused, took a breath and broke off to the left tunnel. It stayed on a level footing and continued for about twenty yards.

Which was when Agamemnon suddenly heard something. He froze. His ears strained to pick up the distant sounds. He could hear vague voices somewhere off in front of him.

Scrapes and shuffles flew at him now, as well. Whatever or whoever was farther down there, seemed headed straight for him.

Agamemnon raised the AK-47 to his shoulder and glanced around before realizing he wouldn't necessarily see a good spot for cover.

He moved to the side of the tunnel and squatted, running his hands over the rough rock. A small depression seemed adequate to at least provide him some measure of surprise for when they reached him.

He could make out two different voices. But they were still too distant to determine who they might be.

It could be Joey and Michael, he thought. He smirked. He might even forgive Joey for running off like this. After all, this tunnel complex was a great discovery.

Agamemnon could bring his men down here and kill whoever lived here. Then they could take them over and use the tunnel network for their base of operations in case things went south.

There was no way the enemy would ever find them. They'd be successfully hidden and safe from snipers and annoying American women.

Agamemnon nodded. Yes, he had much to thank Joey for.

The noises grew louder now. They were getting closer.

Agamemnon raised his rifle and leaned closer to it, trying to sight down the barrel. The voices grew louder. It sounded like an argument.

That seemed strange to him. And yet…

The voices were arguing. And speaking English.

He strained to listen and caught snippets of words.

"…go back…"

"…get out of here…"

"…should have known…"

"…forget her…"

And then the voices were suddenly much closer. Agamemnon stood, feeling confident he had the superior position on whoever was coming toward him.

"Stop!" he ordered.

The voices halted immediately.

Agamemnon took a breath. "Come toward me. Slowly."

He heard shuffling as their feet walked closer. Agamemnon wished he'd remembered to bring a flashlight with him from camp. But then again, he hadn't imagined he'd be underground in a tunnel. And he hadn't planned on using a flashlight in the jungle, either. He would have made himself into a target by doing so.

But now it would have come in handy.

"Who's there?" a familiar voice said. The voice had an accent. A Filipino accent.

"Eduardo?"

"Agamemnon?"

Agamemnon laughed. "My God, it is you!"

"Yes, sir. I was kidnapped by some type of tribe of crazy warriors who kept us imprisoned down here."

"Us?"

"Yes, sir. I'm not alone."

Agamemnon frowned. "Who else is with you?"

"An American."

"American? The woman?"

"No, sir. We left her behind."

"Where?"

"Back there. She told us to escape."

"So who is with you?"

"The sniper."

"What?" Agamemnon couldn't believe his ears. "The man who killed Luis?"

"Yes, sir."

"I should shoot you." He raised the rifle and tried to visualize where Eduardo would be standing. But then he heard another voice.

"We called a truce until we could escape. Otherwise, we'd all be dead by now. And what good would that do?"

"Eduardo, you should never have made a pact with this man. You were supposed to be hunting him," Agamemnon said.

"I did hunt him. And while I was, we were being hunted, as well."

"By this tribe you speak of?"

"The guide we used. He betrayed us."

Agamemnon couldn't believe what he was hearing. The sniper was so close, he could touch him. He raised the rifle and fired.

The explosion tore into the relative silence of the tunnel and echoed repeatedly as it traveled throughout the network.

Agamemnon dropped the rifle back on its sling as he grabbed at his ears, momentarily deafened by the gunshot.

"Oh, that was smart." The American's voice was laced with sarcasm.

Agamemnon wanted to kill him so badly he could feel his heart thundering in his chest.

"Thanks for telling those clowns exactly where we are." There was a pause. "This is the guy you follow orders from?"

"He's my leader," Eduardo said.

"You're all idiots."

"We've got to get out of here, sir."

Agamemnon realized that his impetuous action had just alerted the tunnel dwellers. "Yes, yes, we have to get out of here."

"It's that dawning realization that makes this such a special moment for me," the American said.

Agamemnon turned back. "I will kill you. Know that. As soon as we get out of this place, I will kill you very, very slowly."

"Yeah, yeah, promises, promises. Let's just get the hell out of here before we find ourselves with a welcome party on our asses."

Agamemnon turned. "I came from this direction. Follow me."

He led them back up the tunnel toward the fork. If he could just remember which option it would be when they got there, they'd be back at the tree trunks in no time. From there, it would just be a matter of getting out of the hole and then back to the camp, where they'd be safe.

They reached the fork in the tunnel.

"Which way?" the American asked.

Agamemnon turned right. "This was the direction I came from."

He heard something then. It sounded no louder than a slight breeze. But in rapid succession, he suddenly heard three soft thunks. One of them much closer than the other two.

He brushed a hand up to his neck, thinking a mosquito had landed on him. Instead, he felt something soft. Like feathers.

Feathers?

He slumped to the cave floor.

26

Annja floated in a gray mist. She felt a breeze passing over her and gulped in fresh air until the fog began to clear.

She heard a roar in her ears and then felt the hard ground underneath her.

Annja opened her eyes. It was still dark.

Dammit, she thought. Something was wrong.

She sniffed the air. A burning smell greeted her. She realized the torches must have gone out while she was out. That's why it was dark. She breathed deeply.

She felt the ground with her hands and then bumped into the body of one of the men she'd killed.

Ugh.

Annja got to her feet. She felt pretty good, all things considered. She wondered where the source of the fresh air was that had revived her. She thought maybe she hadn't been poisoned after all. Maybe the torches had been giving off some sort of fumes that had knocked her out.

She ran her hands down her back, searching for wounds.

There was a tear in her clothing and a tender spot, but otherwise, there were no signs of serious damage to her anywhere.

There'd be time for a better assessment later. Right now, she had to find a way out of this place. She had to hook back up with Eduardo and Vic.

Annja stumbled toward the exit of the cavern, the way Vic and Eduardo had gone when she'd told them to leave her behind.

The tunnel was still all rock. But Annja felt a breeze of cool air circulating throughout. It felt great on her exposed arms. Annja took fuller breaths, still trying to flush her system with good oxygen.

It felt great to have all her senses back again, now that the fumes had been purged from her system.

But which way to go?

She followed the tunnel until it came to three more openings. Annja's gut told her to go down the left tunnel and she obeyed the instinct.

Ahead of her, she thought she could make out some flickering light.

Torches?

Perhaps Vic and Eduardo had managed to find some more to help them wind their way throughout the tunnel complex.

She heard something now.

Music? Chanting?

She frowned. She wasn't heading toward Vic and Eduardo at all. She was heading right to where the tribe of warriors was assembling.

Perhaps she'd be needing the sword again before too long.

Annja crept down the tunnel, feeling more confident as the ambient light grew from the light cast off by the torches that must have been farther down the tunnel. She could make out shapes and the dimensions of the tunnel. She could stand up if she wanted to, but Annja kept her profile low. The closer she could get without anyone seeing her, the better.

She moved slowly, keeping her upper body balanced over deeply bent knees. The position afforded her greater balance and she'd be able to duck lower if she suddenly needed to.

The music and chanting grew louder. The walls of the cave thundered as the heavy drumming sounds echoed off and traveled down to Annja's ears.

She smelled something burning.

She wrinkled her nose. That smells awful, she thought.

She wondered what was for dinner. A thought crept into her mind that she didn't much like thinking about.

Vic. He was in danger. She was sure of it.

She had to move faster.

Annja closed her eyes and saw the sword hovering.

She wondered why.

The chanting and drums grew louder in her ears. The air tasted acrid. Smoke billowed down the cave, obscuring the limited amount of vision she had. She worried she'd pass out again.

Annja used her hands to paw at the cave walls. She moved farther down the tunnel.

She was getting close.

The light illuminated the smoke, giving the entire cave the look of an old Hollywood set with overflowing fog covering everything.

Annja pushed through it.

And then suddenly, the tunnel was behind her and she stepped into a huge cavern.

The walls were red. Torches hung everywhere, jumping and throwing shadows and light everywhere. Annja gazed down upon the floor of the cavern, some thirty feet below her.

There must have been hundreds of warriors down there.

She saw women and children now. All them were covered in elaborate body paint. They chanted in a language she couldn't understand.

In front of them, a ledge had been carved out of the rest of the cave.

Hector, the old man, stood there, decorated in some type of costume with a feather-laden headband on his head. He held his arms high overhead, urging the chanters on to greater volume.

But it was what was behind him that made Annja gasp.

Vic, Eduardo—and Agamemnon, the terrorist leader.

They were suspended upside down over a pit bordered on all sides by a giant bonfire.

And with every beat of the drum, the rope lowered them deeper toward the gaping pit.

27

Somewhere off in the distance, Agamemnon heard the steady throb of drumbeats invading the darkness of his mind. The more he tried to ignore it, the louder the noise grew until at last he cracked his eyes open and saw the world in front of him turned around.

His hands were bound behind him, and he felt a throbbing in his head from being suspended upside down over a black pit far below. He glanced up and saw the knots binding his feet were secured to a rope that looked to be made of hemp.

Where am I? he wondered.

Memories flooded his consciousness. He remembered the tunnel and the cave. He thought of Eduardo and the American sniper. He remembered chastising Eduardo for forming a truce with the enemy.

And then the noises. The dart in his neck.

I must have been knocked out.

He turned as the rope creaked above him. It looked strong enough, but the sounds of it creaking didn't do much for Agamemnon's faith in its ability to last long.

Next to him, dangling in similar fashion, he saw Eduardo and the sniper. Agamemnon smiled. At least the sniper would die. But he had to figure out a way to free himself.

And Eduardo.

They had to get out of here.

He looked down at the rock ledge and the man whipping his followers into a frenzy. Judging from the costume and the chanting, he was the man in charge.

"Hey!" he shouted.

Agamemnon's voice was drowned out by the roar of the crowd. He could see the men, women and children all chanting and clapping their hands in time to the drummed beat.

What is going on here?

Agamemnon glanced down at the pit. The fire that ringed it cast only a little bit of light farther down. Making out anything in detail seemed impossible. But since they were slowly descending toward the pit, Agamemnon found himself concentrating on what it might contain.

Spikes? Hot, molten lava of some sort?

He shuddered. Whatever it was, it couldn't be good. And he had to somehow get free and get out of here.

He had a city to vaporize.

He twisted on the rope, straining at the knots that bound his hands. He shrugged his body and tried flexing his muscles. But every time he tried, he only succeeded in making the knots bite into his skin.

A small dribble of blood fell from his wrists and sank into the black pit.

And then Agamemnon felt something move next to him. Eduardo's eyes fluttered open. "Sir?"

"Eduardo."

Eduardo struggled with his bonds. "What is this?"

"We seem to be suspended above a pit ringed with fire. Every time they beat the drum, the rope lowers us a little bit more."

"What's in the pit?"

"I don't know."

Eduardo struggled with his knots again.

"They're tight. I already tried to get loose," Agamemnon said.

Eduardo relaxed and looked around. "I see they took us all. Probably in the tunnel, huh?"

"What's the last thing you remember?"

"I heard something. And then felt a prick in my back."

"They got my neck." Agamemnon frowned. "They also got your newest friend, I see."

"He's not my friend, Agamemnon. I was forced to make an alliance with him and the woman. Otherwise, they would have left me there and I wouldn't be able to serve you any longer."

"I suppose that makes sense, then. But it was awfully dangerous of you to risk compromising our mission."

Eduardo glanced at the sniper, who still seemed to be unconscious. "We shouldn't talk about that right now. Not with him so close to us."

Agamemnon smiled. "We're all hanging here. Even if we get free, there's no way I'll allow him to survive this ordeal. He's as good as dead."

Eduardo nodded. "Good."

Agamemnon glanced up at his feet. He could see the rope vanish up into the rock ceiling. Somewhere up there, they must have had a series of levers. But who was holding the rope?

Agamemnon looked back down at the ledge. He scanned the crowd and finally spotted three men standing off to one side. Each of them held a rope. And every time the drum sounded, they let another fistful of rope go, lowering Agamemnon, Eduardo and the sniper closer to the pit.

"That's them," he said.

"Who, sir?"

"The men holding us up. They control our fate. If we're to get out of this alive, we need to figure out how to get to them."

"With our hands tied behind us? I'm not sure how we could hope to pull that off."

Agamemnon nodded. "Give me some time to think it over."

"Time doesn't seem to be a commodity we have that much of."

Agamemnon smiled. "Even the bleakest situations can have some good in them. It's just a matter of looking at it from all perspectives."

"If you say so, sir."

"Anyone ever tell you guys that you talk way too much?"

Agamemnon turned and saw the American sniper's eyes were now open. He looked pained and as he considered his situation, Agamemnon looked him over. He was obviously extremely fit. The camouflage face paint he wore couldn't disguise the fact that he had a hard face. He was accustomed to killing. In another life, Agamemnon would have loved having a man of his talents around.

But they were enemies now.

The sniper eyed him. "Hey, I know you. You're Agamemnon, right?"

"How do you know me?"

The sniper actually grinned. "Oh, we've got lots of photographs of you back in Manila. Seems like you've pissed off a good number of people, buddy. Your time on this planet is severely limited. I'd get a will in order if I was you."

Agamemnon chuckled. "I don't think any of us are in an enviable position right now."

The sniper grinned. "Fair point."

"So, you were sent to kill me?"

"Not this time. Only your second-in-command."

"What about the next time?"

The sniper shrugged. "Who knows? It might be me. Could be someone else. It's a crapshoot. Lots of talented shooters around."

Eduardo spit at the sniper. "You will all die."

The wad of spit missed its mark and plummeted into the pit.

"Do you have any ideas on how we might get out of this mess?" Agamemnon asked.

The sniper eyed him. "You want me to help you?"

"You and Eduardo had an agreement. We might be better off extending it to include me, as well."

The sniper laughed. "Since we're all in exactly the same position, I don't know how much help I'll be."

"Look," Agamemnon said, "those men down there hold the ropes that keep us from falling right into the pit."

He watched the sniper follow his gaze to where the three warriors clutched the ropes.

"They don't seem very tired."

"I imagine they have some sort of lever system in place up there that makes holding us fairly simple."

The sniper nodded. "All right, so what's your plan? You want to attack them with our psychic abilities?"

"I'm not sure yet, but I did want to make you aware of the all the factors I've been able to fathom."

"Okay." The sniper looked at his feet and Agamemnon watched him rub his ankles together trying to break the knots.

"They're quite tight, I'm afraid."

"Seem to be. How about your hands?"

Agamemnon flexed his wrists again and felt the knots cut deeper into his wrists. More blood pooled and then dripped off him. "The same," he said.

"Damn."

Eduardo kept looking at the pit beneath them. "How long do you think we have before they lower us all the way into the pit?"

"We're descending at a slight pace." Agamemnon looked at the chieftain. He seemed unhurried. "I'd guess he still has some work to do to get his followers riled up to the point that this thing climaxes."

"I give us ten minutes," the sniper said.

"Agreed," Agamemnon said.

Eduardo struggled again with his knots. The more he exerted himself, the weaker he looked. Agamemnon could see the fear in his eyes. "Calm down." he advised.

Eduardo looked at him. "How can you say that?"

"Because fear paralyzes you. If you can reason things out, then there's always a chance something good will come of it."

"What happens when we get into that pit?"

"I have no idea."

Eduardo glanced back down. "The fire doesn't let me see anything."

"All I see is darkness," the sniper said.

"Perhaps that is deliberate on their part," Agamemnon said.

Eduardo frowned. "Why would they do that?"

Agamemnon looked around the cavern. The walls were streaked with red. It looked like blood. He could make out a series of paintings on the far side of the cavern, but smoke from the bonfire obscured his vision.

"Do you see those?" he asked.

"What?" Eduardo strained to look.

"The paintings over there. I can't make out what they depict."

Eduardo turned himself around and tried to right himself to get a better look. After a moment he collapsed and swung on the creaking rope. "I can't see them any better."

"I can."

Agamemnon looked at the sniper. "You can see them?"

"Yep."

"So, what are they?"

The sniper looked at them both and a slow smile spread across his face. "You sure you want me to tell you?"

"Yes," Eduardo said.

"It'll ruin the surprise," the sniper said.

Agamemnon frowned. "Just tell us."

The sniper nodded. "They show some kind of giant creature. It's eating the people who get dropped into the pit."

"Creature?"

"I can't figure out what it is," the sniper said. "But I think it's a pretty safe assumption that we're on the menu for dinner tonight."

"That painting could be hundreds of years old," Agamemnon said. "There's no reason to believe that such a creature exists."

But, as if in response, a sound emanated from the pit below them. Agamemnon heard what sounded like a low, grumbling roar.

He felt himself being lowered closer to the pit.

28

From where Annja crouched behind a big rock at the entrance to the massive cavern, she could see the ropes holding Vic and the others twisting under the weight. She followed the rope up into the rocky ceiling and then to where they reemerged and fed down to three warriors holding the ropes.

With each drumbeat, they let another fistful of rope go, lowering their captives closer to the pit.

If I attack them, they'll let the ropes go, she thought. And then they'll drop right into the pit and be dead.

She needed another plan. She had to somehow get over to the ledge and take control of the ropes herself.

Or at least Vic's rope. She had to be honest, admitting to herself that she didn't much care if Eduardo and Agamemnon lived or died. But a part of her still wanted to remain faithful to the pact she'd made with Eduardo.

Agamemnon was another story altogether. She could still see the look on his face when he'd suggested he was going to have her decapitated and videotaped. It was hard to find any sympathy for the situation he was in now.

What's in the pit, though? she wondered.

And what was this tribe, anyway? The longer she had contact with them, the more she doubted they were related to the famous Moros at all. Even though the warriors she'd killed earlier had been armed with the deadly kris knives, that didn't necessarily make them Moros, did it?

She knew the Moros had been traditionally thought of as being Muslim. But this tribe clearly wasn't worshiping Islam at all. Judging from their primitive cave paintings, they prayed to a different god altogether.

One that very clearly had a taste for human flesh.

Annja looked at the elaborate painting on the wall across the cavern. She hoped that the monster wasn't drawn to scale, because it looked as if it must have been over twenty feet in length. It reminded her of a dinosaur, with rows of serrated teeth that it used to disembowel its victims.

Was it waiting for Vic and the others in the pit?

If so, it might be merciful to simply drop them in and let the fall kill them before the monster could. She reminded herself she didn't believe in monsters.

Annja took a deep breath. The chanting was growing in urgency. The drums sounded louder and the acrid taste in her mouth seemed to be caused by a mixture of plants they had cooking over open flames throughout the cavern.

The crowd itself was getting more and more worked up. She'd seen this happen at church revivals. The preacher in charge could whip his flock into a frenzy where they would believe anything he said, do anything he ordered and just generally fade out of reality.

Annja didn't think she'd necessarily have to fight the entire crowd of people. And she certainly didn't want to fight any children.

But the men holding the ropes on the ledge and the head priest, Hector, if that's what he was—they would be trouble.

Annja crept farther into the cavern, trying her best to keep herself low. She didn't think anyone would notice her, what with the environment. But she couldn't take a chance on being seen, infuriating the high priest and hearing him give the command to drop Vic and the others into the pit.

A winding path led down to the main cavern floor. Annja avoided it and concentrated on working her way around the periphery of the cavern, using a lip in the rock that was partially obscured from view by stalactites.

As she worked her way around closer to the ledge, she tried to figure out a plan. But her options were sorely limited.

If she risked a head-on assault, they could drop the ropes. And even if she grabbed one of them in time, she wouldn't know whose rope it was. She might end up saving Eduardo or worse, Agamemnon, while Vic plunged to his death.

Annja reached the end of the lip and found herself still fifty yards from the ledge where the rope holders stood.

And now Vic and the others hovered just twenty feet from the open pit. Flames shot up into the sky as the fire ate into fresh boughs of wood. It crackled and popped and sent sparks into the air. The smoke was thick near the ledge, as well. Annja could taste the fumes from the plants and stifled a cough.

She had to stay quiet.

She closed her eyes and made sure the sword was ready to use. She'd need it soon enough.

A breeze blew through the cavern, causing smoke to swirl.

It enveloped her instantly. Annja used the diversion to make her move. She jumped as far as she could.

There was a roar in her ears.

And then she was out of the smoke, on the ledge.

She was behind the men holding the rope. They hadn't noticed her yet, but they would soon.

Already people closest to the ledge could see the sword and someone screamed.

So much for surprise, Annja thought.

She knocked the first rope holder on the back of his head and he dropped while Annja clutched at his rope. The sudden amount of weight she took on jarred her and she had to drop to her knees to keep from being pulled off her feet.

She had no idea whose rope it was.

She struggled to her feet and wrapped the rope around the closest outcropping of rock.

The two other rope holders turned and faced her, still clutching their ropes. The high priest was screaming something in the strange language he spoke. His followers were shouting now, as well. Annja could see some of them trying to get up on the ledge.

She'd have to make this fast.

"Annja!"

She glanced up at Vic. "Hey!"

"Nice of you to join the fun."

She almost chuckled but at that moment, a painted warrior leaped onto the ledge, blocking her way. He raised a long knife and Annja swept her blade out in front and cut his legs out from under him. He dropped and rolled off the ledge.

Annja stepped closer to the next rope holder. His eyes were wide and terrified. Annja flicked her blade at him and he screamed and let go of the rope and jumped off the ledge into the seething crowd.

Annja threw herself forward and grabbed for the rope, but she was too late. She saw Eduardo's body plunge through the air and into the pit.

Annja expected to hear a thud.

Instead, she heard a splash. The pit was filled with water?

The third rope holder tied his rope to a rocky outcropping and then grabbed a wooden club. He swung it overhead and charged at Annja.

Annja dropped to her right knee, extended her foot and tripped him, sending him right off the ledge, as well.

She grabbed the rope and released it. Vic's body came down slowly. As he got within range, Annja grabbed him and swung him over to the side, cutting his bonds as she did so. Vic sat on the ledge for a moment, letting the blood rush back into his lower body.

"Thanks," he said.

"Don't mention it."

"Get me down!"

Annja looked up. Agamemnon still twisted from his rope. Annja glanced at Vic, who just shrugged. "What the hell," he said.

Annja helped him down and Vic got him onto the ledge.

Another two warriors jumped up and tried to rush Annja. Unfortunately for them, the entry to the ledge was wide enough for only one of them. Annja speared the first man through his heart and he fell back into the second.

Agamemnon knelt by the pit and fished his hands around. Annja looked and saw that he'd managed to haul up Eduardo's body.

"Is he alive?" she asked.

Agamemnon shook his head. "I don't know."

Vic helped him pull Eduardo out of the water. He looked lifeless, but Agamemnon started rescue breathing and soon enough, Eduardo coughed and vomited some water.

Annja watched the front of the ledge and staved off another attack from a very determined woman who had jumped on to the ledge with a four-foot staff in her hands. Annja pirouetted as she attacked, and smacked the flat of her blade against the woman's head. She fell off the ledge.

The drums and chanting stopped. No more warriors jumped onto the ledge.

Annja stood with her sword poised to attack anyone who did. Out of the corner or her eye, she saw the high priest regarding her.

"You are very skilled," he said.

Annja looked him in the eye. "Who are you?"

"I told you my name is Hector."

"And you're the high priest here?"

He smiled. "We prefer to think of ourselves as caretakers."

"Caretakers of who?"

"You mean, what."

Annja narrowed her eyes. "You're not going to kill us. I won't allow it."

Hector nodded. "I can see you won't be an easy person to kill, but we've had others here we thought were troublesome at first. Soon enough, they all died."

"Well, things are different this time," she said defiantly.

"Are they? And where will you go? There's no escape for you. I have many followers, as you can see. And while you've killed some of them, I have no doubt that we can eventually overpower you."

"You'll lose many in the process."

"Perhaps. But they are committed to the ideals we worship. Dying would be a reward of sorts," Hector said.

Vic muttered under his breath. "Sounds like friends of yours, Agamemnon."

Annja ignored him. "And you're willing to sacrifice them?" she asked.

"Of course, but I don't think that will even be necessary."

Annja glanced around the cavern. From the back she could

see a commotion as people seemed to part and move out of the way. She could see a group of warriors heading toward the ledge.

"Why not?" she asked.

Hector smiled and pointed at the group moving toward them. From behind her, she heard Agamemnon gasp.

She turned. "What is it?"

Agamemnon pointed. "Those are my men they're herding in here. Joey and Michael. My trackers."

29

Annja watched as Hector's men herded Joey and Michael through the crowds. As they moved closer to the ledge, the chanting began again. Annja frowned. These people wanted blood.

And Hector seemed poised to give it to them.

She glanced at Agamemnon, who seemed almost genuine in his concern for the safety of his men.

Joey and Michael were herded onto the ledge. Joey looked at Agamemnon. "Sorry," he said.

Agamemnon shook his head. "It was your family. I understand."

"Enough!" Hector spread his arms and the entire cavern quieted down. Smiling, he looked at Annja. "Now, you see what it is that I hold in my possession. Your choices are simple—surrender or die."

"If we surrender, we will die," Vic said.

Hector laughed. "The will of our god cannot be denied. He demands sacrifice."

"Who is your god?" Annja asked. "I don't recall hearing of any tribes in these jungles that still worshiped a pagan deity."

"There is nothing pagan about Jajuba."

"Jajuba?" Annja asked.

"Yes." Hector pointed at the cave painting on the opposite wall. "He is as old as the earth itself, born out of the fires of her belly into the waters of her world. He is the giver of life and the taker of souls. Without his protection, we would perish."

"How so?"

Hector frowned. "Jajuba would descend upon us and destroy us all."

Annja caught Vic's eye. "You believe this?"

He shrugged. "I was suspended over the pit, but I didn't see anything."

Annja frowned. Running into a monster in this place wasn't exactly what she'd been hoping for. But then again, facing down a hundred crazed zealots didn't ring her bell, either.

"Does Jajuba live here?" she asked, deciding to play along for the moment.

"In the pit behind you," Hector said.

Annja stared into the inky-black depths. Did something just move? She couldn't tell for sure. She looked back at Hector. "I don't believe you," she said.

Hector grinned. "Very well." He turned and shouted something to his followers. There was a screech from the back of the crowd, and a young woman decorated in elaborate braids and streaks of paint up and down her body pushed through the crowd.

Hector looked at Annja. "Now you will see."

The woman jumped on to the ledge and bowed once to Hector. Then she faced the edge of the pit, closed her eyes and stepped right off the lip, vanishing almost instantly from sight.

Annja heard the splash and rushed to the side.

In another second, the woman's upper body popped back up to the surface, but her face was drawn back in a grim visage of agony. She screamed and her wails echoed up out of the pit and filled the cavern.

Annja kept watching and saw a row of teeth appear next to her, chomping down on the woman, splashing bright red blood across the surface of the water. In another second, the carnage was over.

The woman was gone.

In the cavern, Hector's followers began a new chant, but this one was lower, a steady humming that caused the room to almost vibrate. They all had wide smiles on their faces.

They were happy.

Annja shook her head. What sort of cult had she wandered into here? She knew about the Moros and the pygmies who lived in the jungles, but this? This was unlike anything she'd ever heard of.

Hector spread his arms again. "Enough."

Again, his worshipers fell silent. Hector looked at Annja. "You believe now, don't you?"

"You've got something down there, sure. I saw it."

"You saw Jajuba."

"Okay," she said.

Hector grinned. "So, will you surrender?"

"No."

"You are willing to see your men killed?"

Annja shrugged. "They're not my men. In fact, they were sent to track me down and kill me. If you want to throw them into the pit, as well, be my guest. You'll actually be doing me a favor."

Hector's eyes narrowed. "You are a strange woman. If these are not your men, then whose are they?"

"Mine," Agamemnon's voice broke out.

Hector looked past Annja. "Who are you?"

"I am Agamemnon. And in my world I am much the same as you are here, a great leader."

Annja looked at him but he ignored her. "I am well aware of the role you played in my other camp and I admire your ability to blend in with us for so long and to remain undetected."

Hector smiled. "So, at last we meet."

"Indeed."

"And you came here, how?"

"By the entrance to this amazing place through the trees. I found the entrance and followed the tunnels down here."

Hector nodded. "I am impressed. You have shown ability I did not expect to see from any of these people."

Agamemnon bowed. "I'm humbled by your flattery, but in awe of your world here."

Hector gestured at Annja. "You are with this woman?"

"No."

"Really?"

"I was hunting her down to kill her. She escaped from my camp and has caused death and destruction wherever she goes. It was my hope that she be dead by now. It was a task I had entrusted to men I thought capable, but who only succeeded in failing me."

"Perhaps your quarry is more adept than you first believed," Hector said.

Agamemnon nodded. "I have no doubt of that. However, my goal remains the same—to see her die."

Annja frowned. "I'm touched."

Hector appeared to be thinking something over. After a moment of introspection, he spoke. "One called Agamemnon, you have greatly impressed me and I have heard much about your work and your vision. It is something I feel could be beneficial to us all."

"Oh, great," Vic said.

Hector ignored him. "Would you betray your knowledge of this place to anyone, should they ask you?"

"Never," Agamemnon said.

Hector nodded. "Then you are free to go."

Agamemnon bowed. "You are most generous, mighty one." He stood again and spread his arms. "Please accept these people as my own sacrifice for the mighty and all-powerful Jajuba. I am sure he will find them most delicious."

Eduardo's eyes widened. "Sir?"

Agamemnon turned to him. "You have failed me for the last time, Eduardo. I warned you what would happen if you did not succeed."

"But it wasn't my fault. They caught us. They took us by surprise. There was nothing I could do. Hector betrayed us."

"Failures cannot simply be explained away," Agamemnon said. "And neither can they be forgiven."

Two warriors stepped forward, one on either side of Eduardo. Eduardo fought to break free, but Annja could see he was still in a weak state from the fall into the pit.

"No!" she shouted.

Annja stepped forward, but a number of warriors jumped onto the ledge. There were too many to reach Eduardo, and she and Vic could only watch as the warriors dragged him to the edge overlooking the black pit.

The warriors looked at Hector.

Hector spread his hands and the cavern erupted into a new chant. Annja's ears hurt from the way the noise reverberated off the cavern walls. But she had to keep her eyes open or risk the warriors in front of her taking advantage of her state to disarm her.

Eduardo still tried to free himself. "I beg you not to do this! Please!"

The chanting grew. Annja could see drops of water leaping out of the pit. The chanting must have called the monster to the pit. Underneath this network of caves and tunnels, there had to be a reservoir or other type of giant watery realm where the monster could live.

"Agamemnon, please!" Eduardo cried.

But Agamemnon's eyes were like stone. A flicker of a grin spread across his face.

He's enjoying this, Annja thought. The sick bastard is actually enjoying seeing the fear on Eduardo's face.

Hector dropped his hands.

The warriors pushed Eduardo into the pit.

He screamed as he hit the water. Annja could only listen as his cries for help were cut short and his last wail gurgled away as whatever lived in the pit devoured him. She could hear the snapping jaws and the tearing of flesh. It was horrible.

In another moment, the churning waters stilled.

Hector smiled and the chanting switched to the low murmur that had happened after the woman had sacrificed herself to Jajuba.

It almost sounds like a cat's purr, Annja thought. Perhaps it soothes the beast so it doesn't get out of control.

Hector looked at Agamemnon. "You are free to go. I will send a guide to show you the way back to the surface."

"Thank you," the terrorist said.

"Agamemnon."

He turned. "Yes, mighty one?"

Hector eyed him. "Do not forget the mercy I have shown you here today."

"I will not."

"And do not ever reveal this place to anyone. Otherwise,

we will come for you. And we will drag you back here for a fate worse than what the mighty Jajuba would inflict."

Agamemnon seemed about to say something, but thought better of it. He bowed again and then turned to leave.

"Agamemnon!"

He looked back at Annja. "Yes?"

"We're not done, you and me."

"It looks to me like we are."

"Not by a long shot."

Agamemnon nodded. "We shall see. Now, if you'll excuse me, I have certain other things to attend to."

"You mean that thing in Makati?" Vic asked.

Agamemnon frowned.

Vic nodded. "Yeah, I heard you talking. You should never assume just because a guy's eyes are closed that he's asleep."

"I won't do that ever again," Agamemnon said. "In any event, it's a moot point. You will die here soon enough and you're much too far away to do anything to stop the inevitable."

He turned and left the cavern. Vic turned back to Annja. "He's right."

Annja shrugged. "Maybe."

Hector eyed her again. "Your last chance for survival is now gone. He might have spared you. He did not."

"I'm not surprised," she said.

"And now," Hector said, "you will all die."

Annja sighed. "Let me tell you something."

"What?"

"We might all die," she said, gripping the sword a little bit harder, "but we're going to take an awful lot of your people with us."

And with a scream that shook the walls of the cavern, Annja leaped into the air, already bringing her sword high overhead ready to strike down.

30

Annja's first strike almost halved the warrior in front of her. Her blade cut through him as if he wasn't even there, and before any of the others could react, Annja had already pivoted and stabbed the guards holding Joey and Michael hostage. As the warriors fell, Joey and Michael armed themselves with weapons from the dead men.

So did Vic.

Annja spun and knocked two warriors right into the pit. She didn't have time to notice if they were being devoured by the creature that lived below, because she was already engaged with a warrior wielding a spear.

He faced her and stabbed right in. Annja parried the thrust and swiped down at his hands.

He backed away, but her blade caught the shaft of the spear and cut through it, splintering the wood and making the warrior drop the pointed part. He spun the half shaft now and swung it at her head.

Annja dropped and cut up on an angle, catching him just

above his left hip. She stepped through, feeling her blade cut deep into his abdomen. Blood sprayed and he fell away.

Vic was holding his own against one of the warriors who had rushed him. Annja watched as he slashed and drove the point of his knife deep into the warrior's throat. The man went down gurgling.

Joey and Michael seemed well versed in knife fighting, easily dispatching two more warriors.

But the ledge was getting crowded.

Annja kicked two more fallen warriors into the pit. Jajuba was going to eat well today, she thought.

But the amount of blood on the ledge was making her concerned. Already she'd slipped twice when deflecting blows. Any more of the blood would make her footing and that of her comrades even less secure.

Annja briefly wondered if Joey and Michael would try to kill her and Vic when they were done, but she disregarded that as silly. Agamemnon had abandoned them to the pit. There was no way they'd fight for his cause ever again.

No, if Annja was able to get out of this intact, they'd be a foursome making their way back to the surface.

If they could find it.

A female warrior jumped in front of Annja and promptly pummeled Annja's hands. Annja felt as if her bones had broken and grunted. She had to hold on to the sword at all costs. If she lost it, she might not be able to fend off the attacks long enough to retrieve it.

She ducked down and drove the blade forward, feeling her hands pulse in pain. But holding on to the sword at least dulled the pain enough to continue fighting.

The woman leaped, brandishing her own set of twin kris blades. She hissed through yellowed teeth. Annja caught a whiff of her breath and blanched. It smelled as if she'd been eating raw flesh.

"I hope you haven't been eating Jajuba's leftovers," she said.

The woman hissed again and stabbed at Annja's heart.

Annja jumped out of the way, narrowly missing bumping into Joey, who had just dodged his own attack from the side. He grinned at Annja.

"Sorry," he shouted.

Annja jumped out of the way to avoid the woman's second strike. "No sweat," she replied.

She pivoted and drove the sword up high, flipping it and cutting down. She caught the woman's collarbone and the blade hit bone. Annja grunted and yanked the blade free and continued cutting through as the woman warrior screamed and then dropped.

Annja nudged her into the pit, as well, careful to avoid the now dying flames of the bonfires that had ringed it earlier.

She heard Vic grunt and turned to see him yanking a knife free of another warrior. The man dropped without a sound. Blood spattered Vic's face, mixing with the camouflage face paint he already wore. He grinned at Annja.

"I really need a shower."

"Me, too."

His eyes danced. "Cool. It's a date, then."

Annja started to say something, but at that moment her instincts took over and she sidestepped, just missing being run through from behind by another spear-wielding warrior. She backhanded him, and then drove her sword into his gut. He seemed to almost shiver as the blade pierced his sternum and slid into his heart. More blood splashed the ledge and he dropped down, as well.

"We're running out of room here," Annja said.

Michael looked at her. "We can't go down there, though. Too many people to worry about," he said.

Annja surveyed the scene. The main cavern was still filled with Hector's followers. She was relieved to see protective parents had taken all of the children away, but a great many warriors remained.

We'll never make it if we jump down there. Joey and Michael were having a hard enough time keeping the throngs from overwhelming the easiest access point to the ledge.

But Hector's position...

Annja glanced over at him. He seemed to be enjoying the fights happening in front of him. He held his hands clasped as if he was deep in thought.

Annja frowned. What's he up to? She wondered.

"Annja!"

Annja ducked as the body of a warrior went flying overhead. He'd launched himself up and at Annja. Joey had called her name just in time. The warrior tumbled, tried to stand and then slipped back into the pit, screaming.

"We can't stay here!" Annja shouted.

Vic dispatched another warrior and moved alongside Annja. "We have to get a better position. They'll keep coming at us until we're either dead or surrender."

"In which case we're dead, anyway," she said.

"Right." Vic looked around. "How did you come in here?"

Annja pointed up at the lip that ran around close to the ledge. "I snaked my way down here following that."

Vic frowned. "There's no way we can use that. They'll cut our feet out from under us. We need something better."

Annja pointed at Hector's position. "What about there?"

Vic frowned. "I don't like the lack of maneuverability but we could grab Hector. If we get to him, it just might take the fight out of his people."

"Agreed," she said.

Annja turned to Joey and Michael, who had just double-teamed another warrior. "We're moving!" she told them.

Vic led the way across the ledge toward Hector. Annja watched as Vic kept himself low and balanced, avoiding the bigger puddles of blood easily and concentrating on getting close to Hector.

Hector seemed completely unfazed by the movement and continued to hold his ground, with a curious expression on his face.

Annja felt a twinge in her stomach.

Something wasn't right.

"Vic."

He turned. "What?"

"Is he suckering us in for something here?"

Vic frowned. "We can't go back. Joey and Michael have already abandoned their position. They're fighting with their backs to us as it is."

Annja turned as Joey stabbed another warrior. "You guys okay?"

"Keep moving," Michael said. "We can't stop here."

Annja turned back, deflecting the warrior who had jumped up to her left and tried to swing a club at her head. She parried the blow and struck down, slashing off his hands. He fell off the ledge with blood spraying from his wrists.

Vic closed in on Hector. Hector still had not moved.

What's he planning? she thought. Why hasn't he tried to escape? It doesn't make any sense.

She heard Michael gasp and turned to see him taking a cut across his arm. Blood ran freely and he backpedaled, trying to get some distance from his attacker. Annja stepped between them and drove the warrior back, cutting and slashing until he missed deflecting one of her moves and found himself cut open.

Annja retreated and Michael breathed a sigh of relief. "Thanks."

"Don't mention it."

Joey was next to her. "You okay?" he asked.

"Yeah."

"They seem to be slowing down," he said.

Annja watched as the warriors who had just jumped on to the ledge were now starting to back away.

"What's going on?"

Joey shook his head. "I don't know."

Annja turned. Vic had reached Hector and he stood behind him with a smile on his face.

Hector was also smiling.

Annja, Joey and Michael raced over to Vic. "You okay?" Annja asked.

Vic nodded. "No problems."

Hector looked at Annja. "You've killed a great many of my warriors."

Annja shrugged. "They shouldn't have tried to kill us. Self-defense and all that jazz."

Hector smirked. "They were doing what they were trained to do. It's their life mission to appease their god Jajuba. Just as it is my mission to ensure his continued survival."

"By sacrificing people to him?"

"Yes."

Annja pointed at the pit. "I'm sure he's done for the day. We threw in countless bodies while we were killing your people."

Hector shook his head. "No. All you did was stoke his blood lust. He will crave more now that he has been overfed."

Vic glanced at Annja. "You think so?"

Annja frowned. "I'd be willing to bet he's curled up some-where now just trying to get over the indigestion."

Hector spit. "You are a foolish woman. You know nothing about what it is that you face."

"Well, I know something," she said. "I know you're in a really bad position right now."

Hector eyed her. "And what would you like me to do?"

"Tell your warriors to give us passage out of here. What you do here is of no concern to us. We just want to get home."

Hector shook his head. "I'm afraid I cannot do that. Jajuba has already told me that you must all die."

Vic frowned. "We could kill you, of course."

Hector shook his head. "That would not matter one bit. Jajuba would still demand his sacrifice. You would still die."

"But your people would let us go if you were dead," Annja said.

Hector frowned. "This has nothing to do with me. It has everything to do with tradition and the needs of Jajuba. Nothing more. Our destiny as a people is tied to his survival. If he lives, so do we."

"And if he dies?" Annja asked.

"He will never die," Hector said. "He is immortal."

"No one lives forever," Joey said.

"That you know of," Hector replied.

Vic looked at Annja. "So, what now?"

Annja glanced at Hector. "We might as well kill him. If it doesn't matter anyway, there's no sense keeping him around," she said, hoping he'd back down from the threat to his life.

Hector laughed. "You are about to see what it is that you are up against."

He brought his hands together, and instantly a different chant came out of his mouth. Annja found herself mesmerized by its soothing melody. And then it changed abruptly, rising in volume until Hector's voice rebounded off every cavern wall.

Now his people began chanting, as well. And Annja could at last make out one word they screamed together.

"*Jajuba!*"

The noise grew.

Vic frowned. "Annja."

"What?"

"Look."

The area around the pit had changed. Something kicked up the water. Huge splashes sounded from below, and then there was a great roar.

And then as she watched, Annja saw something emerge from the pit.

Jajuba had risen.

31

Hector's chanting continued. And the effect was immediate.

Jajuba wasn't quite the monster Annja had imagined, but it was still a huge beast. As it squatted on the ledge eyeing them, water dribbled off its leathery reptilian skin. It used its long, sharp snout to nose the air as if sniffing for its next meal. And the rows of sharp teeth were coated with blood and gristle from its most recent feedings.

"That's no monster," Vic said. "It's a saltwater crocodile."

"It's huge, though," Joey said. "It's got to be twenty feet long at least."

"With plenty of room, it would seem, for many more bodies," Michael said.

Annja regarded the crocodile. She didn't even know they lived in the Philippines. But here it was, hissing away at the five of them on the ledge.

And Hector continued to chant.

Annja glanced over at him. His joy was clearly evident. He stopped chanting and eyed Annja. "I told you."

"I hate to tell you this, Hector, but you're here with us. I don't think that bodes very well for you."

Hector shook his head. "I can leave any time I want to. As can my followers. Jajuba knows who we are. And he knows that we protect him. He won't harm any of us unless we fall into the pit."

Vic cleared his throat. "You have a plan, Annja?"

"I'm thinking."

"Better think fast," Hector said. "Once Jajuba rises from the pit, he usually only takes a moment to decide who he's going to eat first."

Joey glanced at the knife in his hands. "Somehow, I think I'm outgunned here."

Michael stood next to him. "If we fight together, we might have a chance against it," he said.

Hector laughed. "Jajuba will devour you all. Your tactics are worthless against his might. He is faster than any of you. And he is very strong indeed."

Annja looked back at Hector. "I'm getting tired of listening to you, old man."

"You should have listened to me before, and given yourselves up. Jajuba can be merciful, as well. Simply jumping into the pit will be enough to signal your desire to be sacrificed for the greater good. Jajuba will end your life quickly."

Annja shook her head. "I never pictured myself dying by way of being eaten by a crocodile, so if it's all the same to you, I think I'll pass."

The crocodile hissed again. Annja watched its movements. She could see the ball eyes rolling around, eyeing everything nearby. The beast seemed to be sizing them all up. Possibly, it was trying to figure out the threat level they represented. As soon as the crocodile decided on how dangerous it was or wasn't to attack, it would make its move.

And it might be too late then.

Annja knew that crocodiles could run at high speed for short distances. But when you're twenty feet long, a short distance is pretty far anyway.

The best thing to do would be to get on its back and cut into its head. If she could get access to its skull, she could pierce the brain with her sword and kill it.

Getting there would be a problem, though.

Hector had taken up his chanting again. It seemed to have an almost lulling effect on the crocodile. As Hector repeated the chant, the crocodile's head seemed to move back and forth in time to it.

"I can't take this anymore," Vic said.

Annja heard a dull whump and turned to see that Vic had clocked Hector over the head. Hector slid to the floor unconscious.

Vic looked back at Annja. "Sorry."

The crocodile hissed again, louder this time, and now all of Hector's followers fell silent, as well. The crocodile stamped around the edge of the pit, regarding it and for a moment, Annja found herself wondering if the beast might actually go back into the water.

But then the crocodile turned itself around again and took two steps toward the group of them.

"Annja," Vic said. "Now might be a good time to let us in on your plan."

"I'm thinking," she said.

"Think quicker, please."

Annja frowned. "I need to get up on its head in order to kill it. If I can stab down into its skull, I think I can end this."

"Great. So how do we do that?"

"I don't know."

Joey and Michael looked at her. "What about a distraction?"

"That's an awfully big gamble you're talking about. If you ness up before I can kill it, it will eat you up."

Joey looked at Michael and then back at Annja. "We don't have a choice, do we?"

"I'll help, too," Vic said. "Not much I can do to help Annja get on its head. Besides, if it's confronting three of us, it will see it as more of a threat than just two. And that might buy Annja the time and positioning she needs."

Annja glanced at Vic. "You'd better be careful."

Vic winked at her. "And miss our date if I'm not? Not very likely, I'll tell you that."

Annja smiled. "All right. How do you guys want to do this?"

The crocodile hissed again and took another step toward them. Annja held her sword out in front, aiming it directly at the beast's eyes. That seemed to stop it momentarily.

Michael pointed over to the lip of the ledge. "We can start making our way there. If it gets too close, we can jump down into the main cavern."

"And it might jump down on top of you," Annja said. "What else do you have?"

"Nothing," Joey said. "There's no other option except for that. We aren't exactly sitting on a big hunk of real estate here."

"They're right," Vic said. "It's the best shot we have."

Annja frowned. "All right."

Vic looked at her. "Give us ten seconds to get a reaction. If he follows us, then you should be able to get yourself onto his back. Just watch out for that tail. I think those things can kill just by swinging it around."

Annja nodded.

Vic turned and got closer to Joey and Michael. "You guys ready?"

The brothers nodded. Together, the three of them brandished their knives and began making loud noises.

The crocodile reacted almost instantly, pulling its head around to face them. It clacked its jaws together, and Annja could see the huge teeth and stringy bits of tissue and tendon still dangling from it like bloody Christmas garlands.

Vic, Joey and Michael took turns screaming. They flailed their arms, while Annja sidled very slowly around to her left.

If she could just keep herself from getting noticed…

The crocodile made a sudden lunge forward and snapped its jaws at Joey's head. Joey ducked and managed to get himself out of the way. The crocodile recoiled and considered its next action.

But Joey was now separated from Michael and Vic.

Annja had to move fast.

She worked her way around to the side some more and then looked at the crocodile's right flank. She would just have to jump up and get on its back. Then she'd have to crawl up to the head.

If she wasn't careful, the crocodile could buck her off and gobble her up in its jaws. And that would be that.

The crocodile seemed satisfied that it had managed to separate Joey from Michael and Vic. Instead of concentrating on the party of two, it settled on Joey.

Joey backed up, closer to the lip of the ledge.

The crocodile stalked him now, moving forward in very slow increments.

Annja waited a second more.

The crocodile snapped its jaws again, and this time Joey had to jump back. She heard him cry out and then he fell off the ledge to the ground below.

The crocodile rushed forward immediately, snapping its jaws again.

But as it did so, Michael and Vic rushed in and stabbed at

its unprotected lower left flank. The crocodile recoiled and screeched as their blades punctured its skin.

Annja caught a whiff of the blood of the beast as it spilled out.

But the crocodile was enraged now. It twisted this way and that trying to get at Vic and Michael. They kept themselves between the crocodile's front and rear legs, but it was far too dangerous. The crocodile could at any point shred them with its claws.

Annja jumped.

As she landed, the crocodile screeched again. Annja stabbed down into the beast's back, trying to saw back and forth to give the creature a wound to worry about as she moved forward.

But the crocodile started bucking like a bronco, and Annja had to clutch on to its hard skin just to keep from being bumped off. She grasped her sword with the other hand, wondering how long she could last.

Michael attacked the crocodile's flank again. But this time, as he stabbed the side, the crocodile reared up and its claw came down.

Annja heard a shriek from Michael and then he dropped and rolled away. The crocodile's claws had torn open his arm and right side. He was bleeding profusely.

Vic kept up his attack and Annja had a moment to work her way forward. She crawled along the back of the beast up toward the head.

She could see the snout waving back and forth in the air as the crocodile tried to get around to attack Vic or dislodge Annja.

She reached the neck. Just a bit farther. And then she heard something.

Hector's voice.

She glanced back. Not now!

But the high priest had apparently regained consciousness

and was chanting again. Worse, his followers had joined in and the beast seemed to be feeding off their energy.

Annja frowned. If she could just kill Hector, then she could take care of the crocodile.

But in her position, even if she threw the sword, there was no way she could aim it properly from the writhing back of the beast.

She concentrated on climbing onto the crocodile's giant head.

Hector's volume increased.

Annja's ears hurt.

She had to do something about him.

"Vic!"

He was busy dodging the crocodile, but still managing to keep himself out of the reach of its claws.

"What?"

"Hector needs to be stopped or we'll all die!"

"Hector?"

"The chanting! The crocodile is feeding off it and getting stronger."

She could see the desperation in Vic's face. Annja couldn't set herself right for a stab to the beast's head. It was moving too much and she would need a moment—just a split second to deliver the killing thrust.

The chanting continued. Annja slipped back onto the crocodile's neck.

"Vic!"

"I can't get to him!"

Annja wriggled onto the crocodile's head. She had the sword in one hand and leathery skin in the other.

She was almost ready.

Hector's voice was now a shout that filled the entire cavern. His followers echoed everything he chanted. The crocodile seemed to almost be growing under her.

But that wasn't possible, was it?

And then, Hector's voice disappeared midway through a shout.

Annja struggled to look.

A kris knife jutted from his throat. He slumped over.

The crowd stopped chanting.

For a brief moment the crocodile froze.

Annja stood. She turned the sword point down.

And drove it home.

She felt the bony skull crack and give way as her blade slid into the brain cavity. She pushed until she could go no farther.

With a final hiss, the crocodile slumped to one side.

Dead.

32

Annja slid off the crocodile's head. "That was one hell of a ride."

Vic leaned against the corpse. "Thank God for all those times in high school when we played dodgeball. Any longer and I would have been shredded."

"Speaking of which…" Annja ran to Michael, who had rolled onto a safer part of the ledge and was wrapping himself up with torn bits of his clothing.

He looked up as they ran over. "Hey."

Vic checked him over. "He got you pretty good, but it doesn't look like there's anything worse than long cuts. There's no real tissue damage, and some stitches should keep you intact. The key is to get it cleaned out. No telling what sort of crap that croc has under its claws."

"That was some shot," Annja said.

Michael looked at her. "What shot?"

"With the knife. Into Hector's throat. That was what enabled me to get the killing strike in."

Michael shook his head. "That wasn't me. I was a bit too busy bleeding to do that."

Annja looked at Vic.

"Don't look at me, I was busy doing the double-dutch."

"A little help over here would be nice."

Annja turned to see Joey clambering up onto the ledge. He was nursing one of his arms. Annja helped him up.

"What happened?"

"After nearly getting chomped in half?" Joey shrugged. "I fell off and banged up my arm. I stayed low until I heard you calling for someone to shut Hector up. I still had my knife, so I figured what the heck."

"Some throw," Vic said.

Joey nodded. "It's my bad arm, too."

Annja examined his wounded arm. "Doesn't seem like anything's broken. I'd say all in all we were pretty lucky."

Michael stood and Vic held on to him. "Not so fast. You've lost a lot of blood. We'll need to take it easy for a while."

Michael shook his head. "We've got to get out of here."

Joey nodded. "Agamemnon has to be stopped."

"Damn, I'd almost forgotten about that," Vic said.

"Forgotten about what?" Annja asked.

"The thing in Makati." Vic looked at Joey and Michael. "You guys know anything more about it?"

"It's nuclear," Joey said. "And small."

"He's going to detonate in Makati?" Vic asked.

"That's the plan. It's being caravanned up there somehow, but we don't know how it's being handled."

"The impression we got," Michael said, "was that someone in his other camp was taking care of it while Agamemnon used us to hunt you guys down."

"Great," Annja said. "So, this isn't over yet?"

Vic eyed her. "Not unless you want to be glowing at the airport."

"No, thanks. I look horrible in ultraviolet."

"We've got to get out of here," Vic said. "And now." He looked at Joey and Michael. "Are you guys well enough to travel?"

"We'll make do," Joey said. "And we want nothing more than to see that guy dead, anyway."

"Should have known he'd sacrifice us at the drop of a hat," Michael said. "When no one came looking for me when Hector's people grabbed me, I started wondering how bad things were going to get."

Joey smirked. "Might be time to retire."

Vic nodded. "Let's settle that later. If we get out of here, can you get us back to Agamemnon's camp?"

"Sure, but I don't think he knows how to reach the people getting the bomb to Makati."

"Why not?"

Michael shrugged. "Standard operational-security thing, I'd venture. Agamemnon gave the order and all he does now is wait for it to be carried out."

Annja glanced around. About twenty of Hector's followers still loitered in the main cavern. They seemed completely unsure of what to do. Some of them were wailing at the deaths of both Hector and their god.

"Well, regardless, we need to get moving. I don't want these people suddenly deciding we're persona non grata and trying to kill us again. I'm a bit worn-out from all the fighting," she said.

Vic pointed. "Back that way, Annja?"

"Yeah. There's the main entrance. And that's how Agamemnon and his guide left."

They jumped off the ledge. Annja still held on to the sword. As they headed up the incline, most of Hector's followers simple folded out of their way.

One of them stood and started to draw a knife, but Annja

merely flicked the sword at him and he jumped away terrified.

Vic leaned into her. "You going to tell me exactly what the hell that thing is and how you came by it?"

She smiled. "Probably not."

"It's almost like you pulled that thing right out of thin air," he said.

"That's ridiculous. But I'm not going to do a tell-all confessional about it just because you happened to see it."

Vic frowned. "I wish you would."

"You going to tell me about all of your classified missions?"

"Definitely not."

"There you go, then."

They reached the top of the slope and Annja paused to let Joey and Michael catch up. Michael's bleeding had at least slowed. And despite looking pale, he seemed determined to keep up with the rest of them.

Joey's arm had turned bluish from the apparent bruising under the skin. Annja examined it again and he flinched.

"You might have a fracture, after all," she said.

"I'll be fine. Let's just get going."

Annja stopped and grabbed torches from up on a bracket. She handed one to Vic and took the other for herself. "I'll bet we'll make good time now instead of crawling around in the dark."

"Probably so," he agreed.

They started for the entrance to the cavern, when Annja heard a noise behind them.

She stopped.

Hector had risen from the ledge. As she watched, he reached up to his bloody throat and grabbed the knife with both hands. Slowly, he started to slide the blade out, retching as he did so.

"You've got to be kidding me," Annja said.

"Doesn't this guy ever quit?" Vic asked. He started to head back down the slope, but Annja stopped him. "Wait."

Hector's appearance seemed to have galvanized the remaining worshipers. As he struggled to stand, the crowd got to its feet, as well. They shouted with joy as he slid the bloody knife out of his throat.

And then something else happened.

The crocodile stirred.

"No way," said Annja. "That's impossible."

Joey and Michael moved into the cavern opening. "I don't know if we should stay around to see how this ends."

More of the worshipers stood up and chanted for Hector and the beast to rise. Annja could tell they were getting worked up again.

Hector stood before them, his back to the crocodile, and spread his arms. When he opened his mouth, instead of words coming out, only a great rush of blood spilled forth.

But the effect was the same.

Instantly, the crowd in the cavern turned and faced Annja and the others.

"Oh, crap," Vic said.

"I was thinking of something a little bit stronger," Annja said.

"Guys," Joey said. "We need to get out of here."

But then as Hector spread his arms and started chuckling, the crocodile reared up and suddenly grabbed him in its mouth. Hector's laughter was choked off as the mighty jaws bit down, cleaving Hector almost in two.

Annja could hear the bones snapping as Hector screeched and blood erupted from everywhere at once. The crocodile chomped down again and swallowed huge chunks of Hector's flesh.

Hector's worshipers screamed.

With a final gulp, Hector disappeared down the crocodile's gullet.

"I can't believe this. That thing should be dead," Annja said. "There's no way it could come back from an injury like that."

Vic grabbed her arm. "I don't think we want to stick around this time. Since we're here, we should get going while the going is still good."

Annja nodded. "Okay."

The crocodile leaped down from the ledge. It landed hard and Annja could see that it suffered from her wound.

But even still, the mighty beast seemed able enough to start attacking the bulk of Hector's followers.

Some of them hid behind rocks, but the crocodile merely swatted its tail, knocking the barriers over. Rocks fell through the cavern. The beast hissed. Its jaws snapped angrily as it devoured people and simply tore others in half.

"I don't think he's happy about being injured."

"Annja," Vic said. "Now?"

She turned. "Okay."

She heard another rumble.

More rocks fell from the ceiling of the cavern. Now the rocks began taking out other followers as the crocodile reared up almost on its hind legs and continued its destruction.

Bodies flew everywhere. Stray limbs did, as well, and the smell of death and blood hung heavy in the air.

A giant rumble issued up from somewhere deep in the earth. The roof of the cavern started caving in.

Annja watched from the entrance as the crocodile lumbered back up onto the ledge and made its way toward the pit. It cast a final look around, its eyes seeming to settle on Annja's for a split second.

And then it slid over the side and back into the murky depths of the pit.

Did it just look at me?

She felt Vic's hand on hers. "Seen enough?"

"Yeah."

"Joey and Michael have the way out already. Let's go!"

Annja turned and followed Vic out into the tunnel. With the torches, everything seemed much clearer now.

Joey and Michael waited up ahead. Throughout the tunnel complex, it sounded as if rocks were caving in everywhere.

"We've got to be quick," Joey said. "I think this entire place is about to collapse."

Michael pointed down another fork. "This way!"

Dust kicked up all around them. Behind in the main cavern, the rocks continued to fall and Annja turned back just in time to see the entrance completely covered with debris.

The main cavern was gone.

She coughed as Vic led her back up the tunnel. Throughout the complex, she could hear people screaming.

More rocks continued to fall. Joey and Michael led the way, surprisingly fast despite their injuries.

And then Annja saw it—the small ladder leading straight up.

To freedom.

33

As soon as Annja broke out of the clump of trees, she felt the weight of the tropical heat descend on her like a four-hundred-pound nose tackle in a football game. After having been underground for so long, she'd almost forgotten the immense mugginess that awaited her back on the surface.

But now she recalled how much she was growing to dislike the jungle. She got an instant sweat on; her clothes felt like an oven, baking her in a skin of her own sweat and stink.

"Yuck," she said.

Joey helped her out of the tree and grinned. "It was nice and cool down there, wasn't it?"

"And how," Michael said as he climbed out behind Annja. "This is going to take a little time to get used to again."

Vic shook his head. "Time is something we don't have much of. Not if we want to head Agamemnon off and save Manila from going nuclear."

Annja looked at him. "Any chance you can get in touch with your people?"

"Not right now. I went dark on this mission, like I said."

She frowned. "No way to call them in, even in an emergency?"

"I know it doesn't make sense to you," Vic said. "But by going dark, snipers can guarantee they won't be tracked by the enemy. Having a radio means you can be triangulated. And everyone has access to that technology nowadays. It's not like it used to be."

"It doesn't make sense to me because in case of emergency—like this—there's no way of alerting folks about the danger we've discovered," Annja said.

Michael sighed. "Well, if there's no way to call them in, then we'll have to make other plans."

"What other plans?" Annja asked.

"We hoof it."

"Fast," Joey said.

Annja wiped her brow. The sweat was pouring out of her body so fast, it almost felt worse now than when she'd first started her journey in this rain forest. "What about water?" she asked.

Michael shrugged. "You've got three people here who can find water easily. Or did you forget that?"

She smiled. "Yeah. How could I?"

Vic stared at the area. "Which way did you guys come in?"

Joey pointed. "Agamemnon made his camp back there some ways."

Annja looked at the small meadow bordered by more jungle. It seemed odd to her that there would be a meadow here at all, but as she studied the lay of the land, she knew it wasn't really a meadow in the typical sense, but more just like a spot of high ground relatively free of vines and trees, except near the border.

"This is a good spur," Vic said. "Perfect for a helicopter to come into. Which, of course, would be really nice."

Michael pointed to the ground. "Agamemnon's tracks."

"Only one set?" Vic asked.

"Yeah."

Annja frowned. "What about the warrior Hector sent with him?"

Joey pointed. "There."

Annja looked and saw the cloud of flies buzzing. Only part of the bloody hand was visible from where she stood, but as she walked over, she could see the multiple stab wounds on the warrior's back.

"He stabbed him in the back?" She shook her head. "There's no low that guy won't stoop to, huh?"

Joey sighed. "Seems not."

"We're lucky to have escaped that much," Michael said. "Now we have a chance to put things right."

"By tracking him," Annja said.

"Exactly."

Joey pointed. "We follow his tracks, we can get a good jump on him. I doubt very much that he can move as fast as we would be able to."

Vic looked at Annja. "How are you feeling?"

"Hot and wet," she said.

"And probably not in a romantic way, huh?"

"Not even close."

Vic smiled. "Can you move?"

"I can move." Annja closed her eyes partway. Looking into the other plane, she spotted the sword, which she'd put back away when she had to climb up the ladder. As soon as she saw it, a spurt of energy helped her feel a bit better.

But she wasn't looking forward to trekking through the jungle. The heat felt a thousand times worse even though it must be early morning. She knew the sun would climb higher during the day and send its sizzling rays down to fry the jungle canopy below.

But she had to go for it. "The sooner we get going, the better," she told Vic.

"Which direction?" Michael asked. "We can follow Agamemnon, or we can make for the coast."

"Which one is closer?" Annja asked.

Joey shrugged. "We could catch Agamemnon probably in about three hours. Or we could abandon him for now and concentrate on getting out of here and being able to warn Manila. If we go after Agamemnon, there's a chance we won't catch him in time to stop the detonation."

"I think," Vic said, "that our choice is pretty clear. We have to get word to the authorities in Manila."

"Agreed," Annja said. "There's no guarantee Agamemnon could even stop the thing from happening anyway."

Michael nodded. "Okay, then we make for the coast."

"Who wants point?" Annja asked.

Joey looked at Vic. "We can take turns. We start out on an easterly heading and that should bypass a lot of obstacles if I remember this section of the country well."

Vic nodded. "East is how I would go, too."

Michael cleared his throat. "I'll take the first shift."

They moved into a ragged line with Michael about twenty feet ahead of the rest of them. Vic eyed Annja. "Remember to stay close to me. If we get separated, we may not find you again."

"The last thing you'll do is lose me. I'm not staying in this jungle any longer than absolutely necessary."

Michael moved fast. By the second hour, it felt as if they'd covered at least four miles, but Annja knew that gauging distance under the canopy was difficult. It took time, even moving fast, to bypass the small rolling hills and the thick carpet of vegetation that sought to mire them in a morass of vines, weeds and downed trees.

They called a rest a few moments later and Vic used his knife to cut into a tube vine. He held it up so Annja could drink first and she greedily lapped up the tepid moisture, feeling it recharge her, but only just a little.

Vic, Joey and Michael took turns taking a quick drink.

"We have to keep moving," Joey said.

Vic glanced at Annja. "How you holding up?"

"I'm holding," she said.

"All right."

Michael said something to Joey, but Annja couldn't hear what it was. She frowned. "You want to share that with me?"

Michael shook his head. "No."

Vic frowned. "Hey, guys, this isn't the time or place to comment on Annja's ability in the jungle. I think she's more than proved herself back there in the caves. She's not used to moving as fast as we are in the bush."

Michael started to say something, but then stopped. Joey patted him on the back and he moved off.

As Vic came forward, he looked at Joey. "What the hell was that about?"

Joey shook his head. "I'll tell you in a few minutes."

Vic shook his head and kept walking with Annja behind him. Joey opted to bring up the rear this time.

As she walked, Annja felt herself grow angry. What right did Michael have to grouse about her lack of energy? He'd been taken captive, as well, hadn't he? And she hadn't seen him take on that crocodile by himself, climbing on to its back and stabbing it in the skull.

Even if it hadn't worked.

She was doing her best. And now she had to deal with his machismo, too? What was it about some guys that they had to complain about an apparent weakness in females? She wanted to strangle him.

She frowned and kept trudging on. Ahead of her, Vic seemed pretty upset, as well.

She heard very little noise from behind her.

She glanced back. Joey was moving through the woods very quietly, but also very fast. He'd drifted back some ways, and she could only just catch flashes of his clothing as he continued to move toward her.

Why had he drifted back so far? Hadn't Vic told her the importance of keeping them in sight?

She sighed. Well, he could probably follow a trail anywhere. He didn't actually need to see where he was going.

She'd heard about some tracking schools located in the United States. Maybe when she got home, she'd look into getting some training. It seemed to be a valuable skill to have.

Annja grinned. Yeah, she'd look into it, right after that drippy, gooey cheese-steak sub and French fries she was going to devour at Bobby Ray's back in Brooklyn. That, a good long soak in the tub and about a month of sleep.

Annja's mouth swam in saliva. "God, I'm hungry," she said.

The thought of getting out of the jungle seemed to lift her spirits. If they could just keep on going, who knew? Maybe by tonight, she'd be in a luxurious hotel room in metro Manila as she waited for her flight home.

That would be nice.

Vic chopped his way through more vines. Even he was starting to look winded. Annja could see how much sweat was pumping out of his pores; his camouflage was stained dark by each cut he made.

At least I've got him, she thought. There's no way I would have survived if we hadn't hooked up.

The thought of decapitation sprang into her head again. She frowned. Agamemnon really needed to be put down, and soon. A crazy megalomaniac like that didn't deserve a place on the planet.

She felt a presence behind her and looked back.

Joey was coming up on her fast.

She braced herself.

As he moved past her, he whispered. "We have to move quickly, Annja. Please."

"I'm going as fast as I can," she said.

"You need to move faster. Trust me."

"Why? Because if I don't your brother will get even more upset at me than he already is?"

Joey glanced back and then urged her on. "Annja, my brother isn't upset at you at all."

"He's not?"

"No."

Vic saw them talking and stopped. "What's going on?"

Annja nodded at Joey. "He wants me to go faster."

Vic sighed. "Joey, ease off, man, okay? I'm sure Annja is going as fast as she can."

Joey nodded. "And as I told her, we have to move faster."

Vic's eyes narrowed. "Why?"

At that moment, Michael reappeared. He looked at Joey and nodded.

Joey frowned. "Agamemnon left us a surprise."

"He did?" Vic asked.

"We've got a kill team on our tail. And they'll be able to fire on us within the next few minutes," Joey said.

"We've got to take them out," Michael said in a whisper.

34

Michael led them farther down the trail until they reached a slight rise in the landscape. Annja could see that ground sloped downward after that and she could hear a river farther along.

"Here?" she asked.

Vic surveyed the area and nodded. "Yeah, I suppose this is as good as any. They won't be able to see us and might get a little jumpy. They should rush over the lip where we'll be waiting."

Annja frowned. More death was not what she wanted to be dealing. She would much rather continue on their journey to get the hell out of the jungle. But that would have to wait.

Vic sighed. "Wish I had my rifle with me. I could take them all down before they even got close."

Michael and Joey huddled around them. Joey drew his finger along the ground, teasing what looked like a beetle of some type. "Michael thinks there's four of them behind us," he said.

Annja glanced at him. "How did you know?"

Michael smiled. "You learn to read the signs. When we started out, I could tell there'd been a lot of activity in the area. Like someone had been all over the place, checking it out."

"You think they were watching us when we got out of the tree?" she asked.

"No doubt."

"Why not take us then?"

Vic shook his head. "They didn't know which way we were going. In order to set a proper ambush, they'd need time to see where we were headed. They couldn't just sit there and hop on us or they'd risk losing some of us back underground."

"So," Joey said, "they waited. And when they saw that we were headed east, they took up the pursuit."

Annja frowned. "Still seems weird they didn't just wait and shoot us back then."

Michael wiped his brow. "Regardless, they're on our tail now and we need to set up."

Vic withdrew the kris knife he carried. "This is going to be close-quarters type stuff."

Annja shrugged. "I'm getting more and more used to that."

"I saw."

Michael and Joey slid their knives out. Even with their respective injuries, they looked solemn.

Vic looked at each of them. "You guys seen combat before?"

They shrugged. "We've seen plenty of death."

"Have you ever dealt it?"

"Once before the fight in the caves back there," Joey said. "But we don't need to go and revisit it. Let's just say we're both prepared to do whatever we need to do."

"It's going to be different from the caves," Vic said. "We're talking about springing an ambush. These guys won't know what hit them. Shock and surprise are our best chance to survive."

Joey nodded. "We know."

"Hit hard and fast," Vic said. "And don't give any quarter. They wouldn't for you."

He glanced at Annja. "You all set?"

"Yeah."

"What about your, uh, sword?" he asked, looking around.

Annja grinned. "I'll be ready," she said.

Vic nodded. "All right, let's get into position."

He moved them off the trail while Michael cut a few branches farther down to make it look as if they'd continued in that direction. They wanted to make sure the men pursuing them believed they hadn't stopped.

Vic positioned Michael off to the left of the trail and Joey off to the right. "The goal," he said, "is to do a sort of pincer move on them. As they come abreast, Annja and I will engage from the front. You two will swing in from behind and take them that way. Since we don't have guns, there's no danger of a cross fire."

Annja looked at him. "We hit them in the front?"

Vic nodded. "Well, you've got that sword and all. Seems like a good idea to me."

"Oh, sure."

Vic and Annja positioned themselves just over the lip. Vic's voice was a whisper. "As they come abreast, we'll cut low. Aim for a killing stab or slash into the upper thighs. If you can get the femoral artery, all the better."

Annja shuddered. "This is so premeditated."

Vic nodded. "Yeah. It is."

"I'm not used to this. I usually only fight when I have to. Killing isn't something I set out to do on a daily basis."

"Sometimes, we can't help what destiny hands us. We just have to make the best of the situation as it unfolds," he said.

"There's a lot of truth in that," Annja said.

"Find the silver lining in it."

She glanced at him. His eyes were dark brown and lively. "Do you always find a silver lining?"

He smirked. "Sometimes it feels more like pewter."

"This one of those times?"

He smiled. "I doubt it."

Annja lay flat on her stomach, trying to quell her nerves. Vic lay next to her, his knees up slightly so he could spring up as the men came to them.

"How long?" Annja asked.

Vic shook his head. "Not much longer now. They'll see the landscape change and hustle. That's what we want."

"You think Joey and Michael are okay?"

"We'll find out."

"That's not very reassuring," she said.

Vic shrugged. "You're never sure until you see how people handle themselves in combat. They did great back in the caves, but that was self-defense, mostly. This is different. It's almost a different mind-set."

"I guess you're pretty familiar with that, huh?"

He nodded. "I have to be. My life depends on me getting that one shot, one kill. If I don't, I might die."

"How do you reconcile it? The premeditated thing."

Vic lifted himself off the ground. "You try to make peace the best way you can. For some guys, it's that whole good-versus-evil thing. They tell themselves if this guy lives or that guy gets away, he'll kill lots more people."

"Better the price of one than many?" she asked.

"Yeah."

"What about other guys?"

Vic took a deep breath. "Maybe they take the human factor out of it. It doesn't become so much about killing a person—it's more just a job. You track and stalk and line up the target. You squeeze the trigger and they drop dead. You go on your way."

"It's a little different from being an insurance salesman, though," Annja said.

"Yeah, it is. But some guys can do that."

"So you do that?"

Vic shook his head. "Me? No. My motivation's a little bit different."

Annja paused. "Want to tell me about it?"

"Now?"

"Why not?"

"Because we're about to spring an ambush, that's why."

Annja shifted onto her side. "You'll tell me later, then, okay?"

"Sure. Just as soon as you spill the beans about where the hell you got that sword."

Annja grinned. "Speaking of which." She closed her eyes and reached into the tall grass beside her. When she opened them, she pulled her hand back and the sword gleamed in her hands.

Vic blew out a breath, "It's really quite beautiful."

"Thanks."

"You've got the advantage of reach with that."

"Meaning what?"

Vic looked at his knife. "You go first."

"Me?"

He smiled. "I'll be right here."

Annja started to say something but then stopped. With the sword, she'd be able to cut a wide swath and hopefully score some good hits before everyone else engaged. It made sense.

"All right."

Vic quieted her and they waited in silence for something to happen.

Annja heard a crack.

Vic froze.

She raised her eyebrows. He nodded.

The men who stalked them were close.

Another twig snapped somewhere about twenty feet away.

Annja felt her heart start hammering. If she'd said anything else, they might have heard her.

A low rustle sounded like a vine dragging over the material of a pant leg. Annja's ears pricked up.

They were so close.

Sweat ran down her neck and she gripped the handle of her sword.

Vic's eyes had gone to stone.

Annja found herself sucking in more oxygen.

And then something inside of her set her into motion. Annja came alive, lifting herself up into a crouch, swinging the sword for all she was worth.

The effect was instant chaos.

The two men in front of her saw her at the very last possible second. Their guns started to come up but Annja was already cutting into them, her sword blade slashing deep wounds in their upper thighs, across their groins and lower abdomens.

The air exploded as the men behind the front two opened fire. But it was undisciplined and the rounds went right into the backs of the front two men, who dropped dead even before the reality of the situation seemed to register.

Annja saw Vic moving beside her and in her peripheral vision she saw Joey and Michael come alive from the edges of the trail, closing their deadly noose on the two rear men.

Joey went low, driving his knife deep into the side of the man in front of him. Michael cut down into the neck of his target, slashing and tearing at the exposed muscles.

Vic finished off the two men in front, delivering deep thrusts to both of their hearts.

It was over in seconds.

Annja sniffed the air and could smell the stench of blood and cordite. The air still smoked from the rounds the men had fired off.

But the noise died as quickly as they did and soon enough, the jungle settled back down.

Annja surveyed the damage.

Four men dead before they knew what hit them.

Vic nodded. "Everyone okay?"

"I am," Annja said.

Joey and Michael checked each other over. Michael looked as if he might have been bleeding a little from the sudden exertion that tore at his wounds. Joey looked as if his arm was bothering him.

But otherwise, they were okay.

Vic cut a nearby tube vine and helped himself to a long swallow of water. He gestured for Annja to do the same. "Store it up. We don't have any time to hang around."

Annja pointed at the four corpses. "What about them?"

Joey walked over and cut into a vine for himself. "Leave them. The jungle will take care of disposing of them."

"They'd leave you there," Michael said. "No sense doing any better by them."

Annja drank from the tube vine. It felt weird just leaving the bodies behind. But Vic was right—they didn't have any time to waste.

She knew that it was right to pay with four men dead than the thousands who would die if Agamemnon's nuclear fantasy was allowed to play out on the streets of Manila.

She took a final swallow, looked one last time at the bodies of the men who would have killed them all, and then took off down the trail, following Vic.

Annja didn't look back.

35

The landscape was changing.

As they'd walked down the trail, Annja's suspicions about there being a river nearby were confirmed. Although not much larger than a creek at first, it soon gave way to a larger tributary that led them down to a river swollen with water. The jungle had little choice but to yield to the wide, fast-flowing water and Annja felt as if they were finally making some progress.

She felt her energy increase as Joey took over on point. He kept his arm near his side, doing his best not to let it bang into any of the bushes or trees as they skirted the banks of the river.

His color had paled some.

Annja caught up with Vic, who was walking faster than he had before. "Is he going to be okay?" she asked.

Vic shrugged. "It's probably broken somewhere. But it might not be detectable without an X ray. He needs medical attention. Come to think of it, we all need it. But he'll make himself keep going."

"Is he going to drop dead, though?"

"I doubt it. But shock can kill. He has to be careful."

Annja sighed. "He shouldn't be on point."

"He and Michael know this jungle better than I do. They won't take a back seat here."

Annja glanced back at Michael. He was even more pale than Joey. But he kept moving forward, his footsteps shuffling through the undergrowth. Once he slipped and Annja started back to help him, but he quickly recovered, got back to his feet and kept walking.

"This is getting ridiculous. We need to stop and rest," she said.

"You can suggest it if you want, but neither of them will listen to you," Vic said.

"But they're dying."

Vic frowned. "Put yourself in their position. If someone had a suitcase nuke and was planning on getting it into the heart of New York City, wouldn't you push on past your normal limits of endurance to try to stop it?"

Annja sighed again. "Yeah. I would."

"This is their country. I can't blame them for wanting to keep moving. But if we suggest they stop, they might think we don't care."

Annja looked back at Michael again. The bandages on his arm were stained a deep, dark brownish red from where the blood had dried and new bleeding had bled through the dressings.

"Michael, you okay?" she asked.

He glanced up and despite looking terrible, his eyes still seemed to be sharp. He nodded. "I'm okay. Looking forward to the beach."

"Makes two of us," Vic said.

"Three of us," Joey said from up ahead of them.

Annja smiled. Despite their different backgrounds, she'd grown fond of these guys. It would be difficult leaving them when this was all over.

The trees seemed to be growing farther apart now and the carpet of thick vines and dead litter was lessening. Annja's ears filled with a roar of rushing water.

Her heart rate increased at the thought of getting out of the jungle finally. She found herself digging even deeper into her own personal stores of energy and pressing to move faster.

Vic grinned as she steamed on past him. "Slow down, Speed Racer."

"Can't help it. I can feel that we're close," she said.

"We are."

She looked back. "You sure?"

He nodded. "About a half mile, I'd expect."

A half mile. Annja wanted to run for it. The river was widening and the flow of the water had slowed a little as farther down she could see it take a sharp bend to the left.

She skirted the bank and looked into the white water that swirled below.

"Looks so inviting," she said.

"I wouldn't," Vic warned her.

Annja shook her head. "Why on earth not?"

"Sharks," he said.

"Sharks?"

"Yep."

"In the river?"

Vic walked past her. "The mouth of the river meets the ocean. It's a feeding ground for them because the river washes a lot of jungle debris down to the sea. Dead bodies, animals that get trapped in the current and can't escape, that kind of thing. And there are plenty of tiger sharks in the seas around the Philippines that would love to take a bite out of you."

Annja stared at the river. "First crocodiles, now sharks. Unbelievable."

"You wouldn't even see them coming. The visibility is probably awful because the two bodies of water are mixing."

"You're a real killjoy, here, pal."

Vic smiled. "Just trying to save your ass again."

Annja continued walking as Michael came closer. His eyes gleamed and he walked as if he had some fire in his soul. "You sure you're okay?" she said.

"Will be soon enough."

"What's that supposed to mean?"

He just smiled and kept walking. Annja caught up with Vic. "You don't think they have a nasty surprise in store for us, do you?"

Vic looked at her. "You're always so suspicious of everyone, aren't you?"

"I have to be. People are always trying to either kill me, or get me to do things for them. It gets a little trying sometimes."

"Yeah, well, I think these guys are fine. Hell, they helped us kill some of the bad guys, remember? If they had any wavering in their loyalty, I think it's all gone now."

"Just checking."

Vic pointed. "Look there."

Annja followed his gaze and the jungle foliage ended abruptly. Suddenly a line of sand on either side of the river mouth could be seen through the remaining palm trees that had sprung up in the last few hundred yards.

"The beach!" Annja exclaimed.

Annja wanted to run for it, but kept herself from doing so. There was no sense leaving everyone else behind. They'd come through all of this together, and together they'd make it to the beach.

Joey shuffled onto the sand and sank to his knees. "Finally."

Vic knelt next to him. "You okay?"

"Arm hurts like hell."

Vic checked it over. Annja could see the skin had turned a nasty shade of dark blue. Bits of it were yellowed from the bruising, but it also looked swollen.

Vic frowned. "It's badly infected. You've got a fracture somewhere, no doubt, but I can't figure out where it would be. And I sure don't want to go poking you and putting you into even more pain than you're already in."

"Thanks," he said.

"Can you keep going? You need a doctor. Bad."

"My brother needs one, too," Joey said.

Vic nodded. "Yep. He does. No doubt he's lost a lot of blood."

Joey got back to his feet with Vic's help. Annja watched the waves crash on the shore.

Joey smiled. "It's always so great seeing the ocean. It rejuvenates my soul. The times Michael and I have worked in the mountains, it's felt like we were dead. But the sea, there's something about it that brings me back home. Always."

Annja smiled. "It's beautiful."

"You should see the beaches of Palawan. They're like pure sugar. Some of the resorts there are like Eden on earth. It's heavenly."

"Maybe we can go there some time. When you and Michael are better, I mean," she said.

He smiled. "Good plan."

"But right now," Michael said, coming out of the jungle at last, "we need to get back to Manila."

Vic looked at him. "You have a plan for that?"

Michael nodded. "Sure do. We head down the beach about a mile."

"Another mile?" Annja groaned.

"Yes," Michael said.

"And what's there?" Vic asked.

"Helicopter."

Annja whipped her head around. "Are you sure?"

"Absolutely."

Joey grinned. "There's a doctor there, too. A clinic where we can get patched up."

"*Patched up* is a bit optimistic for you two," Vic said. "I think a hospital stay is in order."

Joey looked at him. "Would you stop if this was your country?"

Vic frowned. "No."

"Exactly."

"Annja and I can handle it, though. You should rest," he said.

"There's no way I could rest knowing you two were taking it on alone. I have to be there when it goes down," Joey said.

"So do I," Michael said. "Let's keep moving."

Annja helped Michael stumble on the sand, which was loose and hard to slog through. Her own feet seemed to sink several inches with every step she took. The sun was also brutal and she felt suddenly exposed.

A mile seemed like forever across the sizzling sand, but as they came around a bend in the beach, she could see scattered rooftops come into view. A few boats bobbed in the waves just offshore.

And she could see kids jumping in the waves.

"Guess the sharks don't bother them," she said.

"We're moving away from the river's mouth," Vic said. "It's safer swimming there. But only just a little."

"I bet you're one of those people who only likes to swim in pools, right?" she asked.

Vic smirked. "How'd you guess?"

Joey did pretty well moving on his own, but Vic stayed close enough to lend him a hand in case he needed it. Twice, he almost fell, but he steadied himself and regained his footing.

I can't believe they've been able to do what they've done with their injuries, Annja thought.

The sun sent rivers of sweat down her face. She had to keep blinking to keep the salt from stinging her eyes. She wanted water desperately.

Michael coughed as he walked. Annja slid an arm around him and he accepted it. "Thanks."

"Forget it," she said.

"You and Vic are okay, yes?" he asked.

"Seem to be. Just exhausted mostly."

Michael nodded. "That's good. That's good."

"They'll help us at this place?"

He smirked. "Oh, yes. They know us here."

"They do?"

"Yes. This is where we grew up."

Vic turned. "This is your village?"

"Yes."

Annja smiled. "Homecomings are always nice."

"They will be once we find the doctor and get to the helicopter."

They stumbled along the beach. And as they grew closer, the children saw them. Annja saw them running down the beach, their deeply tanned skin in sharp contrast to the white sand around them.

Joey carried himself higher now. Michael pulled away from Annja.

"You sure?"

He nodded. "I have to walk in on my own two feet."

As they walked down the last hundred yards, Annja saw something else that buoyed her spirits. The rotor blades of a helicopter sitting on its own pad could be seen farther off down the beach.

Her time in the jungle was finally over.

36

From the air, metro Manila looked pretty smoggy. Annja could see a thick blanket of brownish-gray air over the city before it finally seemed to dissipate farther out. As the rotors above her head beat a steady *whump-whump-whump,* she looked down at the various towns and cities dotting the landscape on the approach. Poverty seemed rampant here, and she could tell just by the rooftops who had money and who did not.

They weren't in the smaller Bell chopper they'd seen back on the beach. Once the villagers had spotted them, they'd gotten the doctor right away. He'd patched Joey and Michael as best he could. Michael refused the transfusion at first until the doctor promised to ride along and do it in-flight, almost squeezing the plasma bag into his veins.

Joey sported a flexible cast on his arm and his color looked a lot better. He'd already washed down a boatload of antibiotics, but he, too, had insisted on coming along.

Vic had immediately gotten hold of a cell phone and called in his people. Once they were airborne, Vic gave the pilots the proper coordinates and they'd flown to a small military base plopped down in the middle of nowhere. From there, they'd had a rushed meeting with a variety of the top brass, as Vic had referred to them, before boarding a Black Hawk chopper bound for Manila.

Across the cabin, Vic worked the radio while plotting out points on the map. He had changed his uniform and grabbed a new rifle from the armorer while they were at the camp. He looked clean and serious and Annja thought he was rather striking.

She had managed to grab a quick shower, as well, washing off the jungle grunge, bits of moldy twigs, leaf litter, dirt, mud and extensive grime. She had bug bites in all sorts of marvelous locations. And she fully expected it would take her exactly forever before her fingernails were ever clean again, let alone her hair.

She was dressed in a fresh set of urban-camouflage fatigues. Along with them on this jaunt was a squad of other soldiers that Vic had referred to as "special-ops guys." They all wore grim expressions as they sat near Vic talking and listening to each other on the radio.

Joey and Michael held a quiet conference with each other, probably comparing notes on their injuries. But every once in a while, Joey would nod at the picture of Agamemnon tacked to the inside of the cabin along with a score of other faces known to be his associates.

The fact was, finding the nuclear device was going to be difficult, if not impossible. Top military leaders on both sides of the Pacific had already been consulted. The government of the Philippines had ruled out notifying the public, saying it would simply create a mass hysteria that they could not control.

Vic had received orders to find and stop the person carrying the device while the U.S. scrambled to get other specialized units in place in the event they successfully cornered the couriers.

"It's a crapshoot," Vic said. "And the odds are piss poor."

"So what?" Annja said.

He had looked at her as they huddled outside the Black Hawk. "So, you don't have to go. I can get you out of the country and back home to the States. There's no need to go anywhere near Manila."

Annja shook her head. "There's no way I'm not going. I need to see this through to completion."

"Why?"

"Because I know what he can do if he's allowed to pull this off. Agamemnon needs to be stopped."

"There's no guarantee we'll even find him," Vic said.

"Yeah, but there's no guarantee we won't, either."

Skimming over towns and villages below, Annja wondered just how they were going to find Agamemnon and his couriers. Joey and Michael had insisted he probably didn't know who would be carrying it out.

"They'd use cutouts, in case one of them got captured, so they couldn't damage the operation," Joey said.

But Annja wasn't so sure. She'd seen Agamemnon up close and interacted with him. She couldn't believe that he would allow something so huge to be out of his control. He probably knew exactly how the device was going to get to Manila and who was carrying it. His ego wouldn't have let him not know.

Find Agamemnon and they'd be able to stop the destruction—she was sure of it.

It was already early evening now and they were only just getting toward Manila. Annja was worried they would be too late, but something inside her told her they still had time.

But how much?

Vic continued working with his team. Annja glanced at them. There seemed to be a free exchange of ideas on how to best run things down. She'd heard special-operations units worked that way, that all ideas—even from junior members of the unit—would be considered.

Still, Vic had operational command of this unit, and the final decision about what to do and how to do it would be his. She didn't envy his job right now.

Actually, she wasn't sure she envied anything right now, except maybe everyone who was oblivious to the unfolding situation below.

Agamemnon's picture fluttered in the crosswind. He had a sneer in the photo that sent a chill up Annja's back. He was ruthless. And what he'd done to his own men reminded Annja that some people simply did not deserve any mercy. The unmistakable fact was that there were plenty of people on the planet who really didn't deserve a molecule of oxygen.

Still, she found it tough being the one to judge who was and who wasn't worthy of it. That was the rub, she decided. Knowing how to be a tool of the universe to help remove the trash without becoming enthralled with the power and going berserk.

She sometimes missed the mundane existence she'd enjoyed before she'd found the sword.

The Black Hawk started to descend.

Annja looked over at Vic. "We're landing?"

He nodded. "Inside the city at the Embassy. We've got a makeshift HQ set up there with agents from a bunch of offices already bringing in good intel."

"Do they know what to look for?"

Vic stabbed his thumb at Agamemnon's picture. "They know enough."

Annja held on to the strap inside the cabin as the Black

Hawk banked and descended even more. It sounded as if the throttle was increasing as the helicopter flew lower.

Annja could see the embassy grounds and the clearly marked helipad in the open ground at the back of the compound. She could see a few military personnel guiding the bird with hand signals.

She looked inside the buildings and saw people rushing everywhere. The place was a hive of buzzing activity.

The Black Hawk flared and then gently set down. As soon as it touched the ground, the doors slid back on their rails and Vic's team jumped out with their gear.

"Stay with me," Vic said, shouting over the whine of the rotor blades. Annja, Joey and Michael followed him off the helicopter.

A man in a suit came running up to him. "You Gutierrez?"

Vic nodded. "Yeah."

"I'm Reynolds. With Defense Intelligence. You and your people can come with me. We've got you set up downstairs in the bubble."

As they walked, Reynolds handed each of them a red badge with the word Visitor stamped across it. At the door, a Marine guard in full combat gear eyed them and then let them pass. Reynolds led them to an elevator and pressed the button.

The noise in the building was loud. Annja could hear footfalls from people running everywhere. Reynolds grinned. "Obviously, people are a little excited about the whole thing," he said.

"Who else knows?" Vic asked.

"Just our people. But word spreads through the Embassy, you know."

"As long as your local employees don't get wind and start notifying everyone. If they do that, Agamemnon will pull the plug on the op and go to ground until he can catch us all unaware some time in the future."

"We've kept a lid on it, and no indigenous folks are allowed in this part of the building anyway."

"Good," Vic said.

Reynolds looked at Joey and Michael. "No offense."

Joey grinned. "None taken. We Filipinos gossip a hell of a lot."

The rest of Vic's team came in and waited for the elevator. When it arrived they all crammed inside and descended.

"Where are we going?" Annja asked.

Reynolds looked at her. "Do I know you? You look familiar."

"Maybe from television," Annja said. "I was on a show."

"That's it! I knew you looked familiar. *Chasing History's Monsters,* right?"

"Yes. But that seems a lifetime away from where we're at now," Annja said.

Reynolds nodded. "Yeah, I suppose so. Anyway, we're going to the bubble. It's a secure room, not really a bubble per se. But our secret communication gear is down there and we can receive direct traffic from Washington via satellite. The folks in power can stay in the loop, and we can get the latest and greatest intel on our targets."

The elevator doors slid open and two more armed Marines met them, checking everyone over before allowing them to proceed. Reynolds led them down a long corridor painted battleship-gray before they came to a heavy iron vault door.

"Just a second," Reynolds said as he punched in a series of numbers and waited for his handprint to be scanned. There was a beep followed by a long hiss as the hydraulic door engaged and swung open.

Inside, the room looked like a nerve center for some science fiction movie. Annja saw banks of computers and huge video displays up on all the walls. The lighting was dim in order to help the folks working avoid eyestrain as they read their screens.

Agamemnon's face looked down on her from twenty feet away. Giant digital maps of metro Manila were displayed on other screens. Annja could see all sorts of dots, code words and numbers appearing and disappearing on the screens.

It was all quite overwhelming.

Vic seemed in his element, though. He turned to Reynolds. "Run it down for me, would you?"

Reynolds nodded. "We've got all the access points to the city under surveillance."

"That's an awful lot of places to check out. You sure you've got them all?" he asked.

"Near as we can. Obviously, we've got limited manpower. And the Philippine government is really letting us run the show on this. They've committed only one special unit from their intelligence branch to the cause because they simply don't want word leaking out about a possible nuke strike in the city."

"What are their people doing right now?" Vic asked.

"Coordinating smaller teams of people using handheld nuke detectors. They've got a bunch of them scattered all over as you can see on the map up there. The areas marked green are covered."

"I see plenty more unmarked," Vic said.

"Yeah, we're getting some aerial-reconnaissance teams up as we speak. They've got birds outfitted with higher-powered scanners that should be able to pick up the residue from the device. There's a good chance we can spot it from the air."

"What else?"

"Your boy Agamemnon was spotted in town earlier today right before you radioed in," Reynolds said.

"He's here?" Annja asked.

"Yes," Reynolds said. "But we don't have him anymore. He slipped his surveillance team near the Robinson Galleria hotel. We don't know where he is now."

"Wonderful," Vic said. "Anything else?"

"That's about it. We've got plenty of intelligence on his known associates, faces mostly, but we figure every little bit can help. If one of the faces comes up from some of our other agencies, then we might get lucky."

"What about the device itself?" Vic asked.

Reynolds shrugged. "Suitcase-size nukes are nothing really new. The Soviets masterminded their development back in the midseventies and finally got them in working order in the early eighties near as we can figure. With the fall of communism over there, a lot of them went missing. That's never really been made public, and we've certainly a good number of them back under control, but more than a few found their way onto the black market, where your boy picked one up."

"And if this thing goes off, what kind of damage are we looking at?" Vic asked.

Reynolds frowned. "Complete destruction of everything within one square mile. And in a crowded place like Manila, that's probably an easy sixty thousand people dead."

"Not including the fallout from the radiation cloud, as well, right?" Annja said.

Reynolds nodded. "It would be even worse if Agamemnon manages to detonate it up high, like say, on top of a skyscraper or something."

"How much worse?" Joey asked.

Reynolds looked at him. "Maybe twice the number of dead."

37

Agamemnon looked out over the skyline of Manila as the sun set. While it lacked the number of buildings that made skylines like those of New York so famous, the city had its own charm.

And it was that charm he looked most forward to destroying in the morning.

From his suite at the hotel, Agamemnon watched the throngs of people flooding the streets far below. Manila had one of the densest populations in the world, with many people packed per square mile. As such, it was a deliciously easy target for a man like him.

He poured himself a fresh glass of wine and savored the taste. His cell phone purred and he picked it up.

"Yes?"

"We're here."

Agamemnon smiled. Miki had managed to come through after all. "Did you have any problems?"

"Increased police presence at the docks, but nothing we couldn't handle. It's amazing what a few well-placed American dollars will do for a tired slave of the capitalist infidels."

Agamemnon smiled. Miki was eager to prove himself. He knew this and played on it. But Miki had already proved himself more than capable of carrying out a complex assignment. Now it was time to stoke the fires of his hatred and turn him into a complete zealot.

"I'm afraid I have some bad news," Agamemnon said.

"What's that?"

"Eduardo is dead."

Miki paused on the phone. Agamemnon could imagine him gripping the phone tighter, rage already seeping into his blood. "How did he die?"

"It was the American sniper he was sent to find. The sniper found him first. I'm sorry."

"Is the sniper dead?"

It was a good question. Agamemnon had no idea if the sniper and the rest had been killed by Hector and his followers or if they'd somehow managed to escape. With the kill team in place, Agamemnon had left strict orders not to contact him. Radio silence was most important at this phase, and only Miki had the number to the cell phone he was using.

"I don't know," he answered honestly.

"I thought you were going to kill him," Miki said.

Agamemnon grinned. He could have lied, of course, and told Miki that the sniper was dead. But it was better to leave it an unknown variable. The thought of the sniper still breathing would help fire up Miki.

"I can't be sure if he lived or not. I had to come here and make sure we saw this out to its completion. Surely, you understand."

"I understand. But for Eduardo's sake, I want to see that man dead."

"Perhaps he's here now. In Manila. He might even be hunting you and your team as we speak."

Miki paused again. "How would he know where to look?"

"He wouldn't. But not knowing where to look wouldn't stop a man like him. He would be duty bound to try to find you."

"Yes, I suppose he would."

Agamemnon could hear it now. The edge in Miki's voice sliced across the airwaves and into Agamemnon's ear. He had to nurse this a little bit more and ensure things went down as he'd envisioned them so many months ago.

"How is our package?" he asked.

"Looking well."

"You've inspected it?"

"Of course."

"And all is ready for tomorrow?"

Miki cleared his throat. "Absolutely. I'm sure there will be plenty of developments when the sun rises."

"And your accommodations?"

"Comfortable. And protected as far as I can tell."

Agamemnon finished his wine and poured himself another glass. "Excellent. You should get some sleep. You have much to do in the morning."

"It's a shame I won't be there to see it when it happens," Miki said.

"Yes, a shame, indeed. But it will be a glorious day for us. And for the people we represent."

"Are you leaving?" Miki asked.

"Of course. I've chosen you for this mission because you are the only one I can trust. You've picked out the courier for the job and I trust that you know he will not fail, that he will not have a change of heart. It's absolutely vital that he carry this out completely."

Miki paused. "I'm sure he will."

"Because if he did have a change of heart, then this would all be for nothing. Eduardo's death would be in vain and the infidels would win. We would become the laughingstocks of the world. The fools who couldn't do anything right, like those bumbling idiots in Britain."

There was a longer pause on the phone. Agamemnon smiled and kept talking. "This is what we've worked for. All of our hard work comes down to this thing. And its success is our success."

"I understand," Miki said.

"You sound doubtful. You have concerns about something?"

"I'm just thinking."

"About what?"

"The courier."

The wine was good. Agamemnon wished he'd ordered more of it, but it wouldn't do to be drunk when dawn broke. He had a plane to catch before the morning rush hour began.

"If you have doubts, then we'll need to take steps to make sure the issues are resolved," he said.

"I'm probably worrying too much."

"Is there such a thing as worrying too much when we're talking about what we're discussing? I don't think so. If you have concerns, then by all means we need to deal with them," Agamemnon said.

"It's just that I'm not sure our man is completely sold on the idea."

"He has to be!" Agamemnon was growing alarmed.

"I think I can talk to him."

Agamemnon fingered the first-class plane ticket to Beijing sitting on the table. He'd heard the weather this time of year was quite nice in the Chinese countryside.

"We're a little beyond the whole talking thing now, don't you think? We need doers not thinkers. That's what it comes down to. Otherwise, that sniper wins. The Americans win. And we lose."

"We won't lose," Miki said, sounding more confident.

"Oh?"

"I'll do it myself."

Agamemnon finished the wine and flipped the room-service menu open. A little dinner would taste good right now. But what? Perhaps some fish. That would go well with the Pinot Grigio he'd just finished. Yes, he'd have the fish. He smiled contentedly.

"You'll do it? Do you realize what you're telling me? Do you know what is expected of you?" He made his voice dramatic.

"I know exactly what I will have to do," Miki said.

"You're sure?"

"Yes."

"Your willingness to do this will make you a hero of our cause. You know that, don't you?"

"I do."

"We will sing your praises every night for many years to come, Miki. Your name will live on in legend, and Allah will reward your devotion to his cause."

"*Inshallah.*"

"*Inshallah.*"

"What time should I set out?"

Agamemnon checked his watch. "Rush hour starts at around seven. I would expect the most people will be out and about by eight-thirty."

"I will start out around seven and ensure that I reach the target by then."

"Good."

"The sniper...if he lived, are you sure he would be in Manila now?"

"Without a doubt. I have reason to believe that he discovered the nature of our mission before Eduardo died. He would be duty bound to report it to his superiors. Knowing how the

Americans work, I'm sure he would be involved in the operation to stop us."

"Then there's a good chance he will be nearby when I make my final quest tomorrow."

"A good chance indeed."

"That makes me happy. If I am able to kill him as I die, then all the better for all of us."

"His death will be your vengeance. And Eduardo will be there to greet you when you arrive in Heaven. I'm sure of it."

"As am I."

"Sleep well, Miki. And don't forget to make your final tape. You will want your message to live on past your final act tomorrow morning."

"I live to serve our cause," Miki said.

"And you die to fulfill your destiny."

"Good-bye, Agamemnon."

"Be brave, Miki."

Agamemnon disconnected and looked out on the Manila night. Lights twinkled all across the city. People enjoyed their dinners and their lives not knowing that come tomorrow morning, a nuclear bomb would bring havoc, chaos and destruction to this city of fattened capitalists.

Agamemnon grinned. He knew he was just as guilty of personal excess as any of them. But this was what it all boiled down to anyway.

Money.

It was the lowest common denominator in any struggle. Every war, every act of rebellion, every cause had its roots in the power of money. Somewhere, somehow, someone was getting wealthy off the work and strife of idealists and zealots.

Agamemnon was no different.

In an offshore bank account based in the Cayman Islands, he had the tidy sum of fifty million dollars ready to use for whatever he desired. And Agamemnon had plenty of desires. Fifty million could buy him whatever he wanted. And he had any number of places he could settle when this was all said and done.

He cell phone purred again and he picked it up. "Yes?"

"Is everything ready?"

"Yes."

"You have your ticket?"

"Right here."

"We are looking forward to seeing you again. You've been away for a very long time."

He thought about everything he'd endured. Plastic surgery. Years in the country learning how to speak the language fluently. Crash courses in human psychology. Weapons, leadership, demolitions and then the small matter of procuring the nuclear device.

It hadn't been easy.

"I'm looking forward to going home," he said.

"You'll be a hero upon your return."

"As long as nothing delays the flight."

"Nothing will."

"This isn't going to be a safe place come tomorrow morning."

"That is why we're getting you out at five o'clock in the morning. Can you be at the airport then?"

"Certainly."

"Excellent. Payment has been made as promised."

"It pains me I won't be able to stay home for long."

"You'll be hunted all over the world."

Agamemnon grinned. "At least until the man called Agamemnon dies. Then I'll be safe at last."

"Another face?" the voice asked.

"It's the only way."

"You have a doctor in mind?"

Agamemnon ran his hand over his face. "The one in

Panama. He did good work before. I think he might be a good choice for my next identity."

"He'll be a loose end."

"Only until he's done with my face. Then he'll cease to be a problem. Like all of the others."

"Have a safe flight."

Agamemnon shut his phone and stared out of the window. Perhaps he would order one more bottle of wine. He was in a celebratory mood.

38

Annja watched Vic as he pored over the various reports that were coming in from all over the city. Most of them were meaningless, and Vic had the task of deciding which ones should be taken seriously.

He looked exhausted. As the clock on the wall marked three o'clock in the morning, Annja poured a fresh cup of coffee and brought it to him.

He looked up and smiled. "Thanks."

"You having any luck with this stuff?" she asked.

He took a swallow of the coffee and shook his head. "Not very much, no. It's all a mass of paperwork, but very little else."

"There's got to be something, though, doesn't there? Some little shred of information you're not seeing?"

"That's exactly what is most frustrating. The feeling that I haven't seen something I should have seen. That and that damned clock ticking away."

"You're sure it'll be today?" she asked.

Vic frowned. "Yeah. We have to figure they'll try and set it off during the rush hour—either morning, or afternoon.

That's when the city core will be filled with the most people. And that's exactly what they're after—maximum casualties."

"All those poor innocent people. Men, women, babies even. They just don't care, do they?" Annja said.

Vic shrugged. "I'm not exactly feeling like I could accurately explain how their minds work. All I care about right now is stopping them. If I fail, I'm probably going to die, as well. We are at ground zero, after all."

Annja smiled. "Yep."

"You should leave," he said.

She looked at him. "You keep trying to get rid of me. Haven't you learned yet that I'm an extremely stubborn woman?"

Vic leaned back in his chair and kicked his feet up on the table. "I know you are. It's part of your charm."

"My charm?"

"Your allure."

"I can accept that," she said, laughing.

"When we get through this," Vic said, waving his hand, "I'm going to take you out for a really good dinner."

"I'd like that." Annja watched him as he closed his eyes. "You never told me how you're able to reconcile what you do for a living," she said.

His eyes opened again. "You sure you want to kill the mood?"

Annja shrugged. "We're in the bowels of the United States Embassy. I'd say the mood's already been pretty well spoiled. This place doesn't exactly rate on the list of the most romantic places on earth."

Vic slid his feet off the table and took another drink of the coffee. "What the hell, right?"

She waited for him to start, watching as the memories seemed to crawl across his face.

"I was just out of sniper training. I'd been in special operations for a while. I'd seen some combat in a few places that were so far off the books they'll never even be discussed. But being a sniper's different. The combat is different.

"When you're in a unit, you have guys backing you up. You depend on each other. You know your buddy has your back and you have his. There's a sense of duty. You won't let anyone kill your pal and vice versa. That drives you, that bond of brotherhood. It makes it easy to do things that you might otherwise find unacceptable."

He polished off the cup of coffee Annja had brought him and crushed the cup in his hand. "Being a sniper is something else entirely. There's no unit. It's just you. You work alone. You've got your rifle and your wits. That's it.

"The first time in the bush, it's like all your worst nightmares come true. You jump at every sound, your heart thunders so much you swear people can hear you coming. They can't, of course, but that's what you believe. Until you learn to handle your fear, you're not one hundred percent. And that's a liability.

"I got my first mission profile about six years back. I was assigned to South America at the time. We still had a lot of drug activity down there and the administration wanted some solutions. Permanent solutions, if you please." He stopped and looked at her with a sad smile.

"What happened?" Annja asked.

"I got dropped via chopper into Bolivia and made my way cross-country to a remote mountainside. I holed up there, living on hard routine for three weeks. Eventually, my target drove up to his vacation compound about a mile away from where I was, as the crow flies."

Vic closed his eyes, probably seeing the whole thing all over again. "I watched that guy for two days. I learned everything about him. That's what it's like being a sniper. It's close. Personal. You see your target like no one else. I watched that guy burp and fart and wink and smile. He was someone. Not just a target."

"That must have made it tough to kill him," Annja said.

Vic opened his eyes and looked at her. "That made it impossible to kill him. Until it was too late."

"What do you mean?"

"I mean when I finally had my crosshairs on his head, I couldn't take the shot. I let him get in his car and drive away."

"You missed?"

"I never shot my rifle. I never lived up to my mission parameters."

"Well, you couldn't really be blamed, could you? It was your first assignment, after all," she said.

Vic shook his head. "I've blamed myself every day since then, Annja. Every day that I wake up, I see that guy's face in my head. And I know that I screwed up."

"You can't ride yourself forever, though," she said.

"I already have. You know what the target did after he left his vacation home? He drove to the house of a government official who'd been making trouble for the drug cartels. He killed him there."

Annja frowned. "I'm sorry."

"That's not the worst of it. The worst part is that this official's son was having a birthday party. This beautiful eight-year-old boy and all of his friends were having the time of their lives playing. And this guy walks in and kills not just the official but every child in attendance. It was a bloodbath."

Annja felt her throat grow tight. "My God."

"You ask me how I reconcile what I do? I don't have to reconcile anything. I have the memory of my failure always fresh in my mind when I go out and take down a target. If I hadn't frozen, if I'd done what I was trained to do that day back in Bolivia, those children might still be alive. They might be in high school now. They might have girlfriends and boyfriends. One of them might have discovered a cure for cancer. Instead, they're dead because I couldn't pull the trigger and end the life of a truly heinous piece of garbage."

Annja heard the ticking of the clock and nothing else. She felt as if the world had stopped turning. Vic's eyes bore into hers with such intensity, she found it difficult to return his gaze.

He took a calming breath and looked away. "Sorry."

Annja placed her hand over his. "No. I should be the one apologizing for bringing it up. I shouldn't have forced you to relive something like that. It was inconsiderate of me to do so."

"You didn't know. Don't worry about it," he said.

Annja leaned back. "Did you ever get him?"

Vic nodded. "When I found out what had happened because of my incompetence, I went into the bush and stalked him. It took me four weeks to get close to him again. But this time, I didn't hesitate. I put a bullet right through his temple and dropped him dead."

"At least you made sure he never lived to do more damage," Annja said.

"He'd done more than enough already," Vic said. "But it was closure of a sort. I could sleep again after that. The memories, though, they don't go away. I don't know if they ever will."

Annja slid her hands behind her head and sighed. "And now you stalk a new target."

"Yeah. And time's ticking away."

The door opened and an analyst walked into the room. "Gutierrez?"

"Yeah?"

The analyst handed him a slip of paper. "Just got a report in from one of our assets in the Chinese embassy."

Vic read the transcript and frowned.

"What is it?" Annja asked.

"The Chinese ambassador has left Manila."

"Is that unusual?"

Vic shrugged. Ordinarily, maybe not. But given what's coming, it looks a little suspicious."

"You think the Chinese are involved in this?"

"I don't know."

Annja frowned. "What would they have to gain from nuking Manila? That doesn't make any sense. They'd be outcasts at the United Nations, and the whole world would ostracize them."

Vic shrugged. "Ours is not to reason why. Ours is simply to figure out and stop things from taking place."

"I guess," she said.

"Come on."

Annja stood and followed him. "Where are we going?"

"The communications room." Vic led her back to the bubble and into the mass of confusion that seemed to envelop the entire room.

A full team of people still worked and every one of them looked as exhausted as Vic. He headed over to one desk run by a young sergeant who looked to be only twenty years old.

"You heading up the cell-traffic surveillance?" Vic asked.

He nodded. "As much as we can pluck out of the air given what we have for interception equipment."

"Is it good stuff?"

"Fair, I guess. It's not latest NSA generation, but it handles the workload pretty well."

"Can you pinpoint cell-phone traffic originating in the Chinese embassy for the last twelve hours?"

"That could be a lot of phone calls.'

"Yes, it could be," Vic said.

The sergeant typed away on his keyboard. After a minute of typing in search parameters, he leaned back. "Looks like there were twenty calls placed within that time frame."

"That's it?" Annja asked.

The sergeant grinned. "The Chinese are a little paranoid about people using cell phones inside their embassy. Some folks don't care and do it anyway. Mostly, they're the higher-ups who think they're untouchable. That works out pretty well for us since the intel is top-shelf stuff if they get lazy."

Vic studied the screen of the times and durations of the phone calls. "What about destinations? Can you narrow down those calls that were made to phones here in Manila?"

"Sure." The sergeant typed a few more keys and then waited for the results to scroll across the screen.

Vic pointed. "There. What's that one?"

The sergeant highlighted it and a new screen came up. "The call originated in the office of the secretary for domestic exports." He grinned. "That's one of our favorites. We think he's actually with the intelligence bureau out of Beijing, here running Chinese assets throughout Southeast Asia."

"Where did the call go to?"

"Hang on, I can get a grid reference." He typed a few keys and a map of Manila showed up on his screen. "There. Somewhere in this area. The best I can pinpoint it is to about a hundred yards square."

Vic studied the screen. "What's there? Anything of importance?"

"You've got the shopping mall, a Jolly Bee restaurant and the Imperial Hotel."

"Hotel?" Vic asked.

"Uh-huh."

Annja looked at Vic. "You think?"

He shrugged. "It's worth a shot. What else do we have to run down?" He looked back at the sergeant. "I think we're going to need your help for a few more minutes."

39

As the sun crested the horizon and the new day began in Manila, Annja was driving down the already clogged streets with Vic next to her coordinating teams on the ground.

"I want a mobile perimeter established. But make sure he can't see you. If he sees us coming, he'll detonate. We can't have that," Vic said.

Between them in the foot well, Vic's new sniper rifle lay wrapped in its carrying case. He hadn't had time to test fire it yet, or zero it, as Vic called it. That meant he'd have to hope that if he needed to use it, the rifle would be reliable.

They knew it was a big gamble. The parts of the rifle could have shifted and might throw his shot off, making him miss completely.

Their driver, one of the State Department regional security officers, swerved to avoid a jeepney crowded with people on their way to work. Annja marveled at the elongated jeeps left over from World War II. The fact that so many of them were still in operation was testament to the ingenuity of the Filipinos who drove them.

Vic looked at her. "Got the latest information on cell-phone activity from that area in question. Looks like he made a call to another number we didn't know about. We're tracing it now."

"He might already be moving," Annja said.

Vic nodded. "We have to hope that if he is, we can find him."

"And how would you do that?"

Vic grinned. "We might just call him."

AGAMEMNON SETTLED BACK into his first-class cabin seat, looking out of the window at the Manila metropolis. He felt the inevitable pull of G forces on him as the jet raced down the tarmac and then lifted skyward.

He'd gotten out just in time.

The ticket in his pocket guaranteed that he would be welcomed back home in Beijing.

He smiled. Beijing. After all these years. He was finally going back to his true home.

He'd spent so many years undercover, and it had been so long since he'd looked at himself in the mirror, the time seemed forever lost.

Still, with the amount of money he'd been paid, he could go anywhere and do anything.

He would, too. Right after he got himself a brand-new face.

He flipped through the magazine from the pocket in front of him. There were several cover stories about high-profile celebrities.

Agamemnon smirked. Perhaps it might do him some good to have a truly handsome face this time. He would then have the luxury of concocting a brand-new life story for himself, just as he had for Agamemnon all those years ago.

Who would ever have suspected that the ferocious leader of Abu Sayyaf was in fact a deep-cover agent of the People's Intelligence Bureau?

Agamemnon hadn't been so sure the ruse would work when he'd been approached so long ago. He remembered the day he was called into the gray masonry building outside of Beijing and met by a gnarled old colonel who sat him down at a desk.

"We've got a mission for you, Comrade Cheng. It's long and will be the toughest thing you've ever done in your life. But if you're successful, we will see to it that you are rewarded beyond your wildest dreams."

He hadn't hesitated. "When do I begin?"

MIKI WOKE UP refreshed and determined.

After speaking with Agamemnon, he'd done as he'd been instructed and made his death video.

As he pulled on his pants and socks, Miki reflected on his life. I'm doing something far greater than anything I've ever done before, he thought. And what a blow this will be for the masses.

He glanced at the unmarked videotape sitting on the table. He smiled. He didn't have much in the way of worldly possessions, but Agamemnon had promised him that his family would receive fifty thousand U.S. dollars for his sacrifice.

That was more than enough to see his younger sister through school.

And perhaps she'd have a better life than the one he'd had.

"My life is about to become a thing of amazement," he said.

He walked to the closet and opened the door. In the back, the blue-and-white backpack rested against the wall. Miki bent down and hauled it out. He checked the detonator and made sure the time was set properly. He started the countdown and then checked his watch.

He had just over ninety minutes to get to his target area.
Miki took a deep breath and slid the backpack on.

He was ready to go.

"WHY THE PHILIPPINES?"

The old colonel had simply smiled. "The country repre-
sents an important alliance with the Americans. If that country
is weakened from within and chaos ensues, we will be able
to exert more influence in the Southeast Asia theater."

"Because the Americans will be too busy helping the Philippines recover?"

The colonel smiled. "You see? We knew you would grasp
the logic of the operation."

"But why me?"

The colonel placed a file in front of him. Inside was every
fact and detail of his life. "You've got no family. Nothing to
hold you back, nothing to look forward to. You're a loner in
your unit—we'll teach you how to be a leader. You could quite
literally disappear tomorrow and no one would ever go
looking for you."

He smiled. "And that's what I'm going to do, isn't it? I'm
going to vanish."

"Right off the face of the planet," the colonel said with a
smile.

VIC LISTENED TO THE VOICE speaking to him and then
glanced at Annja. "We got the trace on the building where
the call was received."

"Are we going there?" Annja asked.

Vic shook his head. "We've got a team nearby already.
They can hit it faster than if we try to get there."

Annja frowned. It was getting right down to the wire.

Vic plugged the phone into a special jack in the car's back

seat. Annja watched him work. "What are you doing?" she asked.

"Patching us in so we can listen when they take the building down."

"They're going in?"

Vic nodded. "Yep. In about two minutes."

"SO I GET A NEW FACE, is that right?"

The colonel laughed. "Well, you can't really pass for a Filipino unless you look the part, now, can you?"

"Yes, but will it be a good job?"

"The man you're going to see is the best in the world at this type of thing. We have used him several times before."

"Really?"

"Believe it or not," the colonel said, "there are times when our best operatives have to disappear. If they've served us loyally for many years, we will gladly make sure they're retired in honor. Many of them live abroad now, living out their last few years in luxury in some remote Third World country."

"It's amazing to me. That's all."

The colonel shrugged. "If it's too much, you can always go back to being in the tank platoon. But I would hate to see such talent wasted on being in an armored cavalry division."

"It's not too much."

"Good," the colonel said. "Then let's begin."

INSIDE THE CAR, Annja listened to the crackling static on the phone as Vic patched them into the greater area network.

"Eagle One to Control."

"Go ahead, Eagle One."

"We're at the staging area. Please advise."

Vic looked at Annja. "They're asking for the final authority to begin their approach to the target."

Annja found her heart beating faster. She could visualize the men getting out of their vehicles, about to step into harm's way.

"Control to Eagle One, you may commence your approach."

"Copy that."

Vic leaned closer to the speaker. Annja could tell he was listening keenly. Even the driver had stopped swearing at the locals as he drove through the streets. Somewhere across town, the special-operations team was about to hit the building where the nuclear device was.

Annja hoped they made it in time.

"THE MOST IMPORTANT THING," the colonel said, "is simply your ability to lose yourself absolutely in the character you are going to portray."

"How so?"

"You must become another man. There can never be a time when you think about who you used to be. Never again will you be Comrade Cheng."

"Is it hard?"

"Is what hard?"

"Letting go."

The colonel leaned across and patted him on the arm. "It has already begun. You don't even realize it yet, but you are already starting to forget yourself. And when I introduce you to the man you eventually become, you will lose a little bit more of yourself. The process may even seem...magical."

"EAGLE ONE TO CONTROL."

"Control, go."

"All units at final checkpoint. We have eyes on the building. No movement. Repeat, no movement."

"Stand by, Eagle One."

Vic looked at Annja. "This is it. Get ready."

Annja leaned close to him.

The speaker crackled again. "Control to Eagle One."

"Go ahead, Control."

"You have the green light. Repeat, you are go for execution."

"Copy that."

There was a pause and then Annja heard another voice come over the speaker. "All units... Execute! Execute! Execute!"

Annja could hear what sounded like several explosions as the teams hit the building. She could almost picture them crashing through doors and windows, trying to get control of the building as quickly as possible.

She heard more shouting and bits of garbled talk on the radios, but nothing seemed clear. She closed her eyes and hoped to God they'd find the bomb.

"What's taking so long?" she asked.

Vic held up his hand. "Give them a second."

"Eagle One to Control."

"Control, go."

"Building secured. All units intact."

"Eagle One, do you have the package?"

There was a pause. "That's a negative, Control. We do not have the package, repeat, no package. This place is deserted."

Annja slumped back against the seat.

The bomb was still out there.

40

"Get me a map of the area, leading from the target building to the center of Makati," Vic said almost immediately after the team had failed to locate the courier and the bomb.

Annja spread out the map of metro Manila that they'd brought with them from the Embassy. Vic took it from her and traced his finger over the area the search team had just covered. From there, he drew a line leading right into the heart of the city.

"He'll want the quickest route. He can't take the chance that he'll be found if he takes a more circuitous route. Every second he's out there adds to the risk."

"Will he drive?" Annja asked.

Vic shook his head. "Doubt it. A car stuck in traffic? Too much of a chance that he'll get bogged down. No, they've got a schedule they want to keep. He's got to be in Makati at the height of rush hour, when there will be maximum casualties."

"So no car. That leaves him walking what—about two miles?"

"About that, yeah."

Vic's phone buzzed. He grabbed at it. "Yeah?"

He listened for another moment and then nodded. "Yeah, send it right over." He hung up and looked at Annja. "The search team found a suicide video left behind by the courier. Calls himself Miki. That ring a bell with you?"

"Nope," Annja said.

"Yeah, well, they've got a still coming in so we can get a look at this guy and see who we're actually after."

"That's good, right?"

Vic nodded. "Very good. Now we have a definitive target."

MIKI WALKED THE STREETS heading to the city center. The sun beat down on his head and shoulders. He hadn't known that carrying the bomb would be so difficult. And the sun's heat didn't help. He already felt all sweaty. The bomb was heavier than he'd realized.

He knew appearances were important. He had to look as normal as possible. And hefting fifty pounds in his backpack wasn't exactly the most normal thing he could be doing.

He stopped at a food cart and bought himself a bottle of water. He drank it down fast, looking around.

He felt scared.

What if they knew he was coming? What if they knew what he looked like?

Miki smiled. How could they possibly know that? His communications had been secure with Agamemnon. No one knew who he was. No, there should be no trouble making it to the target area.

Miki shifted the weight, tightened the straps and continued on his way.

ANNJA STARED at the picture on the screen on Vic's phone. "He looks young."

"They always are."

"Always?"

Vic nodded. "Disillusioned with society, they're natural recruits for extremist philosophies. It's easy pickings for someone who knows how to do it the right way."

"And you think Agamemnon chose him for this job exclusively?" Annja asked.

Vic frowned. "Knowing Agamemnon, he probably had a number of candidates picked out for it. But he lost some of his men in the jungle."

"Thanks to you."

Vic shrugged. "I don't know if Luis was his choice for courier. Luis was known. Agamemnon would want someone we didn't know about. A lower-level soldier who was impressionable and eager to make a name for himself."

Annja leaned back. "So, how do we play it?"

"We find an interception point. And then we stop him."

"Stop him?"

Vic looked at her. "Yes."

MIKI HEADED EAST, tracing his way along the route he'd memorized earlier. It was the quickest path into the city. The only problem was it kept him outside in the brilliant sunlight.

Sweat soaked him. It almost felt as if he was back in the jungle. He smiled. Who would have thought that he would have this chance to do something this great for the cause?

Certainly not him. Maybe not Eduardo, either.

Miki frowned. Eduardo. My poor old friend. Shot and killed by the American sniper. Well, this is for you, my dear pal.

Miki kept his legs moving.

Slowly but surely, he advanced toward the target.

"THE TRICK WILL BE positioning myself where I think I can get the best shot off without any collateral damage."

"Collateral damage?"

Vic shrugged. "It's unlikely. The ammunition I use has been specially modified to stop once it enters the brain. It won't exit and cause another wound. It should just drop him like a bag of cement."

"How?" Annja asked.

Vic tapped the back of his skull. "It enters here and demolishes the stem of the brain where all the life functions are controlled. Everything stops and the target literally drops into a puddle of nothing."

Annja shook her head. "He seems so young."

Vic shook his head. "We can't think about that, Annja. That kid has a nuke strapped to his back. And besides, he's twenty-one years old according to the intelligence we've got on him."

Annja glanced at the data sheet that had just come over the car's fax. Miki Felemenana had been born on Cebu and graduated from high school just before his recruitment into Agamemnon's gang. He had a large family left behind.

"They might be counting on him," Annja said.

"For what?"

"Money?"

Vic frowned. "Annja, you're letting this get to you on a personal level. You have to shut it off and concentrate on the mission. Right now, that mission is making sure we stop the bomb. I'm sorry this kid is so young, but he knows what he's doing. "

Annja sighed. "I know it. I just wish there was another way."

MIKI CROSSED THE STREET with the throng of people, blending into the crowds. A police motorcycle flew past him with its siren on.

Miki gasped.

A girl nearby glanced at him with a strange look on her face. Miki smiled. "Sorry, I thought that guy was going to hit me," he mumbled.

"Well, get off the street, then," she said. She frowned at him and walked away.

Miki made it to the sidewalk. Ahead of him, he could see the taller buildings that were the gateway to Makati. Beyond, the heart of Philippines wealth lay ready for him to destroy it. He saw the innumerable banks and high-priced condominium complexes. A number of embassies were housed there, as well.

Miki grinned. Soon enough, they would be no more.

"THERE."

Vic pointed at an area on the map. Annja peered closer.

"You're going to position there?" she asked.

Vic leaned forward and showed the driver the map. "Yeah. It will give me the largest field of fire."

"Are you sure that's how he'll come into the area?"

Vic shrugged. "We don't have a lot of choice, do we? If he's trying to get there in the shortest amount of time, then the route we drew is the one he'll take. We've got to get to him before that bomb goes off."

THE BOMB FELT HEAVIER. In the distance, Miki heard more sirens.

He frowned. The police activity seemed more than it was normally. Granted, he'd been in the jungle for the past week, but he'd been here enough to know what was normal and what was not.

The number of sirens he heard was definitely not normal.

He paused. They might know about him.

The timer would detonate the bomb in just twenty minutes. But twenty minutes was a lot of time. And if the cops knew about him, they could grab him and then defuse the bomb. Then the entire mission would be a bust.

He glanced around. To his left, a small bus station offered rest rooms.

Miki headed for it.

VIC FIT THE EARPIECE into his ear. "Radio check."

Annja nodded. "Good."

She heard the command center at the Embassy come back and announce they had him loud and clear.

Vic grabbed his rifle. "You ready?"

Annja nodded.

Vic opened the door and they slid out. Two Filipino cops waited for them. Vic introduced himself, and together they rushed into the large building in front of them.

"You're sure this is the best location?" Annja asked.

"It'll give me the angle I need," Vic said. "You coming?"

Annja sighed. "Yeah."

MIKI REEMERGED from the bathroom and pocketed the remote detonator. He felt much better now. He'd turned off the bomb's timer and would use the remote-control switch to set it off instead.

That way, if the cops did know he was coming, he could simply blow it up right before they grabbed him.

And the mission would succeed.

He smiled and turned left, continuing to head toward Makati. He had a quarter of a mile left to travel. Already, the number of people swirling around him had grown exponentially. Ahead of him, thousands more entered the buildings that ringed this portion of the city.

So many people, he thought. So many who would die instantly.

He felt almost godlike.

VIC SPREAD THE BLANKET on the roof of the building and then unzipped his rifle case. As he slid the rifle out, Annja could see his face switching to game mode. Vic was now starting to enter the zone.

"You okay?" she asked.

He glanced at her. "Just running it down. I've got a checklist in my head I have to go through."

"Anything I can do?"

He nodded. "Take the binocs and start scoping out the scene below. Let me know if you see our boy. I've got to adjust for windage and elevation before I can shoot."

Annja took the binoculars and looked down from the roof. The scene below was chaos. People swarmed everywhere.

How in the world were they ever going to find a single man carrying a bomb?

41

Annja scanned the crowd. How would Miki carry the bomb?

"He'll have a backpack," Vic said as if reading her mind. "It's the only way he can carry it in. Look for a backpack and you'll find him."

Annja kept her eyes on the binoculars even as she heard Vic sliding a magazine into the underside of the sniper rifle. "Are you almost ready?" she asked.

"Almost."

Annja's eyes continued to search the crowd. He had to be out there somewhere. But where? All she could see were thousands of people crushing into the streets and sidewalks. Buses whipped past. Small motorcycles zipped down the streets. She heard car horns blaring, almost communicating in some unspoken language.

How was she going to find him before it was too late?

MIKI FELT RELIEF as he spotted the wide, gently sloping entrance to the main concourse at the Galleria Mall. On either side of the steps leading into the ritzy shopping area,

fountains arced gracefully through the air, spraying water
into a receptacle on the other side. Pink rosebushes lined the
steps, and the marble columns at the top perfectly framed the
entire picture.

There was something inherently beautiful about it.

Miki looked at the mall and hefted the backpack again.
That was where he would die.

He and everyone else.

"I'M SET."

Annja slid out of Vic's way. He settled himself with the
barrel of the sniper rifle eased over the edge of the roof. His
fingers found the scope sitting atop the barrel and slowly clicked
off a few settings on two of the dials. "I've got a good picture."

Annja continued peering through her binoculars. Miki had
to be down there somewhere. He had to be.

But where?

"There."

She heard Vic's voice and her heart jumped. "Where? You
see him? Where is he?"

"Dammit. False alarm," Vic said.

Annja breathed again. She glanced right. Was that a
backpack? She turned back and refocused her eyes.

"Oh, my God."

MIKI TOOK THE STEPS SLOWLY, savoring his last conscious
decisions. Who would have thought that his life would boil
down to these last few minutes? That everything he had
worked so hard to accomplish would become this distilled?

He breathed deep and tasted the smog-laced air tinged
with the delicate scent of rose petals. The combination simultaneously repulsed and attracted him. Was this what his life
had become—a synergy of diametrically opposite sensations?

He missed his family. The thought washed over him.

Could he really kill these people? Could he really detonate this bomb? He'd be responsible for thousands of deaths, and lingering sickness would infect thousands more.

Was this what God had planned for him?

"I SEE HIM."

Vic's voice floated out on the wind. He made another correction to the scope. "Yeah, I've got a good picture here. His angle's wrong. I need to wait until he turns around."

He could see Miki standing there on the steps.

Once he turned around, Vic could fire and take him out.

One shot.

One kill.

"Good eyes, Annja."

He frowned.

"Annja?"

He looked up from his scope.

She was gone.

IT WAS WEIRD that doubt would creep into his mind at this moment. Miki frowned. Certainly, this was a natural thing. Probably all suicide bombers experienced this self-same realization right before they blew themselves up.

Still, it would be nice if he could have seen his family one last time.

He wasn't even supposed to be doing this. Eduardo was the chosen one. He was the one who was supposed to carry this bomb into the hearts of wealthy Filipinos. He was the one who was supposed to bring them to their knees and subject them to the horror of what their money had wrought.

But now he was here.

He took a breath. It was time.

"Miki."

He turned. And saw a woman.

ANNJA COULD SEE THE FEAR in his eyes. He doesn't want to do this, she thought. He's scared.

"Annja, what the hell do you think you're doing?" Vic's voice was like a harsh whisper in her ear.

"Get out of the way so I can take the shot."

"Not yet," she said.

Miki frowned. "What did you say?"

Annja spread her arms. "I'm not here to hurt you."

"We've never even met," Miki said.

"I know, but I was in the jungle camp."

Miki's eyes widened. "Agamemnon told me all about you."

"Did he? Did he tell you how he kidnapped me by accident and how he was going to cut my head off?" she asked.

Miki nodded. "Some sacrifices have to be made for the greater good."

"Is that what you're doing here?"

"Yes."

"Is it? By killing so many innocent people, you think that will help you achieve anything?"

"We will achieve much with my action," he said.

Annja shook her head. "No. It will mean only the deaths of many people who don't deserve to die. Not even you," she pleaded.

Miki frowned. "Agamemnon told me he would look after my family in Cebu. That he would give them a lot of money. They will be free of the poverty that enslaved me."

"He told you that?"

Miki nodded. "Yes. And that is why I must die."

"DAMMIT!"

Vic slid along the roof, trying to get a better angle on Miki. What the hell was Annja trying to do? She was blocking his shot.

"Control to Sierra One, do you have the target in sight?"

"Stand by, Control," Vic said.

Vic shifted again. He could just make out he side of Miki's head beyond Annja's shoulder.

"Get out of the damned way!" he shouted.

"Control to Sierra One?"

"Stand by, Control, stand by!"

Vic moved again. He had to get the right angle to make the shot.

"YOU DON'T have to do this."

Miki shook his head. "There's no other way. This is my destiny. I'm supposed to do this for the greater good."

"No greater good comes from an act like this. Only the devastation and misery that you'll bring to all these people and families across the world."

Miki sighed. "You don't understand."

"Make me understand," she said.

Miki shook his head. "There's no time left."

Annja started to speak. Then she heard something off in the distance. Police sirens.

Miki heard it, too. He looked at her. "My time is at hand."

He reached into his pocket.

Annja jumped toward him.

She saw Miki's hand start to pull something out of his pocket.

And then she saw his entire body shudder as an invisible hand seemed to reach out of nowhere and slap him hard.

She heard the bullet report a second later.

"SIERRA ONE to Control," Vic said.

"Go ahead, Sierra One."

Vic swallowed. "Target eliminated. Repeat—target eliminated."

"Control to Sierra One…we copy. Good shooting."

ANNJA KNELT next to Miki's body. His eyes were open but bloody. Vic was right; the bullet hadn't exited his skull, but stayed there and caused massive damage inside.

He was dead before he even hit the ground.

Annja looked at the detonator that he'd barely managed to pull free. He would have detonated it, she thought. He would have.

Behind her, she heard the sirens wailing and tires screeching as the cars and trucks drew to a halt. And then she felt a tangle of arms lift her back away from Miki's corpse as the soldiers, agents and scientists rushed to make sure the device would not explode.

It was over.

42

"That was some stunt you pulled back there in Manila."

Annja looked at Vic. He looked a thousand percent better now that he was clean and face-paint free. The close shave did him justice, as well, showing his strong jawline and the laugh lines she'd suspected were there, but hadn't yet seen much evidence of.

"He was too young to die," Annja said. "He was just a boy."

"A boy who knew exactly what he was doing," Vic said. "He would have detonated the device—you know that."

Annja nodded. "I didn't want to believe it, but yes, he would have. I saw it in his eyes and the final act of trying to get the detonator out of his pocket. I think in that split second, I realized I'd made a mistake."

"Luckily, as soon as you started to jump forward, you cleared out of my way and enabled the shot," Vic said.

Annja sighed. "I wish I could be happy about that."

Vic laid a hand on her shoulder. "You don't need to be happy. You don't need to be upset with yourself about not being happy. This kind of thing—it comes with the job."

"It's not exactly a job I want," Annja said. "I was happier doing other things."

Vic nodded. "Yeah, well, hopefully soon you'll be back to doing what you love."

"And what about you?"

Vic smiled. "Me? I'll be back to doing what I do, too, I suppose."

"Traipsing through jungles?"

"Living out of a backpack and humping a rifle all over the place. Yep." Vic shrugged. "It's a living."

"If you say so."

He looked at her. "Are we going to argue about whose existence is more meaningful now?"

"I hope not."

Vic took a deep breath. "I heard there was quite a shake-up in Beijing after the Philippines government confronted them about their involvement in the averted nuclear terrorist act."

"Oh?"

Vic nodded. "Word is that a very senior colonel in the Chinese army was executed for his rogue status in planning and executing the entire operation."

"So, officially, the Chinese weren't attempting to cause a huge ecological disaster in Southeast Asia?" Annja said.

"Supposedly no."

"And you believe it?"

Vic smirked. "This kind of thing happens more than you might want to know. Governments are always trying to gain the upper hand. And they'll sink to the lowest depths in order to do so. There's no such thing as a good government. Only a motivated one. And one government's motivations are always at odds with another."

"And the people?"

Vic nodded. "They get caught in the middle. And usually get squashed for it."

"That's a pretty optimistic viewpoint," Annja said.

"Let's change the subject. By the way, you look quite beautiful today. Did I mention that?"

"No," Annja said, smiling.

Vic came up behind her and gave her a kiss on her neck. "Well, you do."

She turned and kissed him then, full on the lips, pressing herself into his body. She could feel how heavily muscled he was, and yet the way his hands wandered over her body, he could have had the lightest touch around.

When they broke apart, Annja gushed. "Some kiss."

"Likewise."

"You have any leave coming up?" she asked.

Vic shrugged. "I could put in for some time off. What'd you have in mind?"

"Nothing tropical. How's that sound?"

Vic smiled. "I could spend some time somewhere cooler. A nice mountain lodge. A roaring fire."

"Late mornings spent sleeping in?" Annja said.

Vic's mouth turned upward. "Yeah."

"Sounds like a plan."

Vic turned and slid on the white coat. "As soon as we're done with this, I think we should catch a plane and go for it."

"You can phone in your leave?"

"Well, maybe."

Annja heard the chirp in her ear, followed by the voice she knew Vic was hearing at the same time. "Heads up—he's on his way in."

Vic looked at Annja. "You sure about this?"

"Absolutely."

Vic slid on his eyeglasses. "How do I look?"

"Fabulous." She smiled. "But you're an almost perfect match, I think. That extra bit of nose putty really helps."

Vic glanced in the mirror. "Shame, actually. I could get used to having a straighter nose. When I take this stuff off, it'll be right back to that rather Romanesque schnoz."

"Which I happen to like," Annja said. "Now, get in there."

Vic stopped by the door. "Showtime."

And then he slipped through. Annja could hear him speaking Spanish to the man waiting on the other side of the door. They exchanged pleasantries and then she heard the man giving Vic a detailed explanation of exactly what he wanted.

Vic laughed and told him it would be no problem and if he wanted to, they could get started immediately.

The man was eager.

"My nurse will be in shortly to get you squared away," Vic said. Annja watched him come right back through the door. "He's all yours."

Annja slid her surgical mask on and then strolled through the door. She looked into the face she'd grown to know so well.

Agamemnon.

Agamemnon was removing his jacket and shirt.

Annja set down the tray she carried and began preparing the hypodermic needle. "You'll be here with us for a few weeks, I understand?"

"Yes, just long enough to get the operation completed and make sure there will be no infections."

Annja nodded and stuck the syringe into the vial. "We're getting you right in there, apparently, so please lay down on the table and allow me to get you relaxed."

Agamemnon had just a robe on and lay down on the table, exposing the vein in his right arm. "Very well."

"You've had a long journey?"

He smiled. "Feels like it, yes. But I'm looking forward to a long rest."

Annja bent over and slid the needle into Agamemnon's arm. She pressed the plunger down and sent the drug mixture deep into his vein.

As she did, Agamemnon looked at her. "You're a very beautiful woman."

Annja smiled. "Thank you."

"You look a bit familiar. Have we met before?"

Annja shrugged. "I don't think so."

She withdrew the needle and turned back to the table. She heard Agamemnon sit up.

"Are you sure?" he asked.

The door opened and Vic walked in. "How are we doing?"

Agamemnon frowned. "Your nurse looks familiar to me."

Vic raised his eyebrows. "Are you sure?"

"I think so." Agamemnon slurred his words now. "What was that you gave me, anyway?"

"Just a muscle relaxant," Annja said. She looked at Vic. "Doctor, is it okay if I take my mask off now?"

"I think that would be fine."

Annja turned and faced Agamemnon. Slowly, she took off her mask. And when she stared at him, his eyes widened. "You!" he shouted.

Annja smiled.

Agamemnon tried to leap at her, but his movements only toppled him off the table onto the floor. Vic got him back up on the table. "Now, now, we can't have you hurting yourself. Not yet."

Agamemnon looked at him. "Doctor?"

"Actually, no," Vic said. He slid off his mask and then tore off the plastic nose putty. Agamemnon's eyes widened again. "This can't be."

Vic laughed. "Yeah, funny thing about that—turns out your pal the colonel knew some interesting things. Right before the Chinese put a bullet in his head, they got him to talk about your vacation plans and all. You know, the trip to see the good doc and get yourself a brand-new face, maybe go back to being Chinese after having been a Filipino for so long. Anyway, as part of their atonement for their rogue officials, Beijing let us have you instead of sending their boys to finish the job."

"Awfully kind of them, wouldn't you say?" Annja asked.

Agamemnon tried to sit up, but his body wouldn't obey his commands. "I wouldn't," Vic said. "That drug Annja slipped you is potent stuff. You've got just enough willpower left to tell us where the money is."

"What money?"

"The fifty million dollars the colonel wired into your account for successfully completing your assignment."

"I don't know what you're talking about."

Annja leaned close to him and whispered in his ear. "You promised Miki that you would send his family money for his sacrifice. Miki's dead. And he would have followed your orders, I know that. So, even though the nuke strike didn't happen, Miki completed his assignment. The least you can do is honor your promise to him. Tell us where the money is."

Agamemnon looked at her. "You'll protect me from Beijing?" he asked.

"Yes," she said.

He sighed. "Very well." He gave Vic the bank information. Vic copied it down and relayed it to the team outside. "They'll make sure Miki's family gets a nice check in the mail."

Vic looked at Annja. "I think we're just about done here. Did you want to go and wait outside?"

"I think so." Annja looked at Agamemnon. "I hope you find

justice in the afterlife. You've committed some pretty heinous crimes against humanity and I hope you're punished for them."

"One thing is for certain." Agamemnon smiled. "I won't be judged by you."

"You already were," Annja said. "And now it's time for your sentence to be carried out."

Vic walked over and held another needle in his hand. As soon as Agamemnon saw him, he started thrashing about. But the relaxant Annja had administered had turned his body into a disobedient mass. He flopped once and then Vic simply held him down with his free hand.

Annja looked at Vic. "I'll be outside."

Vic nodded. "I'll be along shortly."

Annja looked one last time into Agamemnon's face. But now, the bravado was gone. And for the first time since she'd known him, she could see the fear welling up in his eyes. Tears started rolling down his face.

"Now you know how all the people you've killed felt in the last few seconds they had on earth."

Vic leaned down, already aiming the needle at Agamemnon's arm.

Annja closed the door behind her as she walked out.

TAKE 'EM FREE
2 action-packed novels plus a mystery bonus
NO RISK
NO OBLIGATION TO BUY

James Axler
Outlanders

JANUS TRAP

Earth's last line of defense is invaded by a revitalized and reconfigured foe....

The Original Tribe, technological shamans with their own agenda of domination, challenged Cerberus once before and lost. Now their greatest assassin, Broken Ghost, has trapped the original Cerberus warriors in a matrix of unreality and alte[...] Earth's great defense force[...] regain a foothold back to the[...]

Available August wherever [...]